VOICE OF POWER

VOICE OF POWER

THE SPOKEN MAGE BOOK 1

MELANIE CELLIER

LUMINANT PUBLICATIONS

VOICE OF POWER

Copyright © 2018 by Melanie Cellier

The Spoken Mage Book 1
First edition published in 2018 (v1.5)
by Luminant Publications

ISBN 978-1-925898-03-3

Luminant Publications
PO Box 305
Greenacres, South Australia 5086

melanie@melaniecellier.com
http://www.melaniecellier.com

Cover Design by Karri Klawiter
Editing by Mary Novak
Map Illustration by Rebecca E Paavo

For Rachel,
for too many reasons to name.
I treasure our friendship.

ROYAL FAMILY OF ARDANN

King Stellan
Queen Verena
Crown Princess Lucienne
Prince Lucas

MAGE COUNCIL

Academy Head (black robe) - Duke Lorcan of Callinos
University Head (black robe) - Duchess Jessamine of
    Callinos
Head of Law Enforcement (red robe) - Duke Lennox of
    Ellington
Head of the Seekers (gray robe) - Duchess Phyllida of
    Callinos
Head of the Healers (purple robe) - Duke Dashiell of
    Callinos
Head of the Growers (green robe) - Duchess Annika of
    Devoras
Head of the Wind Workers (blue robe) - Duke Magnus of
    Ellington
Head of the Creators (orange robe) - Duke Casimir of
    Stantorn
Head of the Armed Forces (silver robe) - General Griffith of
    Devoras
Head of the Royal Guard (gold robe) - General Thaddeus of
    Stantorn

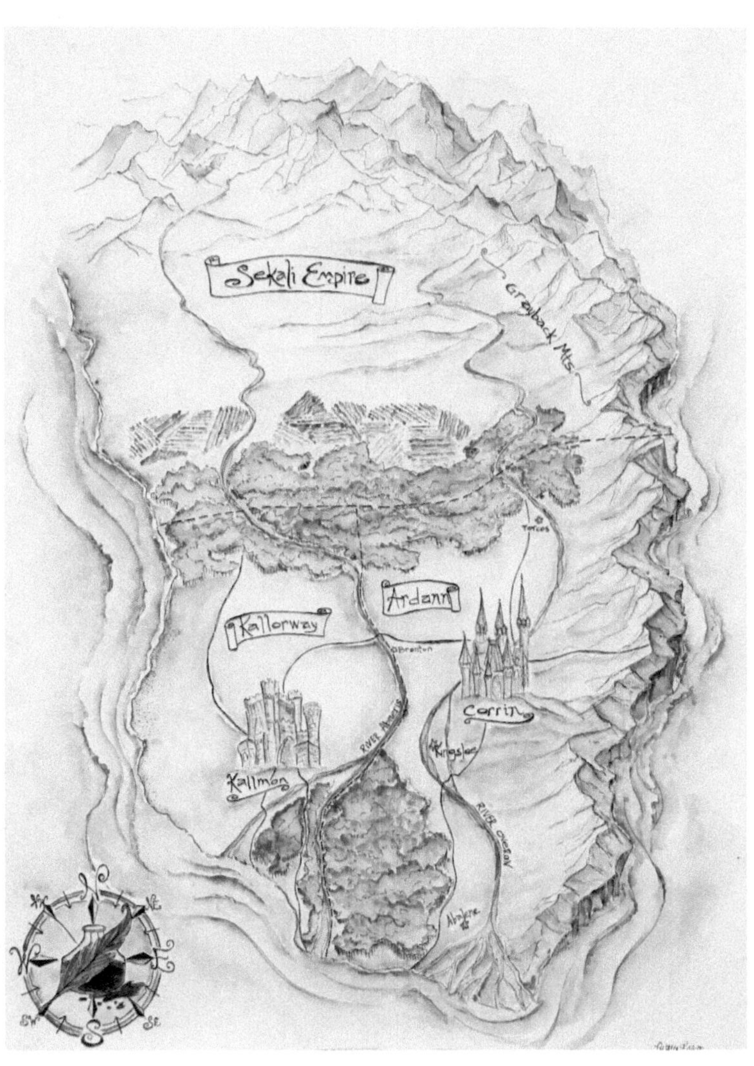

Sekeli Empire
Greyback Mts
Kallorway
Ardann
Corrin
Kallmon
Kingslee
RIVER Amathir
RIVER Cheslav
N
NE
E
SE
S
SW
W
NW

CHAPTER 1

I was hurrying home along the dirt road, already late, when I heard the cry. It clearly came from a young child and was too loud to miss and too pained to ignore. With a sigh, I slowed and tried to pinpoint the source. I had spent longer in the woods than I usually did on my herb-gathering expeditions, and the sun was already drawing low. But I was well outside the village now, so no one else was likely to hear or intervene.

An angry voice followed by another cry sent me around some bushes and onto the flat patch of ground bordering the small river that flowed past our town of Kingslee. A small child who I vaguely recognized—not more than three years old—cowered in the dirt away from a boy and girl my own age. I leaped in, placing myself between the child and his attackers before my brain caught up. I shot a pained look at the girl in front of me.

"Really, Alice?"

She winced. "We had to step in, Elena. He was endangering us all. You would have done the same."

I turned to glance at the boy who now clung to my leg. He didn't look dangerous. Tears ran down his cheeks, one of which bore the distinct red mark of a hand. I turned back to glower at the other two.

"I really don't think I would have."

Alice winced again. "Well, maybe not that. Samuel got a bit carried away, perhaps…"

"No, I did not." Samuel narrowed his eyes at me. "That boy needs to be taught a lesson, and even you should know that, Elena. Isn't your family's house just down the road?"

I rubbed my head. I was too tired today for riddles.

"What are you talking about, Samuel?"

Samuel just pointed at the scuffed dirt beside where we all stood. I looked helplessly across at Alice.

She leaned over slightly, pointing more closely. Reluctantly I bent down as well, frowning at what appeared to be a single short, curving line drawn in the dust, deeper than the other muddled depressions.

"It's a…line?" I picked up the crying child, who was now attempting to climb my leg, and settled him on my hip. "So he's been drawing in the dirt. What of it?"

"Yes, just a line. Thanks to us." Samuel stepped forward, his posture belligerent, and I fell back a step. But only because of the boy. I didn't want Samuel taking another swipe at him.

Samuel ignored the child, however, pointing instead at something on the other side of us. It appeared to have been pushed aside and partially concealed by a bush during whatever scuffle had occurred before my arrival. The half page still visible was enough to show what it was, though—a single sheet of printed parchment.

I gasped and jumped back instinctively, nearly dropping the boy.

"What—? Where did that come from?"

Samuel crossed his arms in front of his chest and regarded me again with narrowed eyes. "And now you see. We've saved us all. And that child needs to be taught a lesson."

"He's only a baby," I protested, my arms tightening around him. "He doesn't know any better."

But I could feel the shake in my limbs as residual fear burned through me. How close had we all come to death? I scrubbed at the dirt with my foot, removing even the faint traces of whatever had been marked there.

"Why haven't you burned it?" I asked. "Before someone else sees it. Like a guard. You know the penalty for possessing writing, let alone the danger…"

Samuel shook his head. "We'll burn it once that boy has learned his lesson."

I stepped back again as he leaned forward threateningly. Alice put her hand on his arm, restraining him.

"I think you've scared him enough, Samuel. Look, he's still crying. Elena is right. We should burn it."

For a moment Samuel and I stood frozen, our gazes locked. But then Alice pulled at his arm again, and he sighed, shaking her off.

"Very well."

As he pulled out tinder and flint, I tried not to look at the parchment. The firm black marks called to me, however, and I couldn't resist stealing several glances. I couldn't read what they said, of course. None of us could. But I knew enough to recognize words when I saw them. Their loops and curves and straight edges fascinated me. What mysteries would they unlock, if only I could decipher them? If only I hadn't been born Elena of Kingslee, daughter of two shopkeepers.

As the first bright lick of flame ignited the paper, the forbidden letters burning away, I shook myself. I wouldn't trade my family for anything. Not even the wonders of the written word and the magical power it could unleash for those with the right bloodlines.

"Well, that's done then," said Alice when the parchment had

turned completely to ash. "We should be going." She looked over her shoulder at the road, clearly eager to be gone.

But uneasiness stirred in me.

"Surely the real question is where did he get it." I looked down at the boy who had snuggled into my shoulder, his tears finally fading at the mesmerizing sight of flames. "Where did it come from? Kingslee doesn't need that kind of trouble." Not when we stood so close to the capital, in all too easy reach of any number of the king's guards.

Samuel grunted. "Didn't you see earlier? A couple of fancy carriages came rolling through on their way to Corrin." He gestured up the road past my house to where the capital lay, far out of sight. "They deigned to stop, and the mages inside even went into your parents' store. I've no doubt one of them dropped the thing, and this idiot found it."

At his angry tone the boy began to tremble, attempting to burrow into me. I hoisted him a little higher on my hip and glared at Samuel again.

"It's not his fault. He's too young to know better. Things like this aren't supposed to be lying around."

"He's obviously a smart one." Alice watched him with sadness lurking in her eyes. "To try to copy what he saw."

"Smart? Ha!" Samuel barked a laugh without humor. "Idiot fool, more like. He could have exploded us all with a single word, you know that."

"Well, he didn't!" I snapped, my nerves having eaten the last of my patience. "And it's getting late. I'm taking him home." I narrowed my eyes, daring Samuel to try to stop me, but he merely glared back.

"Do you know where he belongs?" asked Alice tentatively.

I nodded. "I recognize him. I'll have him home soon enough."

Neither of them moved, so I took off, winding around them. I would have preferred to walk behind them, out of their sight, but

I didn't have time to wait around. Not now that I would have to return to town before heading home.

I walked quickly, the boy's weight growing heavier by the minute. I considered putting him down and letting him walk, but the slow pace would have killed me. Instead I pushed on, stopping only once to switch hips.

So someone from the mage families had passed through today. It made sense since no one else would have written words with them. If I hadn't been out gathering, I would have seen them for myself. Spoken to them even, perhaps, if they had come into the store as Samuel said.

What would they have been like? It was one thing to learn the facts of them in school. How they alone could control the power that written words always unleashed, and therefore they alone could be trusted to read and write. About the way they built the kingdom with the power of their written compositions. Even about the different color robes they wore to signify their various disciplines. But that wasn't the same as knowing what they were like as people.

Proud, haughty, and disagreeable? That was how I always imagined them, and how the ones who occasionally rode through Kingslee usually looked.

But what if they had instead seemed normal? Friendly even. A person just like me, only wearing fancier clothes. Would that be worse? To know that no more than an accident of birth separated us.

I pushed open the door of a small cottage, set a short way back from the main road, without knocking. A young woman, her eyes red, looked up and gave a small shriek.

"Joseph! There you are!" She rushed forward and snatched him from my arms, wrapping him in her own. I had thought he looked like Isadora's boy, although I had forgotten his name.

She regarded me with wide eyes. "Where did you find him, Elena?"

I shifted from one foot to the other. "Down by the river."

She shrieked again and squeezed him so tightly that he protested and tried to wriggle free. I only just refrained from rolling my eyes. This was a lot of dramatics for someone who hadn't even been out searching for her child.

I wanted to hurry away, but something kept me locked in place. I cleared my throat.

"He wasn't in any danger from the *river*," I said and instantly received Isadora's full attention.

"What do you mean?"

"He didn't show any inclination to go swimming. Perhaps because he'd found something." I glanced around but could see no one else in the small two-room house. I lowered my voice anyway. "A piece of parchment. With words. Samuel thinks someone in those carriages from earlier must have dropped it. Joseph had found it and…" I paused. "He was trying to copy some of it. In the dirt."

I had been sure my revelation would earn another shriek, but apparently it had shocked Isadora into silence instead. She looked round-eyed between me and her young son.

"And…" Her voice wobbled. "Samuel knows of this? He was never one to know when to keep his mouth shut."

"Don't worry," I said quickly. "Joseph is practically a baby still. And we burned it. I'm sure Samuel won't stir up any trouble, no matter what he says." I hesitated. "But you need to make sure he understands—" I bit my lip. "He must be very smart. Has he…has he ever tried anything like that before?"

"Of course not!" She looked offended this time. "He's never even seen words before. Where would he? But he loves to draw. He's always trying to copy the shapes from the pictures at the market, and from the signs…" Her words trailed off, and she dashed her hand across her eyes. "He's smart like you say." She shot me a look. "Like your brother, Jasper."

I smiled, but it felt false, tension still radiating through me.

"That would be fortunate indeed for him. For you all." I refrained from letting my eyes run over the poorly kept interior of the cottage. "But first he has to live long enough."

Isadora shuddered. "It's been burned, you said?"

I nodded.

"Well…" She sighed. "Hopefully that will be the end of it." But I could see the fear lurking in her eyes as she watched Joseph who had managed to work himself free and run off to play on the other side of the room.

"Yes." I inched toward the door. "I'd better be going…"

"Of course, you'll be wanting to get to your dinner. Thank you, Elena."

Joseph looked up, as if on cue, and repeated, "Thank you, Elena," his high voice mangling the words slightly. His mother's face melted, and even I couldn't resist a smile.

But it fell away as I jogged back out of town. Isadora should have been more careful. Should have been watching her son more closely. He was old enough now to understand. I shivered. Or perhaps he wasn't. I could hardly remember Clementine at that age, let alone what it had been like to be that age myself. Still. A whole village had been lost only last year. One big bang and the whole thing had disappeared. No one knew exactly what had happened, of course. Not after the fact when there was nothing left.

Just that the explosion had been untrained, out of control. Deadly. Someone had been writing. A commonborn without the control to shape the power that flowed out of them as soon as they began to form written words. A commonborn like me and every single other person in the kingdom not born to a mage parent.

And that could have been Kingslee. Nearly had been, perhaps. I swallowed and veered off the path to collect my leather satchel which I had abandoned in the bushes when I rushed to defend

Joseph. Jasper would scold me as he always did if he ever heard of it, telling me I was far too protective.

"And you're not even the oldest, Elena," he would say, pulling affectionately on my hair. "Aren't I supposed to be the protective one?"

I always smiled and played along, but we both knew the truth. Jasper was our shining light. The one who was going to lift us all out of poverty. The genius with perfect recall who could compete even against the mages when it came to academics.

One day he would secure a lucrative position and take us to the capital. Which meant it was left to me to do the protecting, of both him and our younger sister Clementine. Although he was far away at the Royal University these days. Too far for either teasing or protecting.

It had always been clear that Jasper would not be accepting our family's conscription responsibility. Any more than there was any question of weak, sickly Clementine being left to go to war.

So if I was to bear the ultimate burden of protecting my siblings, why not start early? Even if my eighteenth birthday was still more than a year and a half away.

When I pushed open the door to our home, my sister greeted me with a glad cry as she always did. Unlike the house I had just left, everything here was neat and in good order, the furniture sturdy and every surface scrubbed clean. Even the curtains looked newly washed. It was larger, too, with two more rooms tucked away, as well as a loft where Clementine and I slept. The reward of my parents' careful running of their small store. That and their willingness to live out of town where there was room for a bigger house.

I tried to smile, but Clementine knew me too well. Her face fell, and she hurried over to take my hand.

"What is it, Elena? Is something wrong?"

I shook myself. "No, indeed. Don't mind me, Clemmy. I'm just tired." And it was true. Nothing was wrong, now. But still I couldn't dislodge the feeling of unease that had settled over me beside the river.

"Oh, poor thing. Of course, you're exhausted, traipsing through the woods all day." She hurried to take my bag from my shoulder, gesturing for me to sit down while she emptied it, laying the herbs out neatly on the table.

"We had some special visitors while you were gone." She giggled. "Well, not visitors exactly. Customers."

I ran a hand over my eyes. "I heard. Mages, were they?"

She nodded, looking a little crestfallen that someone had beaten her to the news. "One of the ladies caught sight of some of our fresh fruit and had a 'hankering that couldn't be denied' apparently."

I rolled my eyes, but Clementine was obviously fascinated by her brush with the upper class. Our oppressors. I pressed a hand to my head. I must be more tired than I realized. Now I was the one getting dramatic.

The mages might wield all of the power and much of the wealth in the kingdom, but they were also the only ones able to control the power. And we did all see at least some benefits from their abilities. If only because their growers and wind workers ensured the crops grew, and their creators built roads and public buildings. Even their healers were available to those who could afford them.

"I hope they paid well," I said.

"That they did," said Mother, bustling into the room. "And extra. As if counting out the correct amount wasn't worth their time." She shook her head in wonder.

"That'll be us one day," said Clementine, pride in her voice. "Once Jasper graduates, and we all join him in Corrin."

"Aye, that it will," said Father, coming in from outside. He picked Clementine up and swung her around, although at eleven she was really too old for such things. None of us protested, however.

When he put her down again, his eye fell on the neat rows of gathered herbs on the table. He raised his eyebrows.

"You did well today, Elena."

I sat up straight and smiled back at him. I had managed a good haul, although the subsequent events of the afternoon had driven it from my mind. I had always been the best at finding the hidden spots in the woods where the rarer herbs grew. The ones that would fetch a good price in the store—either fresh or dried.

My family would miss me when I turned eighteen and signed up to go away to war. I knew they would. But better me than Jasper or Clementine. No one said it, but we all agreed on it. And the law was clear. One child from every family must sign up to join the army when they turned eighteen. And if no one stepped forward to volunteer, then the youngest would be forcibly conscripted on their eighteenth birthday.

I had heard it debated from time to time, but no one seemed able to agree which position was less enviable—to be an older one, forced to choose, or the youngest, without a choice at all. I saw the sadness and the fear in my mother's eyes sometimes, when she watched me. Most families sent their brawniest son and hoped he could survive the three years until he had served his term and was free to return home.

I sometimes wondered if that was why Mother had fallen pregnant again, a full five years after my birth. It had been clear by then that Jasper was special, and that he could not be wasted on the front line of a never-ending war. My parents had already begun to save their coin, in fact, knowing how much tutoring he would need once he finished in the Kingslee school at age ten.

Perhaps my mother had hoped to bear more sons, who might have been better suited than me to surviving in battle. But she got Clementine, the sweetest—and weakest—of us all.

I had never actually had the courage to ask, though, so perhaps that had not been it at all.

"Did any of them drop anything?" The words were out of my mouth before I realized they were hovering on my tongue.

"Who?" Father looked confused.

"The mages, you mean?" Clementine tipped her head to one side, regarding me quizzically. "Why?"

"Oh, them." Father returned to packing up the herbs.

"Not that I saw," said Mother. "Although from the careless way of them, it wouldn't surprise me one bit. Why do you ask? Did you stop by the store and find something?"

I shook my head. "Not me. But young Joseph—Isadora's little boy—found something it seems." I hadn't meant to tell them what happened, but I couldn't keep it to myself—not with the way it weighed on me. The story wanted to escape.

Plus Samuel had been there. I didn't trust him to keep his mouth shut, and once he started talking, it was hard to know how others would react. I just hoped he hadn't recognized Joseph or seen which house I went into to return him. Thankfully he wasn't the sort to pay attention to details.

"Something valuable?" asked Clementine. "Do you think they'll miss it? The mages, I mean."

"I certainly hope not." I sat up, drawing in a breath. I hadn't even thought of that. "It was words. Some sort of printed dispatch or something."

All movement in the room stilled.

"And young Joseph found it, you say," said Father, after a breath.

I nodded. "Samuel and Alice found him down by the river. We burned it. But..." I took a deep breath and finished in a rush. "He was trying to copy it. In the dirt before I arrived, apparently. They only just stopped him in time."

"Trying to copy the...the letters?" Clementine stumbled over the words, her face white.

"If he'd managed a whole word…" Even my father looked afraid.

I swallowed and nodded. "But he didn't. That's what I keep reminding myself. He didn't. And he's only a child, too. Perhaps… perhaps the power wouldn't have grown strong enough in him to do much damage."

No one responded to my hopeful suggestion. Because we all knew the power of words. Words had the power of life—and the power of death. Written words shaped the power, released it from inside us out into the world. But only the mage families could control that power.

Certainly not people like us. Or young Joseph. If any of the commonborn wrote so much as a word, the power would come rushing out in an uncontrolled explosion of destruction. Just like in that poor village up north. In one instant gone forever, wiped off the map. How many letters had it taken? And who had written them? We would never know.

I might hate the system that trampled us into the dirt, but I understood it. There was a reason none of us could ever be permitted the wonders of reading and writing. Without the bloodline that would enable us to control the power once we accessed it, it was just too dangerous. One slip up, and…

The door banged open, and we all jumped.

Thomas, the young boy who sometimes helped in the store now that Jasper had left, leaned against the doorframe, panting.

"What is it, Tom?" asked Father.

"Trouble," he panted out. "Trouble at the store. Something about those mages."

CHAPTER 2

e all looked at each other with wide eyes, and then Father was out the door, me close on his heels. We ran together, as fast as we could sprint. The short distance into town seemed endless, but as soon as the road hit the edge of the village, we could see the commotion ahead of us, despite the fading light. Several men milled around the front of the store. And they carried torches.

Somehow we both ran faster.

Father jumped right in among them, elbowing and shoving them aside and apart from each other. I sped around the men instead, positioning myself between the locked front of our store and the small group.

It didn't take more than a moment—and a single smell—to tell they had been drinking. I should have guessed it, anyway. They wouldn't have been acting like this otherwise. They knew my parents, and liked them, even. And all of them were customers in our store.

But something had riled them up, and it wasn't hard to guess what. Cries of, "Mages," and, "Reading" sounded amid the hubbub.

"Going to kill us all," one of them said to my father who fixed him with a disdainful look.

"What are you talking of, Murphy?" he snapped, as if he hadn't just heard the full story from me only minutes ago.

"The mages are going to be back down on us, the guards with them." Murphy sounded obstinate, fear lacing his words. "They don't bear with no one trying to teach themselves to read."

"And fair enough, I say," called another voice. "I don't want to be burned in me bed because some fool had delusions. Reading leads to writing. We all know that."

"No one in Kingslee is trying to learn to read, I'm sure," said Father, his voice a calm oasis in the chaos. "And what does it have to do with my store, anyway?"

"They was here," said Murphy, frowning. "We all saw them, talking pretty and paying coin. It had to do with them." He frowned, as if struggling now to work out how the story pieced together. "I'm sure that's what the boy said. They left words behind at your store, and now people are *reading* them."

A chorus of outraged voices supported him, and he seemed to rally despite having no clear idea of what exactly had happened. But his mention of a boy had been enough. I ground my teeth together. Samuel. He'd been in the tavern, no doubt, talking his head off. And he'd managed to rile up a bunch of drunk men. Filled them with fear and left them with the vague idea that our store was harboring words, of all things.

I would wring his neck next time I saw him. I could only be glad he apparently hadn't known to give them Joseph or Isadora's name. Better they face off my father and me than a frightened woman and small child.

But my confidence waned at a further loud cheer from the men. Several of them pushed forward, approaching the store, despite my father's efforts. He couldn't hold them all back.

Fear lanced through me. These men had received a scare—just as I had, so I understood how much it could shake you—but they were looking for some sort of physical outlet. I could see it in their eyes. And they had decided that our store was harboring the most dangerous thing in the kingdoms—written words.

Our store. My family's only livelihood—at least for the three more years until Jasper completed his study.

My father roared loudly, shocking them into stillness for a moment.

"Don't be fools!" he yelled. "We have no words in our store. Go home to your families before you bring real trouble down on your heads."

For a moment I thought his words would work. But then someone at the back yelled something indiscernible, and they all surged forward again. My father grabbed Murphy's arm, and Murphy paused to shout something to him. But the other men still rushed toward me on either side of them.

One of them drew back his arm—the one that held the torch —his eyes fixed on one of the store's windows. Fire.

Energy coursed through me, and I lifted up onto my toes. For a moment I felt the same exhilarating feeling that had gripped me when I looked down at those written words, and their curving shapes floated before my mind's eye. Then I shook the thought free and screamed, "Stop!" as loudly as I could.

For half a second he still drew back his arm, undeterred by my shout, and then power pulsed out of me in a vast wave. I couldn't see it, but I could feel it as it crashed against the small crowd in front of me, dousing their torches. They all froze, clearly as shocked as I was.

Only they remained frozen in place. My father still gripped Murphy's arm, although his face was turned toward me. And the man in the front still held his now extinguished torch back as if preparing a throw. I gulped and stared at them all. They all stared back at me. But still none of them moved. It was almost as if my single word had forced them all to...stop.

I took a shaking step backward, colliding with the store's

closed door. And then the power—or whatever it was—broke, exploding outward and shattering the glass in the store windows.

I ducked, raising my arms to protect my face, although the power had blown most of the shards back into the store. When I straightened the men had all begun to move again. They still spoke over one another, but I could see in their faces that the shock had sobered them more effectively than a cold bath.

"What was that, Elena?" asked Murphy, his voice rising over the others.

I shook my head, my back still pressed against the door. "I don't know. I just yelled for you all to stop, and then…"

"One of them must still be here," called a nervous voice from the middle of the group. "One of those mages."

Several men looked shaken at that possibility.

"Lurking around watching us!" said another.

"Well, if that's the case," said Father, somehow remaining calm in the middle of everything, "you'd better all be getting off home. Before he marks you, or some such."

The men needed no further encouragement to scatter—some back toward the tavern, but most in different directions, heading for the safety of their own homes, no doubt.

"Marks them?" I wished my voice didn't shake, but I kept reliving the feeling of the power rushing out from me.

"Who knows what those mages can do?" My father shrugged. "Anyway, it worked, didn't it? They've all gone." He looked around us before raising his voice. "They've gone, and you've our thanks, whoever you may be. You can come out."

Darkness had well and truly fallen now, and no voice spoke up to disturb it. No one appeared to join us, either.

"Well, then." My words rushed over each other. "I suppose we'd better be heading back home ourselves."

My father frowned, still scanning the darkness, so I took his arm and propelled him down the road. A bobbing light ahead of us caught both our attention, but it turned out to be my mother, bringing a lantern to meet us.

"What of this trouble, then?" she asked, looking around at the empty street. Then her eyes fell on the windows of the store. "The glass!"

I looked back over my shoulder. I had forgotten the windows.

"Don't worry," Father said. "I'll bring back some planks and board it up straight away. But I doubt anyone will be troubling the store tonight regardless."

"Oh?" Mother looked skeptical.

"There's a mage about," Father said. "And for whatever reason, he chose to step in and help us. Murphy and some men from the pub were set to torch the store in a drunken rage."

"Torch the store? A mage?" Mother looked between me and my father, but I just shook my head helplessly.

As we walked slowly back home, he told her the whole story to many exclamations and gasps.

"Sounds like we were lucky to lose nothing more than the windows," she said at last, and my father grunted in agreement. But he seemed distracted, and I could still see him peering furtively into the darkness, as if expecting the unknown mage to leap out and accost us.

"Clemmy wanted to come, too, but I made her stay. That's what held me up." Mother paused with her hand on our front door. "She'll be dying to hear the whole thing." Her eyes fastened on me. "I'm glad you weren't hurt, Elena. Or...wait..."

She held up the lantern. "It looks like you've got a cut. Must have been from the glass. Thank goodness it's only a small one." She pushed inside as she spoke, rushing over to fetch water and a fresh cloth.

I dabbed at the dribble of blood from a short gash on my forehead, but she batted my hand away. I hadn't even felt it.

Clementine rushed forward and demanded an explanation, and Father repeated the story.

"A mage saved us?" Clementine clasped her hands together, her whole face alight. "How terribly exciting." She turned reproachful eyes on our mother. "You should have let me come."

"It wasn't…" The words barely squeezed past my tight throat.

"What's that, Elena dear?" asked Mother, still distracted by my cut.

I took a breath and tried again, although the words still came out shakily.

"I don't think there was a mage." I looked up to meet my father's eyes. "That…whatever it was…it came from me."

"Impossible," Father said, for what might have been the hundredth time. He had certainly said it enough last night, and now he had only restarted the refrain with first light.

I hunched in my chair, my untouched breakfast before me. I wanted to give in and say that perhaps I had been mistaken, and it hadn't come from me at all. But I couldn't. Because I had relived the moment in my head too many times, and I was utterly sure. Whatever wave of power had locked all those men in place had burst from me.

I could understand his disbelief, of course. And his fear. I shared both. Because what had happened was totally impossible, just as he said. And yet, it had happened.

Clementine knelt in front of me, and the fear in her eyes rocked me even more than my father's terror.

"Are you sure, Elena?" She examined my face.

I couldn't bear her scrutiny and looked away before nodding.

"Well, then," said Mother. "It either was or it wasn't. And it seems to me there's no way for us to prove it one way or the other. In fact, there's nothing for us to do about it at all."

"But—" Father's protest cut off as he met her eyes across the room. "I suppose you're right. There's nothing to do but wait, and see what happens."

No one asked him what we were waiting for because we all knew without needing to voice it. The mages and the soldiers. If I had truly let out a burst of wild power, then they would be in Kingslee today. There were mages and squads whose whole job was to find any hints of uncontrolled power. And any signs of anyone learning to read. The Grays. Those were the same mages who had conducted the investigation after that village went up in one giant ball of fire.

Had it haunted them afterward? They had failed, and too many had paid the price. But none of *them*, of course. No one from any of the mage families had died in that remote village. So perhaps it hadn't bothered them so very much. Except as a matter of professional failure.

But I knew I was only trying to distract myself from the thing that scared me most. I had shouted the word *stop*, and those men had frozen. The power had been unstable, ricocheting back on me quickly enough. But it hadn't been uncontrolled, exploding indiscriminately. No one had died—instead they had done as I commanded. And that was even more impossible than my wielding power in the first place.

"She has witnesses, at least," said Mother, the slightest wobble in her voice. "She was right up the front of that whole crowd, you said. They all saw that she didn't write anything."

My father nodded, but I could see his slight grimace.

I sighed, my head heavy with exhaustion. I had slept only in fits and starts all night.

"They were all drunk, Mother. All except Father and me. I can only imagine the stories that are already spreading through the village. If any of them can remember clearly what happened, I'll be more than surprised. They won't exactly make reliable witnesses."

"Maybe that's a good thing," said Clementine, the only one

who was managing to eat anything—no doubt buoyed up by a childish optimism. "The story will be so muddled up that no one will even think to connect anything to Elena."

My parents exchanged another glance, but none of us corrected her. Let her keep her optimism for as long as possible. If the mages came, I could only imagine they would have more exact ways of pinpointing the source of the power than interviewing the drunken locals.

But when she had scrambled up to the loft to finish dressing for the day, my eyes followed her.

"What if—" I lowered my voice. "What if someone does come for me? What if they think I've been reading and they...take me away?" I winced at the foolishness of the euphemism, but I couldn't bring my mouth to say the word *execute*. "What will happen to Clemmy?"

The thought had haunted my night just as much as any concerns over my own fate. Jasper's chance was gone—he had turned nineteen only three weeks ago. If he signed up for the army now, he would be considered a free recruit. Every family must send an eighteen-year-old. So if the mages came—if they killed me—then in six and a half years, on her eighteenth birthday, the soldiers would come for Clemmy. And she wouldn't last a month in the army. She wouldn't even need the enemy to seal her fate. Not given how prone she was to catching every illness that passed through the village.

"That won't happen," said Mother, but I could hear how she tried to inject certainty into her voice that she didn't really feel. "You've done nothing wrong. You've never read a word in your life, let alone tried to write one."

I nodded, but my mind flew unbidden to that parchment and the alluring black marks that had filled it. She was right, so why did I still feel guilty? Mages couldn't read your mind, could they? And the desire to read wasn't forbidden, anyway—so long as you didn't act on it.

As if in response to my guilty thoughts, a loud banging sounded on our door. Clementine's head poked out from the hole up into the loft, her expression reflecting the fear that filled me.

Slowly my father got to his feet and crossed the room. The banging continued.

When he pulled the door open, he revealed a guard poised, his hand raised to knock again.

"Yes? Can I help you?" Father's gruff voice sounded nothing like his usual tones. My mother moved slightly to place herself between me and the door, but I stood anyway. There would be no hiding from whatever was coming.

I noticed with detachment that the man didn't bear the insignia of one of the elite squads who hunted down rogue readers. He was a guard, not a soldier. But I didn't know enough to know what that meant.

A taller man, dressed in a dull red robe, pushed past him and into the house. I could see a flicker of my own confusion cross my father's face at the sight of him. The presence of a mage wasn't unexpected, but he wore the colors of a general enforcer of the law. A Red. Not the special charcoal gray worn by the mages whose specific role was to sniff out readers. The ones who investigated uncontrolled bursts of power.

Someone had come for me, evidently, but not who any of us had been expecting. I moved to step around my mother, but the sound of the mage's voice made me falter.

"Where is the mage? He—or she—must surrender themselves immediately for inspection and review."

CHAPTER 3

"*M*age? There is no mage here." My father spread out his arms, as if inviting the man to look around.

"Please." The man sounded bored. "Don't try my patience. We tracked the use of magic to this house." He peered around, as if taking it in for the first time. "Although I can't imagine why one of us would want to hide out here."

I stiffened in time with my mother, but neither of us spoke.

My father shrugged. "I don't know what to tell you. There is no one here but my wife and two daughters." He gestured up at Clementine and then across at me.

"Look. That mage is ill or injured and in desperate need of assistance—or in equally dire need of re-training. Stands to reason if the backlash could be felt all the way to the capital." I could tell from his face which he thought it was—and that he wasn't impressed with being dragged out to Kingslee at the crack of dawn.

"I don't—"

The mage cut my father off. "You really don't want me to have to ask again." His face had changed from irritated to dangerous so quickly that I nearly fell back. But I forced myself to stand firm.

"That blast was so uncontrolled, some at the Academy wanted to send the Grays." The derision in his voice was clear, but I couldn't tell if it was intended for those who had wished to send someone else, or for the mages who wore the gray robes themselves.

"Send the Grays." He shook his head. "Even the greenest trainee could tell that blast had control in it." He raised an eyebrow. "However poor the control may have been."

We all stood silently, unsure what to say in response to that. The mage gestured the guards forward with a flick of his fingers, and they joined him inside, spreading through the house. Clementine almost leaped down from the loft to cower against my side as they even climbed the ladder to poke through our bed space.

"No one wants that sort of poor control let loose on the kingdom," the mage said, his eyes following his men. "We'll ensure this mage is cared for and their skills re-honed. Such a thing is in everyone's interest." He turned to glower at us all. "It's not only non-bloods who can cause flameouts, you know. There's a reason all our children must attend the Academy. A poor composition has the potential to wreak considerable destruction."

Non-bloods? Was that what the mages called us regular people?

"There's no one else here, My Lord," said one of the guards, saluting the mage.

"I told you—"

Once again the mage cut my father off, although this time with an irritated gesture. Frowning, he plunged his hand into his robe and pulled out a small curled scrap of parchment. Despite myself I swayed forward, trying to catch a glimpse of any words written on it. But the man ripped it without fully unfurling it, shoving the scraps back into another part of his robe.

Glittering dust rose from around him and hung for half a second in the air. Then it began to move, forming into a stream that wound around my mother and fastened on to me. I held out my hands, turning them over in both fascination and terror. The dust had settled in a film over my skin, so that I was the one who now glistened.

The mage's eyes widened, and he growled at my father.

"What is this? You said she was your daughter!"

"She…she is." My father faltered before the mage's anger.

"Who is her mother, then?"

"I am, of course." My mother put her hands on her hips, managing to look offended, despite the fear I could feel rolling off her.

"Impossible!"

The mage's word rang through the room in an echo of my father. Impossible. I was impossible.

"This girl is a mage, my composition cannot lie. She has recently composed a working of her own." He marched over and gripped me by the arm, giving me a small shake. "What are you doing here? And why are these people lying to me? Clearly you are no daughter of theirs." He peered down at me. "And no wonder your composition was so poor. You barely look old enough to have started at the Academy, let alone finished. You should know better than to be practicing out here."

He began to haul me roughly toward the door.

"Wait!" My mother hurried to intercept us. "What are you doing? Where are you taking her?"

I shook my head at her, not wanting anyone else in my family to suffer for my incomprehensible aberration, but she ignored me.

"Back to the Academy, of course. They can sort her out. Dealing with recalcitrant trainees is not part of my job." His eyes narrowed as his gaze moved from my mother to my father. "I don't know what game you're playing here with your lies, but I can assure you that the Academy will soon get to the bottom of it. And mayhap they'll be sending me back out here."

The threat hung clearly in the air, but still my mother lunged forward to grip my other arm. For a mad moment, I thought she meant to engage the mage in a tug-of-war, with me as the center-piece, but instead she leaned forward to speak quietly into my ear.

"Whatever they tell you, you are my daughter. You under-stand? They placed you in my arms the moment you were born, and I could never have mistaken another for you after that. You are born of my body and your father's blood. I don't understand anything else, but that I know."

I could see the burning certainty in her eyes, and I nodded, since she obviously wished for some sort of acknowledgment. As soon as I had, she dropped my arm and stepped back, the mage pulling me the last of the way through the door.

I had nothing with me but the clothes I wore, and no chance even to say goodbye. The mage shoved me into a carriage, slam-ming the door behind me before mounting a horse. I peered out the window as the vehicle lurched and took off, my last sight of my family Clementine's tear-streaked face as she burst outside, calling my name.

The carriage must have been brought in case the mage they sought really was ill or injured because no one else rode in it with me. The red-robed mage and the guards rode in two columns on either side of me, an easier feat once we joined with the main paved road. The South Road ran from the coast in the south of Ardann through the center of the kingdom to Corrin, the capital. Kingslee might be the closest town to Corrin, but we weren't big enough to warrant a paved road of our own.

And most of us—including me—weren't important enough to

have ever visited the capital either, despite our proximity. Some chose to take their wares to the bigger markets of the city, but few produced enough excess to make the trip worth it. A couple of the wealthier families would sometimes visit for one or other of the festivals, but we had been saving every copper for as long as I could remember. Attendance at the Royal University wasn't cheap, even if you were clever enough to secure official patronage. And on top of that, to win that position, Jasper had been regularly trekking into the capital for tutoring ever since the age of ten, when regular commonborn children finished schooling. Each stay lasted a few weeks, and between his board and the tutor's fee, the visits ate through the coin.

I had often longed to accompany him, just to see it for myself. But no one wanted to waste money on board for me as well—not when it was already expensive enough to keep sending him in— and my mother didn't want me walking back alone.

My parents certainly didn't have the time to go. Not when the store needed minding every day. They had been in once and once only, leaving me behind with great reluctance to run the store. Jasper had gone along to guide them, having been home at the time for an unusually long period since we had decided to use the coin that should have gone to his latest round of tutoring to take Clemmy to a healing clinic, instead.

I had been so excited for their return, only for them to arrive home late that night, exhausted and downcast. All the coin they had carefully saved had barely been enough to cover the healing of her latest bout of the common cold. Her underlying issue was complex, the healers said, requiring diagnosis and treatment by a senior healer. The figure named had been too vast to even contemplate.

And so we had returned to our old ways. All our coin went to Jasper, along with all our hopes. And the rest of us stayed in Kingslee.

As the miles passed, I watched out the window as our stream

joined the larger River Overon, our path taking us across a wide bridge. This was the furthest I had ever traveled from home, and yet I couldn't take any of it in properly. I kept reliving everything that had happened in the last twelve hours, finishing with my mother's impassioned words and Clementine's heartrending cry.

I had been too shocked to consider it earlier, but I could understand my mother's concern now that I had a moment to reflect. The idea that I might be some sort of foundling or changeling—or even that my mother might have been unfaithful to my father—was an almost logical conclusion. But I had known my mother my entire life, and I had looked into her eyes as she assured me of my blood. I believed her.

Besides, I could neither read nor write. Even if I were a secret member of one of the mage families, that didn't explain how the power had burst from me at a single spoken word. No. Something inexplicable had happened. The only question was what would happen when the mages realized the truth?

It took Jasper three hours to walk into the capital, but the carriage and horses made better progress than he did, and the first buildings of the city appeared well before two hours had passed.

Even my confusion and fear couldn't entirely suppress my curiosity as the carriage rumbled over cobblestones. I had dreamed about the day we would move here to join Jasper, and we had even discussed shutting the store for a single day and walking in for the next Midsummer Festival, so we might visit him. But all the imagining in the world couldn't prepare me for the size. At first the houses and streets looked not unlike those in Kingslee, with the exception of the paved roads. But as we continued deeper into the city, it soon changed.

The houses grew closer together and taller, some visibly sagging from old age and the weight of the top levels. Most were made from a weathered gray stone, mixed with the occasional free-standing building of red sandstone. These appeared to be public buildings of various types and had much higher levels of traffic than the houses.

Some large, windowless buildings must be warehouses—although whether they held wares belonging to the mage families or to the wealthy elite among the commonborn, I didn't know. These commonborn merchants struggled to maintain equal footing beside their mage counterparts with their written records, and I had often heard Jasper complain about the ways they were cheated by the mage families.

His tutor had retired from business, but he was a university graduate himself and had for decades held a senior position with one of these commonborn merchants. Just the sort of position Jasper would soon hold with the kind of family willing to pay an eye-watering sum to anyone who could allow their business to keep up without the advantages of writing.

We passed two market squares, set back slightly from the road, and even two small parks, the leaves on the trees already red and orange with the hues of autumn. Few flowers remained, but many of the houses had flower boxes, and I could only imagine how bright the streets must look in spring and summer.

As we continued to jolt along the streets, the houses gave way to storefronts, although they all looked far grander than my parents' version back in Kingslee. Even the smallest of them was much larger, with enormous smooth windows of clear glass. And when the stores petered out, the houses that replaced them bore little resemblance to the earlier ones. These each stood alone, railings and gates separating them from the road. I could catch glimpses of green grass, fountains, and either red sandstone or marble through the rails, as well as see ornate second levels rising above.

I didn't need a guide to tell me that these were the houses of the mage families. The sight of them nearly made me draw back away from the windows, a stark reminder of the power that awaited me at the end of this drive.

But curiosity still won out. I hadn't seen the palace yet.

I knew that the South Road continued all the way through the city, finishing in the courtyard of the palace itself, but before we arrived there, the horses took an abrupt left turn through gates far more ornate than those even on the mage houses. And this building was surrounded by a solid wall, too high to see past, rather than a mere railing.

As we turned, I got a single glimpse of the palace, only a short distance further up the road. It sat perched atop the hill that housed the capital, and I had heard enough stories to know its grounds extended all the way down the other side to the northern city wall. The Overon lay on the other side, protecting the northern approach to the city.

But I only had time for an impression of glimmering white marble and tall towers before we had stopped inside the courtyard of our destination. It didn't take me more than a moment to realize this must be the Royal Academy of the Written Word. Known more commonly as the Mage Academy—or just the Academy. The place where my fate—and that of my family—was to be decided.

CHAPTER 4

$\mathcal{A}$ guard yanked open the door of the carriage and gestured for me to descend. When I didn't immediately respond, he hesitated, and I remembered that I had temporarily acquired the status of a mage. Even a trainee mage ranked well above a guard.

The red-robed mage had no such compunction, however, and when I failed to appear, he pushed past the guard and grabbed my arm, nearly flinging me from the carriage. Clearly I was not forgiven for ruining his morning.

He kept a firm grip on my arm as he towed me across the courtyard and up some stairs to a double wooden door. The building itself was several levels high and made of the same marble I had glimpsed at the palace. But whereas the palace had been elegant and graceful in design, the Academy looked almost utilitarian, a large square block rising above me.

Only the wrought iron and carvings of twisted vines on the doors gave it a more refined appearance. But the door flashed past even more quickly than the large courtyard had done, so I had no opportunity to examine the carvings in any more detail.

In the corridors of the Academy, young people hurried past us dressed in the white robes of trainees. I tried not to stare at them. I had never felt so out of place, despite most of them looking close to my age.

Jasper had been the only Kingslee resident in living memory to be accepted to the Royal University, but no one from our mage-less town had ever become a trainee. Because while perfect recall could—with great effort—allow you to keep up in academic studies with those who could actually read and write, nothing but blood could bestow on someone the ability to control the flow of power.

Impossible. The word still echoed through me. I was impossible.

All of the trainees watched our passage with interest, but only one stood out to me. Perhaps because he looked uninterested compared to the rest—haughty, disdainful, above curiosity. I had never seen anyone who so perfectly fit my mental image of a mage.

And perhaps that was why his dark, almost black, hair and intense green eyes remained seared in my mind after I was tugged out of his path. Even the loose waves of his hair held themselves perfectly in place, as if they wouldn't dare to cross his will. They stood out beside the more close-cropped style that the other boys we passed seemed to prefer.

The mage with me showed no interest in the trainees with the exception of the green-eyed boy. He received a nod on the way past which only heightened my curiosity. But all thoughts of others dissipated when I was propelled into what appeared to be some sort of waiting room and told to sit in no uncertain terms.

"And don't move." The mage disappeared through a door on the other side of the room. He didn't bother to close it completely behind him, so snippets of voices floated out to me, although I could see nothing. I tried not to shake as my mind raced through all the unknown possibilities of what might happen next.

"My dear Romulus, I didn't expect to—"

"Student? I don't think…"

"…not my problem…keep a tighter rein on them, Lorcan…"

The door swung back open, and the red-robed mage reappeared. He moved quickly across the room, his stride pausing briefly as he passed me. But he apparently decided I wasn't worth any words, only shaking his head before continuing on.

"Come," commanded the second voice from inside the room, sounding weary despite the still-early hour of the morning.

I looked around, but there was no one else in sight. I couldn't pretend he didn't mean me. Rising shakily to my feet, I drew a deep breath and walked through into the next room.

A magnificent study at least four times the size of the waiting room appeared. It had tall windows that looked out over the rear of the Academy and bookshelves that lined two of the walls. Despite the anxiety that gripped me, my eyes were drawn to them instantly. So many books. So many words. I couldn't even imagine…

"You are not one of my students." The astonished voice snapped my attention to where it should have been from the start —the man behind the broad mahogany desk.

He wore a black robe, as did the instructors at the University. I could only assume he must be the head instructor here at the Academy. Lorcan, I thought the other mage had called him. His gray eyes gave life to his lean frame and face, assessing me with a curious expression.

I forced myself to stand straight and tall. My family was relying on me. If I stepped wrong here, we could all suffer the consequences. If the mages decided our family had been reading, they wouldn't hesitate to execute us all.

"No. I tried to tell the other mage that, but…"

Lorcan frowned. "Romulus has never been one to listen much to others. I remember when he was a trainee here himself, and—" He cut himself off. "I'm not surprised he wished to be done with you at the first opportunity."

He stood suddenly, bracing himself with both hands on the desk and fixing me with a look that caused me to fall back a step, despite my intentions.

"But he has always been more than competent with his compositions. He told me he used one, and that you were the source of that surge of power we felt last night. Your age made him assume you were a runaway student of mine." He shook his head. "No student has ever run from the Academy."

His look turned calculating. "And you are no student of mine. Nor have you ever been. How old are you?"

"Sixteen." I refused to back down again. I needed to make this man understand that I had done nothing wrong…That I had certainly not intended anything wrong, at any rate.

"Sixteen? Then you should be here. Who are you?"

"I'm Elena. Elena of Kingslee. My parents are shopkeepers there, and—"

"Impossible!"

I gritted my teeth. I was fast becoming sick of that word.

"Impossible," he repeated. "There are no mage families in Kingslee. Do not lie to me, girl."

"I'm not lying!" The words came out more heated than I had intended. "I swear to you that I have never set foot beyond the bounds of Kingslee in my life. I am no mage. Nor do I know anything of reading or writing."

Lorcan held my eyes for a long moment and then collapsed back into his seat.

"Perhaps Romulus has grown lax now that he is no longer under my tutelage, and you were not the source of the working, after all. I suppose I shall have to work a composition of my own."

He withdrew a tiny scroll from the top drawer in his desk. It looked much like the one Romulus had produced hours earlier, although I couldn't see the words. He ripped it with tidy precision, letting the pieces fall into a small receptacle on his desk.

I expected to see the same glittering dust as Romulus had produced, but instead a gust of wind swept from Lorcan across the room. It bore down on me with eerie precision, swirling around me and whipping out my hair, so that the long brown waves danced around me.

Lorcan's eyes widened, and he stirred restlessly. Then, muttering under his breath, he produced a key from a chain around his neck and opened the bottom drawer of his desk. For a moment his fingers flicked through the hidden contents, and then he withdrew another small scroll and another, each no taller than one of my fingers.

He picked up one of them but paused with it in his fingers, his eyes once more on me.

"This is a valuable truth composition, Elena. I will be most displeased if you cause me to waste it."

I swallowed. "I'm telling the truth. My Lord." He probably had a more lofty title than the generic one awarded to all mages, but I still didn't know his official position.

His eyes narrowed again, and then he ripped the scroll in one clean movement. This time, instead of discarding the pieces, he let them fall to the surface of the desk. A golden glow surrounded them, and his eyes fixed on it rather than me.

"Your name?" he asked, although he had called me by it.

"Uh…Elena."

The glow didn't change, and he nodded once. "Now I need you to lie. What is your age?"

Lie? But he had just told me to tell the truth. "Sixteen? My Lord. I don't…"

He shook his head impatiently, his eyes still on the torn scrap of parchment. "A lie, I said, girl. A lie."

"Oh. Um, fifteen?"

This time the glow darkened, turning a sickly, oily black. I shuddered. After a moment it returned to its previous gold, and I realized we had been conducting a test of the enchantment itself.

"Well then, all seems to be in order." Lorcan looked up and pierced me with a curious look, as if I were a phenomenon he had been called upon to study. Which, I supposed, I was.

I licked my lips. That had been the test of the enchantment. Now began the test of me.

"Who are your parents?" he asked, his eyes flicking back to the glow.

"My parents are shopkeepers in Kingslee," I said, my own eyes fastened on his desk. "As were their parents before them. Shopkeepers and farmers."

When the light remained golden, Lorcan drew in a sharp breath.

"Do you have any mages in your ancestry of which you are aware?"

I shook my head.

"Out loud, girl."

"No."

He frowned at the still-golden glow. "That you know of," he muttered to himself. "It only proves that you speak the truth as you know it." He looked up. "But that raises a more important question. If you were raised the daughter of a village shopkeeper, how did you learn to read and write?"

I drew myself up. "I cannot read or write. I have never attempted to do so. I have never had more than a passing glimpse of words in my life. I am not so treasonous—nor so foolhardy."

The glow remained a steady gold.

"It cannot be. It cannot." Lorcan fell back into his chair and raised a hand as if to sweep the scraps of parchment from his desk. A hand that shook.

But he stopped himself and looked at me again.

"Both Romulus and I worked separate compositions. The power cannot lie. It clings to you. Perhaps we were wrong when we felt control within the working. Perhaps..." His eyes fastened on the second parchment still tightly scrolled on his desk. "I had hoped not to use…But this…This is…"

He scooped up the second roll and ripped it with shakier hands than previously. I only just stopped myself from stepping backward again. It must be a powerful and valuable enchantment if he was so reluctant to use it. Or was it merely a painful one?

But no sooner had the terrifying thought crossed my mind than a bright light shot out and enveloped me. For a moment I couldn't see anything amid the brightness, and then it faded—or rather moved—from me to an empty part of the room.

Images appeared in the light, and I swayed, gasping. Lorcan gestured me to one of the chairs facing his desk without taking his eyes from the scene playing out before him.

The figures were insubstantial and smaller than in real life but clear all the same. I watched in horrified fascination as my father grappled with Murphy, and I stood off against the crowd. I could see the flicker of the flames on their torches and see the anger and fear in their expressions. No sound accompanied the images, but the scene didn't need sound to make clear what was happening.

I saw the man stretch back his arm to throw his torch, and I saw my own mouth form the word, "Stop." And then I saw a silvery wave—the power visible as it had not been in real life—burst out from me and sweep over the men, freezing them in place. It held for a long moment while the image of me looked around in astonishment, and then it shattered, blowing back against me and sending glass shards flying.

I clenched my hands into fists, my nails digging into my palms. It looked different from the outside. I looked confused and scared, as I remembered being. But I also looked…powerful. I could think of no other word for it. I stared at my own image until the light faded and the room around me returned to normal.

"That was incredible," I said softly, forgetting for a moment where I was and who I was with.

"No." And now it was Lorcan's voice that carried fear and confusion. "It was impossible."

I looked across the desk, and our eyes held.

"What I just saw was completely impossible. I was watching your hands the entire time. You wrote nothing. Neither did you release a stored composition."

"I told you." Somehow his confusion made my own voice more certain, more sure. "I have never written a word in my life. All I did was say *stop*. I have no idea how it happened."

"Impossible," he muttered again. "It is impossible to access the power without the written word. Just as it is impossible that you —a non-blood shopkeeper's daughter—can control it at all. And yet..."

His eyes wandered the room before fastening on the golden glow that still hovered above his desk. His gaze sharpened and steadied.

"Have you ever accessed power before? Have you ever done a working of any kind?"

I shook my head and then remembered I had to speak aloud.

"No. I have never dreamed of such a thing."

"What about your family? Have any of them ever—"

I cut in before he could finish. "No. No one in my family can read or write. No one in my family can compose. No one has ever even considered it."

He swept up the still glowing fragments of parchment into his fist, crushing them and the glow with them. He dropped them into the same receptacle as previously, and then ran a hand across his eyes.

"And you are sixteen. The age at which our ability to control power finally stabilizes. A coincidence? Perhaps. Further study will be needed." He gave a hollow laugh. " A *great deal* of further study. They shall wish to know of this at the University, of course. Perhaps there are ancient records." He sat up straight. "And the palace. I must—"

He broke off abruptly when he noticed me still sitting in the chair across from him.

"But first, what am I to do with you?"

"Let me go home?" I asked because I couldn't resist.

He actually laughed. "If only it were that simple. No, you are a marvel, Elena. Something unseen, something..." He shook his head. "You cannot understand what this could mean. But while you may be something new, you are also something I have seen many times before. An untrained sixteen-year-old with the power to destroy a great many more people than just yourself. You must be trained, taught to control the power." He drummed his fingers against the desk. "And this is the role of the Academy. No one can dispute it. Oh, I have no doubt the University will try..."

He looked up suddenly, a twinkle in his eye. "No, your place is here. Welcome to first year at the Royal Academy of the Written Word, Elena of Kingslee."

CHAPTER 5

I still hadn't properly processed his words when I found myself in a large room on the opposite side of the ground floor, being handed a pile of white material.

"If you need more robes, come to me," said the girl who had delivered them into my arms after taking my measurements with her eyes. "This should be enough, though." She smiled at me. "We don't usually have any late starters, so you're fortunate I have so many left. But it's an unusually small intake this year, so I have more robes than I know what to do with."

Unable to form words, I managed to nod an acknowledgment before the male servant who had led me here gestured me back out of the room.

"It's true enough," he said as we approached a broad staircase and began to climb. "There are only eleven first years, if you can believe it." He paused and glanced at me apologetically. "Twelve, sorry. I was forgetting for a moment."

"I'm not…"

"Not a first year?" He chuckled. "Well you're certainly not a second year. None of the years are that big, I assure you. I know all the students by name."

I tried again. "I'm not a mage."

That earned another chuckle. "Well, not yet, of course. That's why you're here, after all. My name is Damon, and I'm the head servant here at the Academy. You need something, you come to me. I've been watching over trainees for two decades now, and I've never encountered a problem I couldn't solve."

He winked at me, and I attempted a tremulous smile in return. No wonder he was so relaxed despite believing me to be from one of the mage families. But how would he react when he learned the truth? I couldn't imagine it would take long for word to sweep through the Academy, despite its size.

"So, being a small year," he continued, "you can have your pick of rooms. Well, not quite that, of course, since the other eleven are already settled. Ten, I should say. His Highness gets a suite in the fourth year wing." He winked at me. "Have to be some advantages to being royal, I suppose."

His Highness? My already whirling mind spun further off course. He could only mean Prince Lucas. But…

I clutched my bundle of robes tighter. I thought I remembered the prince being a year older than me. Surely he wasn't a first year. Surely Lorcan was not expecting me to actually join the ranks of these mage children. To pretend I was one of them. To study alongside the *prince*.

But Romulus's veiled threats still whirled around my mind, along with Lorcan's promise that the most powerful among them would wish to study me. Who knew what fate I might bring on my family if I refused to comply with their plan—however insane it might be?

And for now I was alive. Which meant I still had a chance of reaching eighteen and enrolling for the army. I still had a chance to save Clementine. So I needed to smile and nod and comply.

I swallowed. I had never been good at that. Shock had helped me so far, but I knew Jasper would laugh at the idea that I could keep up the mask for any length of time. I could almost hear him in my mind and feel his hand ruffling my hair.

As soon as you see some injustice, you won't be able to bite your tongue. I know you.

But I refused to believe his phantom voice. I could do this. I had to do this.

Apparently Damon had continued to speak because he fixed me now with a questioning look.

"I'm sorry," I said. "I didn't catch…"

"Don't worry," he said, lowering his voice. "You're not exactly the first nervous newcomer I've shown to their room, though most of them try to hide it. The mages have yet to compose a working that will get rid of nerves." He chuckled again. "And a good thing, if you ask me. Best to be on your toes at the Academy."

I swallowed, and my eyes must have widened, because his lips twitched.

"You'll be fine, My Lady."

I shook my head quickly. "It's just Elena."

He smiled broadly. "That's the spirit. Now would you prefer a larger room, or a room with a view? The back ones are on the smaller side, but the windows look out over the rear of the Academy."

He paused again, and I realized that he wanted me to choose. Me. Have a hand in choosing a room of my own in this magnificent building. I shook myself before I could forget the truth. It was only for now. There was still the testing to come, and then who knew what after that.

But for now I was to have a room. "I'd like a view, please."

"Good choice." Damon finally stopped ascending, and gestured to the right, down a broad hallway. "Second year rooms are down there. First years down here." He led me to the left. "Third years have suites on the level below, and fourth years on the level below that. The next level down is instructor suites and classrooms. And then of course the ground floor has offices and workrooms like where we got you those robes. You'll find the dining hall down there too."

I tried to make my overwhelmed mind absorb his words. It felt almost impossible to imagine myself trotting along to class and meals in the dining room when I hadn't even been outside Kingslee before this morning.

Damon stopped before one of the closed doors and withdrew a large key ring. With some hemming and hawing, he selected a key and unhooked it. Handing it to me, he gestured for me to open the door. I juggled the robes into one hand and obeyed without thinking.

The room on the other side of the door made me catch my breath. Hadn't he said it was small? It looked enormous, the single bed leaving plenty of room for a large chest, a wardrobe, a sturdy desk, and two chairs. Bright rugs covered the floor, and thick curtains obscured the windows.

Damon crossed over and flung them wide, letting light stream into the room. I gasped again and rushed over, my load dropped heedlessly on the bed. Far below us, gardens gave way to an expanse of green grass and several fenced areas of packed dirt. Behind them sat something that could only be a mini arena, sloped seating surrounding a large oval floor. Something shimmered around it, but I didn't examine it for long, my eyes drawn onward. We were high enough up to see over the city wall, and endless fields and rolling hills stretched out as far as I could see, the glitter of the river the only barrier between us.

"It's beautiful," I murmured.

Damon nodded at me approvingly. "Like I said, good choice. Some of the students don't appreciate it—I suppose they see better at home every day. But I never tire of coming up here."

Yet another reminder that I could not be more different from the other trainees, despite whatever strange aberration had allowed me brief access to a burst of power.

"Lorcan told me you're in something of an unusual situation and have had to come without luggage." Damon looked sympathetic and surprisingly incurious, although perhaps he just hid it well.

Whatever expression crossed my face, he misread it.

"Oh, we don't stand on ceremony here. You'll find all the instructors go by their names, even to us non-bloods." He used the term I had first heard from the mage this morning easily and without rancor. "No one has time to waste around here. Not like up at court." He laughed again at his own joke. "Some of the students find it a bit of an adjustment. But they learn quick enough."

Interesting. So his familiar chatter had been a first test of sorts, then—how easily could I adjust to the ways of the Academy? Of course, in my case there was no haughty offense to be swallowed. I wondered how the green-eyed boy had fared. It was hard to imagine even Damon daring to joke with him.

"Don't worry about classes for today," Damon continued. "You just get yourself settled, and I'll have some basic supplies sent up for you. You'll find the dining hall on the ground floor, as I mentioned. Come along for the evening meal—all the first years will be there. And then tomorrow you can join them at classes."

And with that he was gone, while I was still blinking. Start classes tomorrow? What sort of classes?

Composition classes. Writing classes. So what would happen when they realized I had no idea how to access or control the power that had burst out of me last night?

I was still pacing my room considering this question when a knock sounded, and a timid servant delivered several large parcels. She began to unwrap them, but I sent her away. I had nothing else to do for the afternoon.

To my relief, she immediately returned with a tray of food, and I sat at the desk to eat before unpacking anything. Even my nerves had only been able to keep the hunger away for so long.

The parcels turned out to contain various sets of clothes—in a practical style but still far finer than anything I had ever owned or worn—and other such necessities. But the smallest of them was the one of greatest interest. It contained a stack of fresh parchment, and a supply of pens and ink.

I placed them on the desk with trembling hands and then stared at them for a long time. Could it be true? Was I really going to learn to read? To write?

When I thought of my family, of the uncertain fate hanging over all our heads, I felt ashamed. But I couldn't deny the longing inside me. The call of the blank page and the memory of the shape of letters. I had always assumed that everyone felt like this —felt the words calling to them. It was our greatest struggle, those of us not born into the mage families. A sacrifice we must make every day to protect ourselves.

But now that the question had been raised, now that the possibility dangled before me...The longing grew stronger and pressed against my will. All those books in Lorcan's study. What must it be like to take down any one of them and discover what secrets it held?

I wished I could sit down at the desk and write a note to my family to let them know I was safe. But the idea was laughable from every angle. Even if I could write such a thing, my family wouldn't be able to read it. And I had no coin to hire a messenger who would memorize my message and deliver it to them. Even if I could get out to a market and hire one. There was nothing I could do for my family except to stay alive and not offend anyone important.

I changed into one of the delivered outfits, but my eyes kept straying to those alluring blank pages on the desk. When a bell sounded through the building, I started, my eyes flying to the window. Sure enough, the light had begun to dim, the sun sinking lower.

Meal time already? I eyed one of the white robes, now

hanging neatly in my wardrobe, with trepidation. I was about to walk into a room full of mages—trainee ones, anyway. The last thing I wanted to do was stand out more than I already would. So would they all be wearing their robes, or not?

They had been wearing them when I saw them in the corridors earlier. But that had been on their way to classes, surely. I sighed and slipped a robe over my head. If no one else was wearing them, I could always take it off, whereas the reverse would require me to hike back up all those stairs.

Slipping out of my room, I hurried down the long staircase. No one else joined me, and I wondered if they were all coming straight from classes. When I reached the lower levels, a few people appeared—their eyes either glazing over me once they saw the white robe, or lingering with curiosity if their gaze caught on my face. I didn't make eye contact with anyone.

My first emotion on reaching the ground floor was relief. It seemed awash with white robes, and they all seemed to be heading in one direction. I slipped into the stream as subtly as I could. But I could still feel the ripple spreading out from me, a disturbance caused by my presence. Whispers hissed and rustled through the corridor.

Damon had said that he knew every student by name and face. How much more must that be true for the trainees themselves, who had no doubt all grown up together as well? I had been foolish to think I had any chance of joining their midst undetected.

The doors of the dining hall appeared, and I rushed through them, only to face a new dilemma. Where to sit. A large number of tables had been lined up in four straight rows. The trainees flowed around me to take their places without hesitation, and I moved forward with tiny steps, my eyes darting around the room.

Finally I directed myself toward the furthest and most empty row of tables. The few students who already sat there looked younger, and many places remained empty. If they sat in year levels, Damon had said first year was a small group this intake.

I picked a seat at an empty table. I knew I should keep my eyes down, but I couldn't help darting furtive glances at the trainees. They all wore the same identical white robes and had their hair in practical styles. My own loose waves still fell about my face, and I let them drop further to shield my expression at the same time as I wished I had thought to tie them back.

All but two of the other students were eyeing me back—with equal curiosity but a great deal more openly. I tried not to think of the accumulated power those eyes represented. And not just their ability to compose. The status and wealth and position of their families hung around them, even if the actual lines of their faces reflected more fatigue than anything else. These weren't like the other youngsters back in my village, and I would do well to remember it.

"Who are you?" A pretty girl with an open face plopped herself into the seat beside me.

I startled, not having seen her coming.

"I'm Elena."

"Yes, but what family are you from?" She sounded impatient. "I don't recognize you. You are a first year, right? That's why you're sitting with us."

I swallowed. "Um, yes?" I wished it hadn't come out sounding like a question. "And I'm from Kingslee."

"Kingslee?" A boy at the next table frowned. "I didn't think there were any mage families in Kingslee. Isn't it tiny? And so near the capital. Why live there when you could just live here?"

I licked my lips. "Not exactly tiny, but it is fairly small, I suppose. And, no, we don't have any mage families there."

"So how can you come from Kingslee, then?" The girl beside me sounded genuinely curious rather than accusatory, so I focused on her when I replied.

"Because I don't come from a mage family."

"What?" Startled gasps sounded from several mouths, and all the trainees in our line of tables were now paying unabashed attention to our conversation.

"Don't say it," I said, my exhaustion suddenly catching up with me. "It's impossible—I know. And I didn't ask to be here, but here I am. Ask Lorcan if you want an explanation." I couldn't face the skepticism and barrage of questions that I knew would come if I tried to explain the situation myself.

Several backs stiffened, and multiple pairs of eyes narrowed. I had just identified myself as well below them on the social ladder, so apparently my attitude wasn't appreciated. I sighed. My brother had been right, even without being here. I hadn't even lasted five minutes without saying the wrong thing.

A new figure approached the tables, moving slowly but confidently through the assembled students. His broad shoulders and air of command attracted attention, despite the fact that he was moving toward the first year end of the room. Many heads nodded at him as he passed, although he didn't respond. His eyes were fixed on us. On me.

I gulped. The boy with the dark hair and green eyes.

His approach silenced the trainees around me, most turning their attention to him as he walked the last few steps and sat down smoothly in the chair across from mine. But despite their attention, his eyes never left me.

As if his arrival had been a signal, servers appeared with trays of food. They went first to the trainees on the far side of the room to us, except for two who broke off from the others to approach my table.

As they laid out various dishes before us, one of them gave a half-bow to the boy across from me.

"Your Highness," the man murmured.

I straightened. The prince. It had to be. Prince Lucas of Ardann. Damon had told me he was here, and I should have known it would be this boy, who stood out so effortlessly from all the others. So he *was* a first year.

What did it mean that he had chosen to sit at my table? Lorcan had spoken of informing the palace. Surely the prince already knew my story, even if he did currently reside at the Academy rather than with his family.

A boy at the next table down the line leaned forward and in our direction. "This girl claims to be a first year and not from one of the mage families. What's Lorcan playing at? Do you know?"

The prince took a calm bite of food, his eyes still not leaving my face.

"That is correct, Calix. She does not come from a mage family. She is—as far as we are currently aware—a non-blood. And yet, despite having no training, yesterday she composed a controlled working. Using only a spoken word."

For a heartbeat silence fell on our side of the room. And then chaos broke out, spilling from our table until it encompassed the entire dining hall.

CHAPTER 6

I could hear chair legs scraping against the ground as people stood, and from the corner of my eye I could see white-robed figures, all leaning this way, trying to peer over each other to see me. But I remained in place, transfixed by the green eyes across from me.

The prince still hadn't looked at anyone else. And now a small smile played across his face, as if he had known exactly what result his words would produce and was rather enjoying it. But as I watched, the smile fell away, and a darker look took its place.

He stood, bracing his hands on the table and leaning across as far as he could. Without conscious thought, I leaned forward as well, closing the gap between us.

"Lorcan may think you belong here, but there are others who can see the truth." His voice was low, his words only for me. And their dark tones held me in thrall, reflecting the threat I saw in his face. "You are not one of us, Elena of Kingslee. Never forget that. We *will* discover your secrets. Sooner or later. You cannot hide."

He straightened and looked away from me for the first time since entering the room. I drew a ragged breath, suddenly realizing I had forgotten to breathe. For a moment I felt only shock. And then anger surged through me, driving away whatever had held me in place.

I shot to my own feet, but Prince Lucas was already disappearing from the room, his meal almost untouched. I risked one glance around at the crowd of trainees milling about in loud confusion, many of them pressing closer and closer to me. The sight was enough to send me speeding from the room.

While I didn't think they meant any violence toward me, I didn't intend to stick around to find out. Not with the anger pulsing through me. I was far too likely to say something I shouldn't.

I took the stairs two at a time, slamming my door behind me and locking it for good measure. Only when I leaned against it, my heart beating as if they had all been chasing me, rather than the solitary run I had actually made, did I take a moment to breathe.

And to consider what else I had seen in Lucas's face. Lurking somewhere beneath the amusement, the superiority, the anger, and the threat, had been another emotion. One that I recognized because I had been feeling all too much of it in the last day. Fear.

And as I climbed into bed for the night, my mind still churned over and over that one thought. How could such a situation ever have come to be? How could a prince of Ardann possibly be afraid of me?

I slept much more deeply than I would have thought possible. So when a bell sounded through the building, I jerked and nearly rolled out of bed. After several breaths, I remembered where I was and groaned. Rolling back into the center of the bed, I stuck my pillow over my head.

But all too soon another bell sounded. Sighing, I forced

myself out of bed and slipped into one of my new outfits. A white robe went over the top. A long mirror had been attached to the back of my door, and I paused for a moment to consider my reflection. My wavy brown hair—neither straight nor curly, dark nor light—hung around my face. I went searching through the supplies provided until I found a tie and quickly secured it back out of my face. With my hair constrained, my eyes seemed to grow large in my face.

They were almost as confused as my hair—unable to make up their mind as to whether they were brown or gold or green. Usually the green only showed when I was particularly excited, but today they looked bright and more green than I ever remembered seeing them. I glared at myself. Being stuck here in constant danger and surrounded by mages was the last thing I wanted. I was not excited about today.

But they might teach you to read, said an insidious voice in the back of my mind. I pushed it away and turned from the mirror. I was not excited. I refused to be.

I had only taken two steps toward the door when a frenzied hail of knocks sounded. I rushed over and pulled it open. The girl standing in the open doorway looked startled and then apologetic.

"Oh, sorry. I wasn't sure if I should knock, only I didn't see you at breakfast, and now we're going to be late, and I thought you might not know where to go." She paused for a breath and beamed at me. I recognized her from the dining hall the night before—the girl with the open face who had sat next to me and asked most of the questions.

I didn't say anything, and she shifted her weight impatiently from foot to foot before stopping and bouncing once on the spot.

"Oh, I'm Coralie, by the way. I think I forgot to introduce myself last night. I'm terrible that way. My family is always scolding me for it. You're Elena, of course. I remember that. And, like I said, we're going to be late for morning class."

I took a breath since she didn't seem to be planning to pause for one. The first bell must have meant breakfast, and apparently I'd dropped back to sleep between the two if I'd missed it. My stomach gave a protesting rumble, but I could hardly go charging down the stairs and demand food now. Not if Coralie said we were late for class.

"Thank you," I said in response to her expectant look. "You're right, I don't know where to go."

"Ha! I knew it!" She smiled and stepped back from the door, and I followed her reluctantly, being careful to shut and lock my room behind me.

As we started down the stairs together, Coralie kept up an almost constant stream of words, although she said little of any great consequence. And apparently she had decided to handle the strangeness of my situation by avoiding any questions. Something I appreciated. In fact, the longer she talked, the more I warmed to her, despite her status. It was hard not to.

She led me straight from the bottom of the staircase to the wide front doors. I had expected us to head for one of the classrooms on the ground floor, but instead we emerged into a large courtyard, the bright sunlight bouncing off a magnificent fountain in the center of it.

"Coralie." I interrupted her stream of words.

She immediately cut herself off and smiled at me, not looking in the least offended. I managed a smile back. I had nearly given her the mage's courtesy title of Lady until I remembered Damon's words from the day before. I had been thrust into this world whether I liked it or not, and if I wanted to survive I needed to play by their rules. And start acting like I belonged.

I cleared my throat and continued. "Where are we going?"

"Morning class, of course." She paused for less than a breath before rushing on. "Oh, of course, you probably don't know what morning class is. We do combat in the mornings, so it's outside. In the afternoon we'll do composition. I much prefer composition, naturally, but Mother told me to make sure I work extra hard in combat. You never know when you might run out of stored compositions and have no time for a new composing. Which do you think you'll prefer?"

A look of consternation crossed her face, as if she'd just remembered that her question violated the no-question rule she seemed to have imposed on herself.

I bit my lip, still trying to adjust to the news I would be expected to do combat training. Or composition training. It occurred to me that they all no doubt already knew how to read and write, and I felt incredibly stupid. Of course they wouldn't be teaching something so basic at the Academy. So how did I admit that I couldn't even read or write, let alone compose a magical working?

"Never mind that," Coralie said quickly when I made no response. "Here we are. First years practice over in this yard." She had led me around to the back of the building and through the gardens. She now pointed at one of the squares of packed dirt I had seen from my window.

I glanced around at the other yards. Only two others were occupied, although I couldn't identify what year level they were by sight. My eyes jumped to the arena, further on, and Coralie's gaze must have followed mine.

"We won't start practicing in the arena until second year." She shivered. "Thank goodness. I'm sure I'll be absolutely crushed." But she followed this up with yet another bright smile as she stepped over the low fence surrounding our yard.

Crushed? What did she mean? What happened in the arena? I looked up at it again, but a barked command from inside the yard made me hop quickly over the fence after her.

"You're late." A tall, hard-looking man regarded us both with a displeased expression.

I expected Coralie to launch in on a wordy explanation, but she said nothing.

"Three laps," he said. "And it will be six if you repeat the insult tomorrow."

"Yes, sir," said Coralie, her tone undaunted. She took off running around the inside of the fence.

When I hesitated, the man raised a single eyebrow at me, and I immediately leaped into motion, scrambling to catch up with Coralie. As we rounded the far side of the yard, Coralie spoke out of the side of her mouth.

"Only three! He must be feeling generous since it's your first day."

I gulped. He hadn't looked generous or sympathetic in any way.

"He's Instructor Thornton," she said, able to hold a conversation while running at a decent pace, despite her claim to dislike the physical half of our training. "The combat instructor. He oversees all the years, but always dedicates the first few weeks to the first years. Everyone says he's the toughest, but Redmond scares me more. He's a Stantorn, and they've always terrified me. I swear that entire family is born dour."

She fell silent as we circled around to run past the instructor and other first years. I pondered her words. Kingslee was too small to have any resident mage families, and even a passing visit like the one that had sparked all the trouble was rare. But even we knew that Stantorn was one of the four great mage families. Queen Verena herself had been a Stantorn before she married King Stellan. Which made Prince Lucas half Stantorn, I supposed.

I stopped myself from turning to look at him. I had been aware enough of his presence ever since our arrival and had been careful to keep my path away from where he stood. He certainly looked dour and haughty enough to be a Stantorn.

I risked a glance at the instructor, at least. Thornton, Coralie had called him. Did the instructors give special treatment to students from their own families? I shrugged off the thought.

Whether they did or not, no one would be giving special treatment to me, that was for sure.

As we once again circled the far part of the yard, Coralie picked up where she had left off.

"Weston and Lavinia are both Stantorns as well. You should steer clear of them. I do. Especially Weston. I swear he views the entire world as his enemy. You'd think he could save that for the Kallorwegians." She said the name like a curse, and I reflexively spat on the ground. When Coralie jerked away in response, I regretted it though.

From her tone, the mages had no greater love for our aggressive western neighbors than us common folk did. But I doubt they spat whenever the kingdom of Kallorway was mentioned. But then they weren't the ones being conscripted to fight and die along our western border. After thirty years of constant war, there probably wasn't a family in our entire kingdom of Ardann who didn't hate Kallorway. But I made a mental note to refrain from spitting in the future.

"They're cousins," Coralie continued, and it took me a moment to remember she must be talking about Weston and Lavinia—whoever they were. Other first years, presumably.

"And very proud of their distant connection to Lucas." Coralie rolled her eyes, and I tried not to look as confused as I felt.

When we circled the yard for the third and final time, she looked over at me sympathetically. "It must be a lot to take in. But don't worry, you'll get them all straight eventually. Just stick close to me for a bit." She glanced back over her shoulder at the rest of the class. "It probably worked out well we have to run since they've already all paired up. Now we'll have to pair with each other."

"Why are you being so nice to me? I'm not one of you." I blurted out the words before thinking them through. But the tension was starting to get to me. I kept waiting for her to drop the facade and reveal her true intent.

She just grinned at me. "I'm naturally curious. I can't help myself." She lowered her voice. "And I guarantee you the rest of them are dying from curiosity, too. A non-blood who can control power? With a spoken word? It's unheard of. Impossible. Incredible." Her smile broadened. "Exciting."

I shook my head. She'd left out a few adjectives. Like confusing and terrifying.

She spoke quickly as we rounded the far side of the yard and approached the group again. "The rest of them are holding back because they haven't decided if assuaging their curiosity is worth any potential loss in status. Plus they're probably waiting to see what official position their families take on the matter of you."

I stared at her in horror. The matter of me? Was she serious about the great mage families taking positions on the subject?

She didn't seem to notice the effect of her words. "But I don't have to worry about that. I don't really have much status to lose." Her smile remained in place, her cheerfulness undaunted by the revelation. "I'm only a Cygnet."

I opened my mouth, and she cut me off.

"Yes, like the bird. And, yes, you've probably never heard of us. We're a small family and not in the least important." She seemed to swell with pride. "Except for Instructor Jocasta. She's the assistant head of the library. And the first Cygnet to ever win an instructor position at the Academy. You'll meet her at some point."

She lowered her voice to whisper her final words. "Araminta and Clarence are both from minor families, too. But Clarence is too focused on books to give much thought to anything else. I can't imagine him striking up a friendship with a new female student." She shook her head laughingly. "And Araminta is too terrified to think of anyone else, poor thing." The laugh dropped from her face as she shook her head. "She's scared she's going to fail, and I would be too if my control was as poor as hers."

The cheerful Coralie shivered, and I bit my tongue as we

arrived back at the class. What did she mean terrified? What happened if we failed?

Just what I needed. Another worry to add to the load.

But I hardly had time to dwell on it. Thornton had us join the existing line of five pairs, facing each other. He didn't bother with explanations, just gestured for us to join the rhythm the others had already established. Coralie's sequenced blows were weak and ineffectual, and I easily blocked them using the corresponding moves.

Thornton regarded us with narrowed eyes for a moment but apparently decided not to comment, moving down the line instead. But none of it fooled me. I had a decent level of conditioning from my frequent forays into the woods and the time I spent helping in my family's store. Running I could manage. But I had never had much time for combat training.

Some of the Kingslee boys had been dedicated to it, practicing with each other whenever they had the chance. The ones who had already been marked to take up their family's conscription responsibility. But by the time I realized that role would fall to me, I was too busy helping my parents—with both Clementine and the store—to join their ranks.

I had watched when I could, of course, and Jasper had shown me the simple moves he knew. But he hadn't devoted time to it, either. He had been focused on a different sort of training.

I had watched the village boys enough to recognize skill level, though, and every trainee here handled the assigned moves as if they were basic and far too easy. Even Coralie was softening her blows on purpose, I could tell. No doubt all these mages had been training since they were children in preparation for attending the Academy.

I had known I would be hopelessly behind on anything to do with reading, writing, and composing, but I hadn't realized that I would be so hopelessly outmatched in yet another area. This whole situation seemed like more and more of a joke all the time. One in which I was the punchline.

Thornton called for us to break apart and begin a series of endurance exercises. And for an hour, I let my mind relax and pushed myself to my limits, glad to be competent at something.

But then he called for us to reform into pairs. When I looked around for Coralie, she was some distance from me, a short, anxious-looking girl gripping her arm and whispering urgently to her. Coralie glanced my way, clearly torn, and then a tall boy stepped into my line of vision.

"Looks like we're partners, Kingslee."

"It's Elena," I said without thinking, half my focus still on Coralie.

"I think it's whatever I say it is." His tone made me force my focus onto him. He was tall and lean, his expression cold and the lines of his face calculating. I swallowed.

"I'm Weston," he said, and it only took me a moment to place his name. The trainee from Stantorn who viewed everyone as the enemy. The one person I'd been most expressly warned to stay away from.

I swallowed again, and a slow smile spread across his face. It had nothing of the friendliness in Coralie's.

Without meaning to, my gaze skipped to the side and met the prince's. For half a second, I thought he meant to intervene. But then he turned away, and I remembered it was more likely he had put Weston up to it. Whatever *it* was going to be.

"Let's spar then, *Elena*," Weston said, just as Thornton called out directions. I recognized almost nothing of what the instructor said, and I was still looking frantically at the other pairs, trying to work out what we were supposed to be doing, when the first blow fell.

CHAPTER 7

"Thornton should have stepped in sooner." Coralie sounded incensed as she helped me limp through the gardens. "That was a massacre."

"Thanks," I said dryly.

She grinned at me apologetically before wincing at the sight of something on my face. I lifted my hand to touch the spot where her eyes lingered and winced as well. That was going to be a large bruise.

"Well you clearly didn't know what you were doing, and he's supposed to be *instructing* us, after all. It's just because he's a Devoras," she muttered. "They're almost as bad as the Stantorns. He thinks we should all be as tough as him and Weston."

"He was testing me," I said.

"Who? Thornton or Weston?"

I shrugged and winced again at a pain across my shoulders. I had aches and bruises in places I had never even felt before. "Both."

Another bell sounded, and I noticed we were the last ones still outside, our pace slower than everyone else's. No doubt the others were already in the dining hall. My stomach rumbled at the thought—undeterred by the pain since I had missed breakfast and most of dinner the night before as well.

But when I stumbled going through the main doors, Coralie frowned and pulled me in the opposite direction to food.

"I think I should take you to the healer's room. We're allowed to go if we're in bad enough shape after training."

My stomach groaned again, but I let her lead me forward. I had never seen a healer before, although I had made my mother describe what their clinic had been like again and again. And now I was to get the chance to see one in action. I wouldn't complain about a release from all this pain either. I had fallen so many times my bruises must have bruises.

"Goodness," said a pleasant-looking young woman when Coralie pushed open a door halfway down the corridor and deposited me on a seat inside. "It is only the first week, isn't it? I thought Thornton was supposed to be easing you first years in gently."

Coralie put her hands on her hips. "Weston had other ideas."

The woman hid what looked like a smile at the Cygnet girl's indignation. "You know what those Stantorns are like, Coralie."

Coralie sighed and plopped into another seat. "This is Acacia, Elena. She's an Ellington, but she comes from Abalene, like my family." She named a large southern city on the River Overon. "She's good people."

"Thank you for that glowing testimony, Coralie," said the woman gravely. She turned her attention to me. "And who might you be? I don't recognize..." Her voice faded away, and her eyes grew wide as she no doubt put two and two together.

I managed a weak smile. "I'm Elena. From Kingslee."

"Kingslee." She whispered the word. "So it's true."

"Which means she could really do with all the help you can give her." Coralie fixed Acacia with a meaningful look, and the healer nodded, although her curious gaze was still on me.

"You're in luck," she said. "I'm well stocked this early in the year, so I'll have you feeling good as new before you know it."

When she smiled and it actually reached her eyes, I wanted to embrace her. After the treatment from Weston, I had been starting to think that Coralie might be the only mage in the kingdom willing to give me a chance. Well, Coralie and Lorcan, the Academy Head. But I was fairly sure his interest was limited to my use of magic and didn't extend to me as a person.

Acacia worked quickly, selecting three different strips of rolled parchment, two the length of one of my fingers and a third a half longer again. She ripped them all in quick succession, flicking her fingers in my direction as soon as she had done so.

A cool mist responded to her movement, flowing over to rest against my skin before sinking in deeper. The first wave came with a sharp pain, but the second brought numbing relief. And within minutes, I felt whole and strong again. I held out my arms and examined them. No bruises or marks in sight.

I looked up at the healer. "That was incredible."

She smiled. "Thank you. Although actually that was quite simple." She frowned briefly down at the scraps of parchment in her hand as if they angered her for some reason. With a quick movement, she tossed them into a small container on the long desk behind her.

"Don't worry, Acacia." Coralie clapped her on the back. "If you were stronger, you'd be working at the front instead of relaxing here with us."

Acacia smiled although a shadow still lurked in her eyes. "I would actually like to be able to help at the front where my services would be most in need, you know. That's why I wanted to become a healer in the first place." She shook her head at Coralie. "But I suppose you lot aren't so bad."

Coralie laughed. "That's the spirit." She looked over at me. "If we hurry, we should still be able to make it to lunch."

I shot up immediately, and both of the others laughed.

"Healing always makes me hungry, too." Coralie propelled me out into the corridor and then took off at a fast walk. I followed close behind. "And you missed breakfast as well, didn't you, poor thing?"

A trickle of trainees already headed in the other direction, but we slid inside and into two seats before the servers reached the first year tables to clear away the platters of food. We both quickly filled a plate and began wolfing it down.

For the first few bites I felt nothing but relief. Then amazement followed. I had never tasted such rich and varied food before. The flavors of the sauces were intricate, and the platters contained three different types of meat. When I bit into the lightest, fluffiest roll I had ever eaten, I almost groaned. Was I really going to be fed like this every day?

But as my stomach filled, I became aware of the room more broadly. Coralie had directed us to a deserted table, whoever had been eating there having already left. But still I could hear whispers around me and feel eyes on my back.

"Is it better if I don't look?" I asked Coralie in a whisper.

She grimaced. "Probably. But don't worry. They'll all get used to you eventually."

I frowned. If I was around long enough for that. Lorcan had said I belonged here—but for how long? I had learned he was definitely the Head of the Academy, which meant he was very important indeed, with a seat on the Mage Council. But he was only one head on a council of ten. And that was without considering the royal family themselves.

The prince had made it clear how they felt, and it didn't seem to bode well for me. I once again fought the urge to look across at the neighboring table where Lucas sat. His eyes no longer followed me like they had the day before, but still I found myself aware of his presence at all times.

Coralie shot me a look, and I could see all the questions lurking in her eyes, straining to break free. She had been more than kind to me, and I wanted to give her permission to ask them, but I held off. I had too few answers myself.

All too soon, Coralie was tugging me back out of the dining hall.

"Quick, the bell will ring any second."

We rushed down the corridor and barreled into a room, sliding into a double desk just as the second bell rang. Coralie breathed a sigh of relief, and then fixed her attention on the front of the room, her back straight. I remembered her saying earlier in the morning how much she preferred afternoon composition classes.

I hadn't absorbed anything in our mad dash, so I took a moment to look around now. The room had several large windows which spilled light into the spacious interior. Four rows, each containing four double desks, faced the front of the room, but only the first two rows were occupied. Coralie and I shared a desk, as did four other pairs of students, only Weston and the prince sitting alone.

Much to my dismay, the prince had the outside desk on the second row which put him next to us. I felt his eyes boring into me, but I refused to give him the satisfaction of seeing that I'd noticed. Instead I examined the other trainees.

In the front row, the anxious-looking girl who had distracted Coralie sat beside a tall, elegant girl who held herself as if she sat alone. The striking contrast held my attention, and Coralie leaned over to whisper in my ear.

"They do look funny next to each other, don't they? Although I shouldn't laugh. Poor Araminta. I'm sure sitting next to Dariela only makes her even more terrified."

Ah. So the anxious girl was Araminta—the weak one from a minor family like Coralie's. The name Dariela I didn't recognize, however.

"Dariela is an Ellington," Coralie said without my having to ask. "I know it's still early days, but if you ask me she's going to lead the class." She grinned. "Weston will hate that—a mighty Stantorn being outshone by an Ellington."

I nodded as if I knew what she was talking about when in fact I had no idea. I might know the names of the four great mage families, but that didn't mean I knew the subtleties of the dynamics between them.

Coralie leaned in closer to whisper again, but a sharp throat clearing from the front of the room made her straighten and assume a serious posture. She might like this class, but I could tell the instructor made her slightly nervous. And I could see why.

He looked around at us all with an angry expression, as if we were an inconvenience on his day. And I was either imagining it, or his eyes lingered extra long on me. He was certainly looking at me when he spoke.

"I am Instructor Redmond of Stantorn. I teach composition."

I nodded and tried to look studious. His voice suggested that he was only bothering with a full introduction because he was confident that I was utterly inept. And sadly, I didn't like my chances of convincing him otherwise despite my having been head of my class in the Kingslee school.

But the Kingslee school only taught students up to ten years old. There we had learned our numbers and what mental arithmetic we were each capable of. We had studied geography—using maps full of symbols rather than words—and learned the history and laws of Ardann by rote. The teacher hadn't needed to teach us the simple system of symbols used to mark signs and marketplaces, those we had already learned from our parents.

Naturally we were not taught anything of reading, writing, or magical composition.

Redmond's gaze swept over the rest of the class. "We have done enough theory now, it is time for you all to make your first attempts at composing a magical working. Naturally we will begin with the enclosing words. We will then produce a parchment that may be used for regular writing. As I have previously explained, this is merely an expansion on the enclosing words."

This time his eyes lingered on Araminta instead of me. "And I expect this to be well within all of your capacities." His tone suggested he believed no such thing.

Redmond moved between the desks handing out a single sheet of parchment to each student. When he reached our desk, I hesitated, but the expression on his face made me snatch one in silence. I placed it down in front of me and stared at the words that filled it. Words. Sharp, curving, black letters. I had never been given the opportunity to look my fill at them before, and I couldn't tear my eyes away.

A sound from the desk beside me—half cough, half choke—made my eyes swing around without thinking. I met the prince's gaze. He looked from me to the sheet in front of me and then slowly shook his head. I could feel the flush rising across my face, and I quickly turned away from him, angling myself toward Coralie.

She had taken a pen and blank parchment from the small supply between us and was staring down at it. Her fist gripped the pen so hard her knuckles had turned white. For a moment the sight reassured me, until I remembered that my problems with this class went far beyond some natural nerves.

I watched with fascination as she lowered the pen to the paper and made several strokes in quick succession. Beneath her tip, words began to form, crossing the page from left to right. Only once did she glance back at the sheet we had been handed— just before finishing her words with a large dot, executed with a flourish. For a second her pen hovered there, above the page, and then she leaned back with a satisfied sigh.

I glanced between her words and the sheet in front of me. Then back again. The shape of her letters was slightly different, but I thought her first line matched the one we had been given. Not that I had any idea what it said.

"Congratulations, Coralie," said an unimpressed voice behind us. "You have made a start."

We both looked up at Instructor Redmond. When neither of us moved, he raised both eyebrows.

"I believe there was more to the exercise."

She gulped, nodded, and bent her head over her parchment. Redmond turned to me.

"Is there a problem, Elena of Kingslee?"

I wanted to say, *Yes. All of the other trainees have had days of theory before this, and you haven't bothered to explain anything to me.*

But I swallowed the words. He was obviously well aware of that, and I suspected he was well aware that no amount of explanation would help me. For the hundredth time, I reminded myself not to blurt out my thoughts in this place.

Instead I took a deep breath and looked down at the desk. "I can't read this, Sir. And I can't write either. I was never taught how."

A slight movement made me glance to the side. I expected to see disgust and contempt on the prince's face, but instead he looked swiftly away, as if embarrassed to be caught showing interest at all.

"I see," said Redmond, drawing out the words. "In that case you have no place in this class. As I have informed Lorcan."

I bit my tongue and didn't move. All of the class had fallen silent now, and many were openly staring at me. I wanted to lash out at them all—it wasn't my fault I couldn't read or write—but I could only imagine how unhelpful that would be.

Redmond gave an exaggerated sigh. "You have no place here until you can read and write. You may seek tutoring from Jocasta in the library. Tell her Redmond sent you." A slight change in inflection hinted that he enjoyed palming me off to another instructor, and this one in particular. Clearly he felt no great affection toward her.

I glanced sideways at Coralie and remembered she had

mentioned a Jocasta earlier in the day. The only Cygnet to ever gain as high a rank as Academy Instructor, or something like that. Which might explain Redmond's delight in sending me to her.

Coralie moved as if she meant to accompany me, but Redmond bent such a forbidding glare on her that she settled back into her seat with an apologetic grimace at me. I shrugged and gave her a tight smile before hurrying from the room.

As soon as the door closed behind me, I took a deep, steadying breath, free from the weight of so many disapproving eyes. I just wished I knew where to find the library.

I wandered down the corridor and then the stairs, wondering if I was breaking any sort of rules by doing so. I certainly couldn't see any other white robes meandering around. But a defiant spark had lit inside me. Everyone kept telling me that I didn't belong here, and they were right. I was behind in every measure. But only an accident of birth was responsible for that.

I was no less intelligent, no weaker than any of them. And if they thought I meant to run away with my tail between my legs, they were wrong. If I was to be granted the miraculous ability to learn to read and write, I meant to grasp it with both hands. I walked past a door that was slightly ajar, the view inside familiar. I stopped and peered into Lorcan's waiting room.

The sight was sobering. I wasn't here because I refused to run away. I was here because I had no other choice. And I had no idea how long I would be permitted to remain. I had no choice in that either.

I straightened. But I did have one choice. I could choose what to do while I was here. And I intended to learn. I intended to learn as much as I possibly could until either they dragged me forcibly away, or I turned eighteen and enlisted in the army.

Damon pulled the door all the way open and stepped out into the corridor, giving me an amused look.

"Shouldn't you be in class?"

I had assumed from his demeanor the day before that he had no idea of my background. But word must have reached him by now, and it seemed to have made no difference to his attitude toward me.

"I'm looking for the library. Could you direct me?"

He smiled. "I'll do one better and show you myself. Didn't I tell you if you needed anything to come to me? You'll never find old Damon at a loss." He chuckled. "Not that finding the library is exactly testing my abilities."

"That's all I need for now," I said. *Well, that and a new pedigree along with a lifetime of training. But there are some things* no one can do.

Thoughts of the family I did have brought a tightening around my chest, and I pushed them away. My family would tell me to seize this opportunity with both hands, I knew they would. Right after they told me to keep my head down and keep us all safe. If only that were possible.

Damon chatted cheerfully about the weather and classes and the students, but I hardly heard him until he stopped in front of a set of double doors and gestured toward them with a flourish.

"The library, as promised."

I smiled. "Thank you, Damon."

"Any time, Elena. Any time."

I pushed the doors open and stepped through, into a place I had never even dreamed existed.

CHAPTER 8

The room itself was larger than any I had ever seen. Stretching up two stories, it expanded away from me in every direction. A large, curved desk stood directly in front of me, but I couldn't tear my eyes from the shelves behind it. They marched up and down the room in straight lines, taking up the majority of the space. Only around the edge of the room, in a giant ring, had the space been left bare of shelves, filled instead with scattered desks and chairs.

And then on the walls themselves, more shelves. These ones reached up the full two levels, although the upper shelves must surely be for show. No one could access them safely.

But none of this was what held me mesmerized. It was the contents of the shelves which I couldn't fathom. Endless books and scrolls stretching out in every direction. I had been amazed by Lorcan's study, but it was a drop in the ocean compared to this. How was it possible that so much writing could exist in the world? How had the entire place not gone up in smoke long ago?

"Can I help you?"

The voice startled me enough that I looked away from all the books and at the short, thin woman behind the desk. She had gray hair, but the smoothness of her face and brilliance of her eyes suggested she had gone gray young rather than from any great age.

"Trainees—even first years—are not permitted to wander around during class time." She drummed her fingers on the desk. "We don't see a lot of first years in the library at all."

I shook my head, still struck dumb. I couldn't imagine why not. I knew I never wanted to leave this place now that I had found it.

Her face softened as she watched me dart another glance at the books. "It is rather impressive, isn't it? Larger even than the palace library. Only the University has a more expansive collection."

I blinked. There were two more such places? And all within easy reach of this building? The thought was almost incomprehensible.

The woman frowned at me. "I'll admit I've never paid much attention to the faces of the youngsters, not until they turn up at the Academy, at any rate. But yours I definitely don't recognize. I'm Jocasta, assistant head of the library."

Her mouth turned down sharply. "Don't tell me you're the common girl Lorcan has insisted on admitting?"

I opened my mouth, but she held up a hand to forestall me. "Of course you are. I don't get involved with all of the maneuvering and posturing—one of the advantages of coming from a minor family—so I have no stake in that game. But I do want to know why you're here, disturbing my library. I have a suspicion I know the reason, and I don't like it one bit."

"Redmond sent me."

"You can't read, I suppose," she said, before I could go on. "It stands to reason. If you could, the Grays would have sniffed you out long ago and made short work of you." She sighed. "And naturally the mighty Redmond wouldn't stoop to teach such a thing. Although I suppose it must be taught if you're to do any studying. And I imagine they're all eager to see what happens when you try a normal composition. I just hope they aren't expecting it to be any time soon. These things take time, you know. Especially if control is their aim, and I can only imagine it's their first priority."

I stared at her. Lorcan had said something about control, and I supposed it made sense. If I could work magic by speaking, we were all in danger until I learned how to control it. And this was the place where mages learned that skill. Of course, my problem seemed to be accessing the power rather than flaming out—something for which I could only be grateful—but the risk still remained.

"I'll do my best," I said, unsure what else to say.

She regarded me for a steady moment and then sighed. "There's a small study room we can use over there." She gestured to my right. "Wait for me inside."

I found the door she meant easily enough and took a seat at the single large desk. Six chairs sat in a circle around it, but otherwise the stone room was empty and plain. It didn't even have a window. No distractions.

I waited for several minutes until I heard Jocasta's voice mingled with several others. I caught my name. Slipping over to the door, I peeked around, listening intently.

"I'm not sure how she's expected to make any progress if she's not to be left alone to study." Jocasta sounded put out.

"The question of whether or not she should be permitted to study has not been settled." The angry man in the gold robe looked unfamiliar.

Lorcan, standing next to him, cleared his throat. "I believe the matter of magical training continues to reside with the Royal Academy of the Written Word and its head. Not with the Royal Guard, General Thaddeus. I find myself somewhat surprised to see you here. Lennox and Phyllida I expected, but you..."

The general drew himself up. "May I remind you that this

building rests only the shortest distance from the royal palace. And that a member of the royal family currently resides within your halls. I assure you that any potential threat is a matter for the Head of the Royal Guard."

I bit down on the inside of my cheek. I should have remembered what the gold robe meant. Only mage officers of the Royal Guard wore them, the color matching the gold and red uniforms of the guards themselves. And this wasn't just any officer, but the head himself. Only the heads—past and present—of the Royal Guard and Armed Forces carried the rank of general. And even I knew that the Armed Forces were led by General Griffith of Devoras. If only so that I could curse his name along with the rest of Kingslee.

Jocasta glanced my way, and I hurriedly pulled back.

"If the testing must be done now, then let us get to it without delay," she said.

"Certainly," said Lorcan. "Any concerns of the general's must be immediately laid to rest."

I hurried back to my seat before Jocasta poked her head in and gestured for me to emerge.

"We can't start right away, after all. A great many important people have shown up demanding answers, so it seems you're to be tested before we begin." She offered no explanation for what that might mean, and I resisted the urge to wipe my sweaty palms on my clean robe. What sort of testing, exactly?

Lorcan nodded to me and led me out of the library and back into the corridor. General Thaddeus had already disappeared. Lorcan, Jocasta, and I crossed a short distance before entering yet another room. This one was a similar size to the composition classroom, although without the desks. Chairs lined the walls, however, and a number of them had already been taken, the room awash with different colored robes.

Lorcan nodded at the gathered mages.

"I had not expected to see so many of you."

"Come, Lorcan," said a lady whose gray hair looked to be legitimately earned by age. She turned keen eyes on me, her face bright with intelligence despite the lines. "We do not doubt the veracity of your compositions. But such a thing! It's unheard of. Can you really blame us for wanting to see for ourselves?"

Lorcan chuckled and shook his head. "Of you, Jessamine, I expected nothing less."

The narrowed eyes of several of the other attendees suggested they felt somewhat less faith in Lorcan, but no one actually voiced such a thing.

Lorcan turned to me. "This is Her Grace, Duchess Jessamine of Callinos, University Head." I noted she wore the same black robe as Lorcan himself.

He pointed to another woman, this time in a gray robe that made me shudder slightly. "And this is Duchess Phyllida, also of Callinos, Head of the Seekers. No doubt she seeks reassurance that her mages have not faltered in their duties where you are concerned."

I licked my lips.

"I have never read a word in my life. Nor written one."

Phyllida, much younger than Jessamine, with her sleek brown hair pulled back tight against her head, merely regarded me with cool eyes.

A man across the room from her spoke, however. "So you say. We are here to see the truth of it with our own eyes."

Lorcan turned to him. "Ah, and let us not forget Duke Lennox of Ellington, Head of Law Enforcement." His red robe stood out starkly in the room of black and gray, only the gold one of General Thaddeus brighter. The general sat several chairs down from the Head of Law Enforcement, and both appeared to have brought an entourage even larger than those accompanying the two duchesses.

This time I did wipe my hands on my robe as surreptitiously as I could. If they were hoping for a display of power from me, they were all going to be highly disappointed. And I didn't want to find out what happened when so many important people were disappointed.

"I assume you've come prepared?" Lorcan looked between the red-robed Lennox and the gray-robed Phyllida. "I have already used two complex compositions to—"

"Oh relax, Lorcan," snapped Thaddeus, "no one is asking you to expend any more of your valuable resources."

"I have come prepared," said Phyllida. "As I'm sure has Lennox. You are not the only one capable of such compositions, Lorcan."

Was that amusement in her calm tone? How much competition existed between the various heads? Still, their words had relieved me. Apparently the tests were to be a repeat of the magical ones conducted by Lorcan on my arrival. In other words, painless, and requiring little from me. I tried not to let the relief show on my face, though. I tried not to let anything show on my face. I wanted to make as little impression on these people as possible.

At least it explained why there were so many of them. Presumably they wished to minimize the use of their compositions by including as many witnesses in one testing as possible. They must require a lot of power—or perhaps just a lot of skill— to compose. I wished the Kingslee school had gone into greater detail on the way magical compositions worked. But it had hardly seemed essential learning for a bunch of village children.

I knew that each of the magical disciplines—law enforcement, the seekers, the healers, the growers, the wind workers, and the creators—had a head, granted the title duke or duchess for life. And that these six heads, along with the Academy Head, the University Head, and the Heads of the Armed Forces and Royal Guard, formed a Mage Council of ten to advise the king and help write our laws. I even knew that only mages from one of the four great families ever had the necessary skill and control to rise to one of these positions. And I knew that the four great families were Devoras, Stantorn, Callinos, and Ellington.

But I knew almost nothing of how they actually composed their workings, or why they would now be poking at one another about the necessary composition for my testing.

"Enough of this," said the red-robed Lennox, rising to his feet and withdrawing a curl of parchment. "Let us hear the truth from her lips." He ripped it into two and threw the pieces onto the floor in front of him. The resulting red glow blossomed larger than the one that had sat on Lorcan's desk.

Lorcan shook his head, amusement lingering around his eyes, and stepped back, leaving me alone in the middle of the room.

Lennox took a single step forward and fixed his eyes on me. This time I was ready for his questions, and ready for the lie when he asked me to give it. As soon as the oily black had faded from the red glow, proving the composition, questions fired at me from every direction.

I answered them as simply as I could. Even when the same ones were asked over and over again, and I had to bite my tongue to keep from giving a sharp retort. So many of the questions centered on my family that their images danced in front of my eyes, making it easier than usual to hold my peace.

"Enough!" said Lennox at last, reaching down to retrieve the pieces of parchment, crushing them between his long fingers. "I begin to think you doubt my composition."

Phyllida, who had asked no questions herself, nodded, as if unsurprised by the results. "I attended her family's home myself."

I drew in a quick breath and focused on her face, barely holding back the questions that wanted to pour from me.

"I interviewed not only her parents, but the midwife who delivered the girl—and delivered both her parents before her, apparently. They all swear the child can be no changeling." She shook her head. "If she has the blood of one of the families in her, it must be far back indeed. And no one else in her family has displayed any signs of control. I have left behind watchers in the village, but I must admit, I'll be surprised if they find anything to report."

I bit my lip. Kingslee had never had watchers. Did the whole town hate me now for bringing the seekers down on them?

Jessamine leaned forward, her black robe swishing around her. "Her blood is only one of the mysteries that has drawn us here today. And it is possible she does indeed have a mage in her ancestry. Although we had thought a much closer blood connection was needed to give the capacity for control, we have been known to be wrong before."

She darted a quick glance at Lorcan, and I saw their faces bore almost identical expressions. This was what she had really been waiting for. This was what had drawn her here, although the University Head had no place in the assessment or restraint of threats against the kingdom. She and Lorcan were driven by curiosity—a visible thirst to understand any new form of magic that might appear.

I shivered slightly. Somehow they scared me almost more than the others. To them I might not be a threat—but was I even a person?

"What interests me greatly," Jessamine continued, "is the assertion that this girl composed a controlled working—"

Lennox stirred, and she glanced at him.

"A partially controlled working, at least. Even you must admit that, Lennox, or we would have sent one of Phyllida's mages instead of one of yours to investigate in the first place."

Lennox nodded reluctantly, and Jessamine went on.

"As I was saying, if this girl has truly composed a controlled working using only spoken words—"

"A single spoken word," cut in Lorcan.

Jessamine shook her head, her eyes still on me. "Incredible. Such control. Such power. And the girl has no training whatsoever. The implications of this...the possibilities..." Her voice trailed away, and everyone else in the room sat up a little straighter.

I fisted my trembling hands into my robe.

"See for yourself," said Lorcan, gesturing toward me, although his eyes were on Jessamine.

She stood, an eager smile on her lips, and ripped her own tiny scroll.

Light surrounded me before rushing off to form a visible image. For the second time I watched the scene at the store unfold. Lorcan had said last time that he watched my hands, and this time I did the same. They hung at my sides, clearly empty, until I rose up onto my toes, a glazed look in my eyes. Then I thrust them out in front of me just before my mouth clearly formed the word *stop*.

The silvery wave of power once again burst forth, holding the men in place before shattering back against the windows of the store. The light faded and the image with it.

"It is as you said." Jessamine's eyes glowed with something that looked remarkably like glee. "Impossible."

CHAPTER 9

$\mathcal{A}$ babble of voices filled the room as each head consulted with their entourage or argued with one another. I watched them all, my gaze scanning the room until it caught on a new figure I hadn't noticed before. The only white robe in the room beside mine.

Prince Lucas sat in a chair near the door, no one on either side of him. When had he come in? How much had he seen? I swallowed and met his gaze boldly. I had nothing to be ashamed of.

His arms were crossed over his chest, his head resting back against the wall. His eyes held mine, a look of deep uncertainty on his face. It was an expression that didn't belong on his confident features, and it shook me. Almost as much as the wonder I saw lurking beneath it.

Even this prince who clearly hated me thought my power incredible. Everyone seemed to think so. But I had no idea where it had come from or how to do it again.

As our gazes held, his face slowly dropped back into its usual haughty arrogance. I nearly turned away from him, but before I could do so, his eyes swung to the side, fastening on the gold-robed General Thaddeus. I had stopped trying to follow the various conversations in the room, but my attention followed the prince's, and what I heard made me falter back a step.

My movement brought Lucas's eyes flicking back to me, but they immediately returned to the general.

"This cannot be allowed," General Thaddeus bellowed. "You all saw it with your own eyes. She unleashed power with a single word. Why, she may give a simple greeting tomorrow and bring the entire building down."

"Do you think so?" Jessamine turned curious eyes on me. "She has uttered many words since joining us in this room, and I have not felt the smallest stirring of power. Have any of you?" She didn't turn to look at any of them, clearly not expecting an answer. "This must be studied, and—"

"Studied? Certainly," interrupted Lorcan. "But she must also be taught control. And there can be no question that the Academy is the place for such an endeavor." He fixed Jessamine with a hard look, and she sat back in her seat with a small sigh.

Had she been about to make an argument for taking me to the University? For a moment the idea filled my mind. Jasper was at the University. But the look on her face made any excitement dwindle into nothing. Here at least I was a trainee. I suspected that at the University I would be nothing more than a test subject. Who knew if I would even be given the opportunity to search out my brother?

"I tell you, she is a threat to our security," cried the general. "She cannot be permitted to wander around the Academy."

"What exactly are you suggesting, Thaddeus?" asked Phyllida, who had so far been mostly silent in the conversation. "She has broken none of our laws. Or have you seen something I have missed, Lennox?" She raised an eyebrow at the Head of Law Enforcement.

Reluctantly he shook his head.

Thaddeus only looked more enraged. "That is beside the

point. The laws are there to protect us all. They serve us, not the other way around. Clearly she is a threat."

"Then, I repeat, what exactly are you suggesting?"

He deflated a little, but the eyes he fixed on me were inescapably cold. "It is unfortunate, of course. As it always is. But uncontrolled power must be dealt with swiftly and finally. There is only one way."

A loud gasp sounded through the room, and it took me a moment to realize it had come from me.

Then chaos broke out again as every black-robed mage in the room protested over the top of each other.

"You cannot truly consider such a thing," said Lorcan, nearest me. "Why, we haven't even begun to understand—"

"Enough." A new voice joined the throng, and everyone fell quiet. Lucas pushed himself off the wall and stood, staring coldly around the room. Although he was only seventeen, every adult present watched him in silence.

"There is no question of executing Elena."

My name sounded shocking on his lips, the first time it had been spoken in this room by anyone except me. Duke Lennox, who had looked almost as incensed as the general, looked away from me. Only Thaddeus continued to glare in my direction.

"But Your Highness…"

"No." Lucas showed no discomfort at speaking in such a way to this collection of important people. "There is much still to be considered here. Even beyond our theoretical understandings of how power can be controlled and worked." He fixed a stare on the general. "I am sure if General Griffith were here, it would already have occurred to him that we cannot afford to let such a new development pass us by without great further study."

Thaddeus's brow crinkled as he considered the prince's words. "My concern must always be for your safety, Your Highness, and that of your family."

Lucas nodded. "And your service is appreciated, Cousin."

I remembered that the queen had been a Stantorn just as Thaddeus was. Perhaps that had even been the reason for his appointment to the role of Head of the Royal Guards.

"You see the threat inherent in this new and alarming development," the prince continued. "As do I. And I find myself considering what the result might be if we are not the only ones to discover it."

He fell silent for a moment, and the whole room paused, considering his words.

"We have enemies at our borders, Thaddeus. You know that as well as I do. We cannot throw away this opportunity to study such a powerful force. Because you can be sure the Kallorwegians will not have done so, if such an opportunity has been presented to them."

Enough indrawn breaths sounded to tell me some at least in the room had yet to consider this possibility. I knew little about the front lines, but the thought of the Kallorwegian forces able to compose with spoken words left me terrified. Terrified, but I had to admit also excited. Could it be possible that there were others out there like me?

"I know Father sent you to assess the threat, Thaddeus," Lucas added quietly after a moment. "But I also know that he would see the same thing I do. Threat—yes—but also possibility. We must let the black robes do their work, and we may yet all yield great reward from it." His eyes swung back to me. "Perhaps even an end to Kallorwegian aggression."

I drew in a breath. I had been held just as captive by his words as everyone else in the room, and now my knees felt so weak I wished I had a chair to sink into. Could it be possible? If the mages here and at the University were able to unlock the secret of spoken magic, could it bring an end to the war before ever I had to enlist? Could I do that? Could I save both myself and Clemmy? The vision felt too alluring to be possible.

"The prince speaks with wisdom," said Lennox, his words

slow and considered. "There have been no laws broken, and no illicit reading. Neither Phyllida nor I have any jurisdiction here. And now that this girl is a trainee, she comes under the authority of Lorcan. I see no further role for myself."

He stood, and after a moment of hesitation, Phyllida mirrored his movements. She looked as if she meant to speak, but instead merely nodded to Lorcan and Jessamine before giving a half-bow to Prince Lucas and moving calmly from the room. Lennox trailed behind her, his Reds in a cluster around him.

Reluctantly the general also heaved himself to his feet. But he paused at the door to speak to the prince.

"Some threats are too dangerous to be played with, Your Highness. It's no good making her your pet. Not when she could be all of our undoing."

I had thought his words would offend Lucas, but the prince merely laughed.

"I am not in the habit of keeping pets, General."

Thaddeus glanced back at me, still frozen in the center of the room.

"I only hope not."

And then he was gone, and I didn't know whether to be incensed or relieved. For a moment Lucas watched me, and I couldn't read his expression. He had spoken up for me. Saved me even, perhaps. But he hadn't done it out of any consideration for me. And yet his eyes conveyed something now that I wished desperately I could understand.

And then he slipped from the room without another word.

"Well, that went as well as could be hoped, I think," said Jessamine from behind me.

"Indeed." Lorcan sounded thoughtful.

"Sending for the prince was an inspired idea," the University Head added. "He tipped the balance in our favor, I think."

"For now." Lorcan sighed. "But you heard Thaddeus at the end there. He wasn't convinced. We'll have a further battle on our hands, I'd wager."

"But that was to be expected." Jessamine didn't sound in the least downcast. "Thank goodness we have such strong numbers in council at the moment."

A throat clearing in front of me made me startle. Jocasta raised an eyebrow and gestured for me to follow her out of the room. I flushed at being caught so obviously listening to the conversation of the two heads.

And yet, as I followed her back to the library, my mouth once again took over from my brain and blurted out the question on my mind.

"What did she mean about having the numbers in council?"

Jocasta looked back at me and sighed. We entered the library together, and she pointed back to the side room I had so briefly occupied.

"I'll be there in a moment."

I didn't sit this time, too full of nervous energy. Instead I fidgeted, pacing around the room and brushing my hands along the backs of each chair. When Jocasta appeared in the door, she raised both eyebrows at me, and I sank into the nearest chair immediately.

Closing the door behind her, she sighed again.

"It's easy to forget how little you must know." She pointed at the parchment and pens she had just deposited on the table. "And this is only the start of it."

I looked at her expectantly, and she rubbed her fingers against her temple.

"You know of the Mage Council, at least?"

I nodded.

"Good. I thought they must teach that much in the schools. Well at the moment, members of Callinos hold four of the positions. Academy Head, University Head, Head of the Seekers, and Head of the Healers. General Thaddeus may talk loudly, but

Stantorn hold only his position and Head of the Creators. No one from Devoras was there today, but generally they can be counted on to side with Stantorn."

She paused and frowned. "Although with the prince's arguments, you never know. General Griffith might be persuaded…" She broke off and shook herself.

"The Head of the Growers also comes from Devoras, so that pits the two sides at equal numbers—four against four. So Ellington is most often the deciding vote these days. And Prince Lucas seemed to convince Duke Lennox. The other Ellington on the council—the Head of the Wind Workers—will follow his lead if he chooses to side with Callinos."

She gave me a considering look. "And that is before the support of the royals themselves. If the prince is right about his father, then it seems your position here is safe for the moment."

"So reassuring," I muttered without thinking.

Jocasta laughed, although it wasn't exactly a friendly sound. "Welcome to the world of the great families. You'll learn to live in it, as the rest of us have."

I glanced up at her. Did she resent it? Did others from the minor mage families? But if Jocasta saw the question in my eyes, she had no intention of answering it. She briskly tapped the pile of parchment in front of her.

"So. Reading and writing. You have a lot to learn."

And somehow, impossibly, the events of the last hour were driven from my mind. Finally I was to unlock the mysteries of the written word.

CHAPTER 10

I soon realized my error. I was clearly a long way from being able to unlock any great mysteries.

I had watched with great excitement as Jocasta first put her pen to parchment, but nothing happened except that black lines appeared where she pressed the tip against the paper. I looked around the room, wondering if I had missed something.

"Elena."

I looked back at her. She rolled her eyes.

"These are prepared parchments for regular writing." She pointed at a line of words already written across the top of the page. "See. Nothing is going to happen."

"I don't understand. Writing releases power. You just wrote. Something must have happened."

She sighed and muttered to herself. "I keep forgetting the basics." Looking up at me, she asked, "How do you think mages prevent the power from spilling out in unintended ways before their composition is complete?"

I blinked at her. "I don't know. I've never seen a mage work a composition. But isn't that the whole point? That they have control? They're the only ones who do."

"We have the ability to control the power, yes. But we still need to learn how to exercise it. We need to bind each composition. The first thing any trainee learns when they begin studying composition is how to compose binding words. Those words hold the power until the full composition has been written. Then it is completed with the words *end binding*. They release the power, ensuring the working takes the intended shape and doesn't just flow into the first few words."

I chewed my lip. That actually made sense. And it explained what Redmond had been talking about in the class. The other trainees had been starting with binding words. My eyes flicked to the written line across the top of Jocasta's parchment.

"Redmond said something about expanding it. The binding. So that the parchment could be used for regular writing. Is that what that is?" I pointed at the line of words.

Jocasta nodded. I felt pleased with myself, but she gave no sign of approval.

"It is possibly the most simple of compositions—an expansion of the basic binding words. In this case, the purpose of the composition itself is to bind the parchment permanently. To make it safe to write on." She gestured at the door behind her. "How do you think we have books and scrolls at all? Any mages who sign up to the creators discipline spend large chunks of their first year at the printers, preparing the paper for the books. An apprenticeship of sorts."

Her mouth quirked up. "As for the rest of us, we prepare our own parchments as needed. That's how mage children learn to write before their control has solidified at age sixteen. Their parents prepare parchment for them."

I stared down at the table, my hands balling into fists. So anyone could write? Without unleashing uncontrolled power? All it took was one of these parchments? For a moment, my vision blurred.

"Then how come we aren't all taught to write using such

parchments?" The words came bursting out of me before I could control them.

Jocasta's eyebrows quirked together. She regarded me silently as I tried to control my breathing.

"There are too few of us," she said at last.

"What?" I looked up at her.

"There are too few mages. We would have to spend all day creating safe parchments and books. And then who would heal or build or ensure the crops grow? Who would defend us against Kallorway's mages? And even if we could do all of that and make enough safe parchment as well, it would be too dangerous."

"What do you mean?" My breathing was still ragged, anger fueling me.

"It's the same reason non-bloods are not permitted to learn to read." She sounded matter-of-fact. "Reading by itself carries no danger and would greatly enhance the lives of many. So why is it not taught?"

She looked at me steadily, and I forced myself to take a deep, slow breath. I knew the answer to this one. This we learned about in school.

"Because reading leads to writing. If a commonborn learns how to read, there's too much temptation to write something. Just once. Or cases of accidental writing. Tracing a word without thinking. That sort of thing."

"Exactly." Jocasta nodded. "And one mistake from a non-blood can level a whole village…Ardann can't take the risk that even one in a thousand will make a mistake just once in their lives. How much worse would it be if everyone was taught to write as well? One absent-minded moment. One slip of the hand on the wrong surface." She shook her head. "No. We are all safer this way."

"But only some of us bear the burden of it," I muttered. But the words were too quiet for her to hear, or else she chose to ignore them.

I swallowed and tried to bend my mind back to the lesson. I knew this was the way my world worked. There was nothing new here, no real surprises. But it still burned inside me.

Jocasta wrote a series of letters, a gap between each one. It didn't look like the words already written on the top of the page, most of which were formed by a grouping of multiple letters. When she finished, she handed the parchment to me.

"This is a list of all the letters we use. When arranged into different combinations, they form words. We call it the alphabet. You'll need to learn this first."

~

"I think it's going to be a long time before I can rejoin the composition class," I said glumly to Coralie over breakfast the next morning. As at the previous meals, the two of us sat alone at one of the tables in the first year row. At least today I had managed to get out of bed at the first bell and make it down to the dining hall in time to eat before class.

"Jocasta is tough, but she's good," she said, mouth half full of egg. "If you spend your whole afternoon with her, you'll be reading and writing in no time."

"If I make it through combat first." I groaned and put my head on the table.

Coralie patted my back. "There, there. You'll survive. I'm fairly sure after he had to step in yesterday that Thornton won't let you pair with Weston again. And I'll try to shake off Araminta more quickly next time, too. She was just terrified she was going to end up with Weston herself, poor thing."

I raised my head and noticed the same speculative gleam in her eyes as had been there at the evening meal the night before.

"Oh, go on," I said with a sigh. "Whatever it is, just ask me."

She bounced on her seat, her eyes shining. "Lucas disappeared part way through composition class. A servant came for him. And when he returned, he looked very...thoughtful. Or something. I'm not the best at reading his expressions. But I heard one of the older trainees say they saw half the council arrive. And someone else said that it all had something to do with you."

She fixed me with an expectant look.

"Was there a question in there?" I asked weakly.

She rolled her eyes and gave me the same expectant look.

"Fine." I sighed again. "Yes, I was called out of the library to be tested. The University Head was there, and also General Thaddeus, and the heads of law enforcement and the seekers."

"Oooh," she said. "The Reds and the Grays. They were serious, then."

I massaged my head and dropped my voice. "Of course they're serious, Coralie. I did a magical composition with a spoken word. Me. A non-blood, as you all say. None of it makes any sense. And I have no idea how I did it, and no idea if I can ever do it again, and I'm just waiting for someone to kick me out. Or arrest my family or something. And I have no idea why any of this is happening!"

I bit my lip and covered my eyes with my hands. I hadn't intended the outburst. Coralie patted my back again until I peeked at her from between my fingers. Her eyes were wide.

"So, are they going to?"

"Going to what?"

"Kick you out?"

I groaned. "No, apparently not. Execute me, maybe. But not kick me out, it seems."

"Execute you!"

My shoulders slumped. "Apparently I'm safe for now. Something about Callinos convincing Ellington and overruling Stantorn and Devoras."

Coralie nodded as if my words were entirely understandable. "That makes sense. I told you those Stantorns are a bad lot." A look of dismay crossed her face. "Except for the queen, of course. I don't mean her. Or the princess. Or Lucas."

"Stop now," I told her kindly. "Before it gets worse."

She groaned and then laughed. "My mother is always telling me to think before I speak—but that's so slow."

This time I laughed. I could relate, although in my case it was speaking up when I should be silent and saying the wrong thing to the wrong person, while in Coralie it seemed to result in a never-ending flow of words. My amusement stopped abruptly when Coralie seized my arm.

"We're almost the last ones here! We'd better hurry."

I looked around and realized she was right. The other trainees had disappeared while we were absorbed in our conversation. Together we hurried from the dining hall and made our way outside, winding around the building toward the training areas at the back. Coralie bombarded me with questions the whole way until I gave her a full account of my testing.

"Wow, that's amazing!" she said. "I wish I could just speak a composition. Think how much easier it would be."

I gave her a loaded look, and she laughed.

"Maybe you're right, that could be a bit dangerous."

"A bit?" I shook my head. "Be glad you don't live in fear of opening your mouth one day and blowing up the Academy."

She just rolled her eyes. "Don't be so dramatic! You didn't blow up anything last time, did you? There's a reason we risk teaching our children how to read and write before sixteen. Even if they make a mistake and write something in the wrong place, it doesn't have as disastrous results. There's always some measure of control. And you're obviously the same." She paused. "But different, of course. I can see why Lorcan and Duchess Jessamine are so fascinated by you."

"Thanks," I grumbled, "but I'd prefer they go be interested in someone else."

"Someone's grouchy this morning," she said, bumping my

shoulder. "It's not all bad. Lucas stood up for you, didn't he? That's got to count for something."

"He didn't stand up for me. He stood up for the value in studying me. Not the same thing."

Coralie waved away my objections.

"He's still the prince."

I gave her an unimpressed look, and she kept going.

"Believe me, there was much private jubilation among our year mates when the news came out about..." She frowned. "I keep forgetting you don't know anything."

I squawked, and she grinned at me. "Well nothing that matters, anyway. It's like this. We all know each other. Even if we don't live in the capital. Everyone's been here for various celebrations or gatherings, so we all take the opportunity to scope out our year mates. Everything is more informal at the Academy than at court, so your years here are your chance to make connections that might serve you later in life. Especially for those from minor families like mine."

She paused for a brief breath before rushing on, trying to fit in as many words as possible before we arrived at our training yard.

"You're supposed to start at the Academy the autumn after you turn sixteen. But Lucas is seventeen already. He was supposed to be in the year above us. Only then the royal family got the chance to send that delegation to the Sekali Empire last year."

I vaguely remembered something about an Ardannian delegation to our vast northern neighbor, but I didn't know any of the details. I had only heard about it at all because the invitation was so unusual. The empire didn't usually show any interest in the affairs of either Ardann or Kallorway. Coralie rushed on, not bothering to stop and explain.

"Naturally they didn't want to risk sending Crown Princess Lucienne—being heir to the throne and all that. Who knows what those Sekalis might do? But they couldn't offend them by sending a delegation without a single member of the royal family. So Lucas went. Which meant he couldn't start at the Academy until this year. Our year."

She shook her head. "Which means we get to call him *Lucas* and spend every day with him for four years. Obviously I have no great hopes of becoming best friends with a prince. But I'm fairly sure Natalya and Lavinia, at least, have visions of themselves as princess one day. And I'm sure Calix and Weston are looking to utilize the opportunity, too. Well, probably everyone really. If they're honest."

Her words cut off abruptly as we arrived at the yard and hopped inside the fence just as the bell rang. We really needed to get better at this running on time thing. Thornton regarded us both with disapproval but said nothing. Instead he instructed us all to run, and I took off with pleasure, glad for the opportunity to stretch my legs.

Several taller trainees soon rushed past me, and I let them without trying to increase my own pace, settling comfortably into the back of the pack. From here I could observe most of the others, freshly armed with the information I had extracted from Coralie the night before.

The tall, elegant Dariela—the Ellington who Coralie had predicted would top the class—led the group. According to Coralie, Ellingtons were generally on the friendlier side, but Dariela seemed entirely cold from what I had seen. And not just toward me. Weston kept pace with her, but neither looked at the other or spoke.

Close behind them came a pack of three, occasionally joking among themselves. Natalya and Calix were twins, apparently, although you wouldn't guess it to look at them, with Natalya so dark and Calix so fair. They were the daughter and son of General Griffith of Devoras, the Head of the Armed Forces. Which meant I would hardly have been searching out their company, even if they didn't both send me poisonous glances at every opportunity.

Their shadow was Lavinia—Weston's cousin and another Stantorn. And Natalya's best friend, apparently.

Behind them ran the two Callinos cousins—Saffron and Finnian. They looked similar, the family connection clear, and their dark gold skin marked them as northerners. I hadn't yet heard Saffron speak, although Finnian kept directing jokes at her which occasionally earned a smile.

Which left only one other trainee in the group ahead of me. Despite all my intentions, my eyes lingered on the prince. He ran with easy strides, and given his tall, muscled form, I suspected he could have pushed ahead of Dariela and Weston if he wished to do so. He seemed content to run in the middle of the pack, however.

As my eyes lingered on his back, I couldn't help my mind running back over the new revelations. Even here in the relaxed environment of the Academy, the instructors gave him special deference. And I had seen him silence a room full of the most senior and powerful mages in the kingdom.

But Coralie's words rang in my ears. *Who knows what those Sekalis might do?* And given that uncertainty, the prince's family had decided he was the one to send. The expendable one. Perhaps there had been no choice. No other option. Although it seemed incredible for a family of the most powerful mages in the land— rulers of an entire kingdom—to be without options. But I knew nothing of the constraints of royalty, and Coralie had said that someone had to go.

In spite of myself, I felt a pang of sympathy. I knew what it was like to have a family constrained by circumstance to view you as the most expendable. The one worth risking. And I didn't like the sense of fellow feeling. Not with an arrogant prince who had known nothing but privilege and power his whole life. Who had never had to watch his younger sister fight to breathe or say farewell to his older brother, knowing he might not see him for years. Who had never been given the chance to be anything in life but an illiterate soldier. And then—if I was lucky—shopkeeper.

No, I had nothing in common with a prince.

I continued my mental review of the first years. The remaining three—the three from minor families—all ran behind me. In Coralie's case because she was trying to bolster Araminta with a constant stream of encouragement. Clarence, on the other hand, was the tallest of the first year trainees, and should have been leading us all. But the pale tone of his skin suggested he wasn't used to spending much time outdoors, and his breathing sounded labored.

Well, that makes one thing I'm not worst in the class at. I shook my head at my own foolishness. I was hardly going to win a place here by running laps.

And that could not have been more obvious as soon as we were called on to pair up again. Coralie managed to extract herself from Araminta, leaving the girl to pair with Clarence. Both looked resigned at the prospect, despite making an odd-looking pair as the tallest and shortest in the class.

But as soon as the sparring exercises began, it was obvious both of them had more experience and training than me. Coralie kept up an almost constant whispered stream of instruction, falling silent only when Thornton loomed over us. I got several bruises while he watched, Coralie wincing in apology each time one of her blows landed.

By the end of the session, I actually thought I'd made progress, however. Thanks to her assistance, of course. That didn't mean I'd managed to land a blow on her, but I felt no need to visit Acacia, at least.

"I'd be lost here without you," I told her as we made our way back to lunch.

She flushed. "Oh, you'd have found your way, I'm sure."

But I could see my words had pleased her. When I smiled warmly at her, she laughed and nudged my shoulder.

"Besides, you can *speak* compositions. One day you'll be the most powerful and illustrious of us all, and I'll get to say I was your best friend at the Academy."

"More like only friend."

"Just give them time. They'll see."

Natalya and Lavinia sauntered past us.

"I can't believe she's still here," Natalya said loudly to her friend. "I keep waiting for someone to admit the whole thing is some sort of joke."

Lavinia nodded, glancing sideways at me. "She can't do anything. Sure doesn't seem like some sort of non-blood prodigy to me."

Coralie wrinkled her nose as they disappeared ahead of us. "Some of them, anyway."

"You know I have no idea how I did that one working, right?" I asked. "At the moment I can't even read, let alone compose."

"You'll figure it out," she said, full of more confidence in me than I felt for myself.

Nothing in the following days seemed to bear out her assurance, however. I felt not the slightest stirring of power inside me, and the progress on my literacy felt painfully slow. After my testing, I had half-expected a bevy of black-robed mages to follow me around, observing every move I made. But it seemed they had all decided I was to do nothing but focus on reading and writing for now.

The seventh day of every week was designated as a rest day without classes, and I had been looking forward to the break. But Jocasta soon enlightened me.

"You won't have combat, so we can work all morning as well as all afternoon."

When I groaned, she fixed me with a sharp look. "This isn't

how I want to be spending my rest day, Elena. I would have expected you, at least, to show some motivation to learn."

I swallowed my dismay after that and redoubled my efforts. She was right, of course. I did want to learn to read. But it was hard to maintain the enthusiasm when, instead of reading books, I was reciting the alphabet or sounding out a list of simple words like cat. At least I would have a day off from Thornton's disapproving looks and Coralie's apologetic blows.

Something I was especially grateful for when I suddenly found myself confronted with Dariela instead of Coralie at the last combat lesson of the week. The tall girl made no extra effort to inflict pain, as Weston had done, but neither did she soften her blows like Coralie. She didn't whisper instructions, either, so I had to watch the other pairs to work out what I should be doing. With the divided attention, I could hardly be surprised to find myself covered in bruises by the end of the lesson.

Dariela just sighed and wandered away as soon as we were released, having not spoken a word to me the entire time.

Coralie tried to convince me to visit Acacia again, but I resisted. Perhaps the bruises would remind me to work harder and pay more attention. Because even if I was never going to be a mage, there was still a good chance I would end up as a soldier. I should be grateful for the opportunity to learn these skills.

Still, after a night of sleeping on my aches, I gladly welcomed Jocasta's sighs and impatient looks over Thornton's glowers and incomprehensible instructions. At least the bruises would have a little time to fade before new ones were added to their number.

By the end of the day, I wasn't so sure, however. My brain felt as if it had been wrung out and then trampled on, and I couldn't even muster the energy to ask Coralie how her day off had gone. Thankfully she didn't need any asking and chattered through the whole of the evening meal about her visit to one of the city markets. Apparently her family were still in the capital after having traveled up from Abalene to deliver her to the Academy.

I wished I could ask her to hire a messenger on my behalf the next time she ventured out, but I still had no coin to pay for a message, nor any way to acquire any. Phyllida, the Head of the Seekers, had said she visited my family herself. Had she given them any news of me? Reassured them at least that I was alive?

Was Clementine terrified now? Did she think she would have to enlist, after all? But as I lay in bed that night, I knew that my sweet younger sister was far more likely to be terrified for me. And while I couldn't send her a message, I could work hard and do everything I could to fit in here. To prove to these people that I had control, that I wasn't a danger. I just needed them to let me stay until I turned eighteen and could enlist.

But before I could start learning how to compose as they did, and with control, I had to learn to read and write.

And so I worked harder than ever—too tired, both physically and mentally, to do more than collapse into bed straight after dinner each night. Until finally the day came when Jocasta announced my penmanship to be legible and my comprehension sufficient.

"And it's about time," she muttered. "I do have other duties, you know."

I was far too elated to be downcast by her attitude. I had done it. I couldn't read every word, and my spelling was atrocious, but I was assured time and practice would improve both of those.

"And for now, you'll only attempt the simple binding compositions. Ones which you can copy," Jocasta explained.

I could barely grip the pen in my hand for the excitement. I didn't care how simple the working. I would finally have the chance to prove myself. To prove that I wasn't a danger, or a threat, or even just unutterably stupid, as most of my year mates still seemed to think.

Pressing down firmly with the pen on the unmarked parchment, I listened carefully to Jocasta's words.

"As you begin to shape the words, you'll feel the power

building around you. Write that first phrase quickly. The one you've been practicing on the safe sheet. As soon as you complete it, you should feel the pressure of the power lessen. It will still be there, but holding in place, waiting rather than building. Well, it's still building but not pressing down trying to break free."

I nodded and waited to see if she had more to say.

"Well, come on then," she said. "Sitting there won't achieve anything."

I took a deep breath and formed the first letter. Just as she had said, I felt a rush of pulsing power as I had so many nights ago in front of my parents' store. My hand hurried to form the rest of the letters of the short phrase, but I had barely finished the first word when the power exploded outward in every direction, and the room came crashing down around us.

CHAPTER 11

*E*verything around me was darkness and pain. A distant sound filtered through, but I struggled to make sense of it through the ringing in my ears. Then the crushing pressure on my legs eased and light pierced my eyes. I blinked, too full of pain to move or even speak.

"I found her! Both of them!" called a voice, and a moment later a cool mist pressed against my skin, seeping in.

"Ahhhh." I closed my eyes, going limp with relief at the easing of the pain.

"Don't move," said a vaguely familiar voice, before cool mist flooded over me again.

Something popped in my leg and in my chest, and I yelped, although it didn't actually hurt.

"Keep still," the voice warned again, and I opened my eyes to see it was Acacia bending over me. "I just need to do one more." She ripped a long scroll, and a third layer of mist settled over me.

I tried to turn my mind from the grinding sensation that filled me by looking around.

"Jocasta? Is she..."

"She fared slightly better than you." Acacia smiled at me. "I already gave her the pain composition, but I'll go finish patching her up now." She paused and turned back to me. "Just remember to take it slow. You might be healed, but your body will still be in shock."

I nodded and sat up, wincing as my head spun from the sudden movement. Jocasta lay prone on the ground, her face white, and a pool of blood around her left arm. I bit my lip and reminded myself Acacia had said she would be fine. The purple-robed healer bent over her and selected a parchment. In front of my eyes the gash healed, the arm returning to its usual color and shape, except for the leftover streaks of red across it.

"Excuse me," said a new voice, and I looked over to find a man I didn't recognize looking at me with some discomfort. He wore a robe in an attractive shade of peach, and it took me several moments to place the color. The creators. Where had he come from?

"Excuse me," he repeated. "Do you think you could move out of the way?"

"Oh." I pushed myself to my feet, swaying for a moment at another head rush. Now that I looked around properly, I could see that many of the larger chunks of stone had already been moved, but the space around me still looked like a demolition was underway.

I picked my way through the scattered pieces of stone and broken furniture, until I stepped through a hole that had once been the wall of the room and into the main library. Several books and scrolls lay scattered across the floor, many of them torn. I bit my lip at the sight of them, even though it looked as if only two sections of shelving had been damaged.

Only two. I shook my head. I was starting to think like them. Only recently that would have represented more books than I had ever seen, or even imagined. I turned back to watch as the creator selected a large number of parchments from inside his orange robe, muttering to himself as he laid them out in a row on a stone in front of him.

As soon as Acacia emerged, supporting Jocasta on her shoulder, he began to rip them in quick succession. While I watched in amazement, the furniture re-formed, the stones flying up into the air and re-joining into square blocks, and the books mending themselves back into wholeness.

"How is he doing that?" I whispered.

"With a great deal of study and skill," said a voice at my side. I wheeled around to see Lorcan also watching the rebuilding. "We can be grateful that such a senior member of the creator discipline was visiting the Academy today."

I bit my lip, glancing between the Academy Head and the destruction I had unleashed. Had he come to tell me I had failed? That if I could not exercise control, then maybe General Thaddeus was right about me?

"I take it you attempted a composition?"

I started at Lorcan's question since he hadn't taken his eyes from the work of the creator.

"Yes," I managed after a moment's pause. "Just a simple binding. But I didn't manage more than a word." I wanted to defend myself, but there was nothing to say. I had done exactly as Jocasta had instructed, and it hadn't worked. There was no more to it than that.

"Interesting. I felt no control in it at all. Not like your previous working."

"That was no poorly executed composition," said Jocasta's familiar and rather caustic voice behind us. Her tone relieved me despite her words. Surely she must be fully recovered from whatever I had done to speak like that.

Lorcan wheeled around to regard her. "I must confess it felt the same way to me. That was the uncontrolled explosion of power of a non-blood attempting to write."

Jocasta nodded. "That it was. And she had barely even

managed one word, as she said. Elena can no more control the power of written words than any other non-blood."

I looked between them. So this was it, then. They would declare me a fraud and—what? Send me home? Execute me? Lock me away?

"Jessamine will want to know of this," said Lorcan, his eyes growing distant. "The puzzle grows more interesting. Does it rule out the possibility of distant mage ancestry? Or could the intervening generations have morphed the power in such a way that—"

"Excuse me," I interrupted, unable to take the suspense. "What does that mean? For me? Am I going to be…expelled?"

"Expelled?" Lorcan looked genuinely taken aback. "Certainly not, although Jessamine would be glad to hear of such a thing, I'm sure. She would have you snatched up and inside the University before either of us could blink. In fact, I'm sure I shall be receiving a visit from her at any moment. There's no way she didn't feel that, and she'll be dying to know if it was you."

He shook his head. "It wouldn't surprise me to have Phyllida descending on us, as well. So I had best excuse myself in preparation." He began to walk away. "Perhaps Jessamine will have some thoughts on the question of—" He broke off suddenly as if remembering me behind him and spun around to regard me.

"Naturally you must refrain from any future writing." He smiled wryly. "For all our sakes. It seems your previous use of power was not merely some small aberration from an otherwise normal mage with a rather unusual background." He shook his head wonderingly. "No, you are something new entirely."

He once again disappeared into his own thoughts before abruptly looking up again. "Which means you must consider yourself under the same strictures as all non-bloods. No writing!" He took a single step and then paused again. "You can continue with the reading, though, of course. No point trying to stop that now, and you have much study before you. I leave you in Jocasta's capable hands." And with that, he hurried from the library.

I blinked at the empty doorway for several seconds.

"Is that..."

"What he's always like when confronted with some new and exciting intellectual stimulation?" Jocasta completed my sentence. "Yes. And Jessamine is even worse. I'm sure he's right that she'll be over here in no time, and then the two of them will be in discussion for hours."

I turned slowly to face her. "I'm sorry, Jocasta. Truly sorry. I didn't mean to..."

"Of course you didn't." Her brisk voice dismissed my apology. "I should have known better than to trust you could do it. I should have set up some sort of shield."

"Could you do that?" I couldn't keep the awe out of my voice.

Her mouth twisted. "It might take me a full page, but I daresay I could have managed something adequate." She watched the last of the reconstruction effort. "I suppose we can just be glad that in one way, at least, you are like a young mage and not a non-blood."

I gave her a questioning look.

"Your flameout was a great deal less destructive than it could have been. Like the occasional accidents of our own children before they turn sixteen and develop the necessary control. Thank goodness Acacia was on hand."

I nodded fervently at that while Jocasta regarded me thoughtfully.

"I had hoped to get you caught up to your composition class, but naturally that will be impossible now. Your reading still needs work." She gave me a knowing look. "Lots of work. But if we are to get to the bottom of your power, I suppose you will need at least a working knowledge of composition as well."

She rubbed a blood-streaked hand across her eyes. "From tomorrow, you may rejoin your class."

I opened my mouth to protest, and she cut me off.

"Not to participate, of course. Don't you touch a pen while you're there, lest you bring the Grays down around our ears. But you can listen and learn. And I'll assign you reading practice to be going on with." She narrowed her eyes at me. "I think I've about earned my afternoons back, don't you?"

I could do nothing but nod, my eyes caught on the red that still stained her clothing and body.

"Oh relax, child," she said, her voice testy. "I've been fully healed. Now be gone with you."

"Elena! What happened?" Coralie jumped on me as soon as I appeared in the dining hall.

I shook my head, but she latched onto my arm and clearly had no intention of letting go until she had the full story. I slid into my usual seat and looked around. We usually sat at the table alone, but this time the next two tables were empty as well. And even the corresponding table in the next row.

"We heard an explosion," said Coralie breathlessly. "And they're saying you—but I told them you would never—"

I nodded miserably.

"Wait. You did?" She stared at me, and I hunched my shoulders forward, filling my plate as quickly as I could.

"So what happened?" She gave an exasperated sigh when I still said nothing. "Come on, Elena girl. Use your words!"

I looked up at her quickly, shock on my face, and she rolled her eyes.

"Not like that. I just mean speak to me!"

I sighed and looked around again before lowering my voice. "I used my words, that's what happened. I tried to compose for the first time, all right? I barely got one word of the binding words down and the room exploded."

Coralie rocked back, for once too shocked to speak.

"So I guess everyone was right. I don't have control. And I am a danger."

"But they're letting you stay?" She looked around wildly as if she expected Grays to come bursting into the dining hall and carry me away.

"Apparently. For now, at least. Lorcan seemed to find the whole thing intriguing more than anything."

My eyes caught on the prince as he strode into the room. His eyes found me quickly, latching on as they hadn't done for weeks now. His step faltered for a brief instant before he continued in to take a seat beside Calix. His look had been accusatory—did he regret speaking up for me to the council members? But something else had lurked there as well. A look that said I was a puzzle he couldn't quite figure out.

I swung back around to Coralie. Well that made two of us. I couldn't work him out and had given up trying.

"So...what does that mean?" asked Coralie, oblivious to the moment that had just passed between Lucas and me.

"It means I'm a regular old non-blood, after all." I stabbed at the food in front of me.

Coralie snorted.

"Well, maybe not completely regular." I sighed. "But no writing for me."

The other trainees had grown accustomed to my presence in my weeks at the Academy, but this new incident had the whispers following me again. Except this time no one leaned forward to look. Instead they all drew back, leaving a wide band of space around me wherever I went.

At combat, a wide space separated Coralie and me from the other pairs, and when we ran laps, I no longer ran in the middle of the pack since even the slowest of the class did their best to avoid me. I ignored them all, reminding myself over and over that I was not a danger to anyone. As long as I didn't try to write, there would be no more explosions.

I hoped.

And since Thornton had introduced staffs to our pair exercises, distracting myself was easier than it would otherwise have been. With a weapon in play, I felt like an untrained idiot again, all my progress with unarmed blows gone in an instant.

But no distraction helped when I stood outside the composition classroom. Natalya and Lavinia walked past me while I hesitated, both giving me horrified glances as they did so. I had needed to stop off at the library for reading material from Jocasta on my way to class, so I was on my own and would no doubt be the last one in. But the bell would ring any second, so lingering out here would only cause more problems.

Taking a deep breath, I pretended a confidence I didn't feel and strode into the room. My eyes fixed on Coralie, and I slid into the seat beside her before I absorbed the rest of the room.

Unlike previously, when only the first two rows of desks had been taken, the students had now rearranged themselves. The desk I shared with Coralie was in the second column of desks, in the second row back, as it had been before. But now the entire front row had moved themselves over to the fourth column of desks on the far side of the room. And Weston, short a desk in that column, sat in the third column in the last row. In other words, they had all positioned themselves as far from me as possible.

I bit my lip and looked down at my desk, willing myself not to flush. A rustle of whispers had greeted my arrival, but when Redmond took his place at the front of the room, Natalya spoke up more loudly.

"Is it really safe for us to be in an enclosed space with her?" She put her hands on her hips. "The Academy is supposed to be a place for those with *control*." Her narrowed eyes turned to glare at me.

I couldn't help responding to her tone, my back straightening as I glared back at her. This wasn't really about what had happened in the library. She had never even considered giving me a chance.

Redmond looked slowly from her to me, speculation in his eyes. How much did he want to be rid of me? Enough to defy Lorcan?

But before he could speak, the door opened, and I remembered we were still a student short.

The prince strode into the room, and this time his steps didn't falter, although he took in the situation in a glance. For a brief moment silence fell over the room as twelve pairs of eyes watched him. He gave no indication of being aware of our interest as he slid calmly into his previous seat directly across the thin aisle from me.

An audible breath sounded from Natalya before Lavinia gripped her arm, and she subsided. Redmond watched Lucas for another second and then cleared his throat and began the lesson. A rustle sounded through the trainees, but no one protested, and I slumped into my seat as Redmond droned on.

Sneaking a sideways glance at the prince, I examined his face. He gave every appearance of earnestly listening to our instructor. Yet once again he had defused anger and threat directed toward me—and this time merely with his presence. Had he known what he was walking into? Had he heard Natalya's words from outside the door?

And if he had, what did it mean? That the royals continued to side with Lorcan, despite what I had done? That I was truly to be permitted to stay—for now, at least?

It took me a long time to focus on the lesson, and even when I did, I could make little sense of it. Unsurprisingly the other trainees had moved past binding words. I looked blindly down at the book I still clutched in my hand. I had been too focused on the upcoming class to take a good look at it when

Jocasta handed it to me, but I tried to puzzle out the words now.

THE. That word was familiar and easy to read. B-A-S-I-C-S. I sounded it out in my head. Basics. Well, thank goodness for that. Clearly I needed basics. OF. Another easy one. The next word was long, but it was a familiar one since Jocasta and I had gone over it many times. COMPOSITION. The Basics of Composition.

My hands gripped the leather binding more tightly. *Thank you, Jocasta,* I whispered in my mind. I promised myself that no matter how tired I felt, I would dedicate all my spare time to puzzling out the words inside the tome. Somehow I would catch up. I might not be able to participate, but I would at least find a way to understand.

CHAPTER 12

To my surprise, composition class ended well before the evening meal. The prince was the first one out the door, but the other students soon followed, leaving Coralie and me alone in the empty classroom.

"Does it always finish this early?" I asked her.

She nodded. "From second year, trainees have to choose two disciplines and pursue further study in them. You can change them each year or keep the same two the whole way through. So the older trainees are all busy studying right now. Mercifully, the Academy takes pity on us first years and we get this time off."

"Unless you have Jocasta as your personal mentor."

Coralie chuckled. "She's tough, I know. But better her than Thornton or Redmond!"

To that I could willingly agree.

"So what are you going to study next year?" I asked her.

"I don't know. I can't decide. I guess I'll keep switching them each year until I find something I love. It will put me a little behind when I eventually join a discipline after the Academy, but better that than being stuck with something I end up hating."

I nodded. It would never come to that for me, of course. Even if I survived my three years of conscription, I would come out the other end in a no-man's land. Neither normal common folk nor graduated mage. But that was a problem much too far away to be worth worrying over. I had a lot to survive before I made it there.

"Do all mages join a discipline?" I asked, still curious, even if it didn't apply to me.

"You don't have to, but most do." She made a face. "I don't suppose someone like Natalya would have to, with her father being general and all. They're one of the most prominent Devoras families and rich as anything. But someone like me?" She shrugged. "I'll need to join one if I want to draw a salary from the crown. My family isn't rich enough to appreciate me lying around doing nothing and earning nothing, and I'd rather be part of a discipline than end up selling basic compositions to non-bloods rich enough to buy them."

"You can do that?" I stared at her in astonishment. Kingslee didn't have any resident mages to purchase such a thing from, and if any of the families who made the trip into the capital had ever bought one, they hadn't mentioned it to me. Likely none of us were rich enough to do so.

"Of course." She gave me a strange look and then shook her head. "You really need to read that." She tapped the book lying on the desk in front of me. "Most mages bind their personal collection of compositions so only they can release them. But there's nothing to prevent a mage composing a more general working. Some of the least skilled mages can't even get accepted into a discipline at all. So they sell all sorts of compositions."

I looked down at the book on my desk. There was so much that I still didn't understand. I had never attempted to read anything but the worksheets Jocasta wrote for me, and the idea of struggling through all the words that must fill the pages in front of me filled me with dread. But another part of me itched to open it and begin.

"Of course, there's also the free spirits," Coralie added. "I had a great-uncle like that. Didn't like the idea of taking orders and was perfectly content to sell compositions. My brother thought he was the family embarrassment, but I always liked him. He made me laugh."

I sighed. Since I couldn't write, let alone actually compose, such a path was hardly open to me. But I knew it would have been the one I chose. I had no interest in a lifetime of taking orders from some arrogant mage who would no doubt look down on me as inferior.

"It's prestige that drives those from the richer families into the disciplines, of course," said Coralie. "There's no other path to a proper title and a seat on the Mage Council. That will be enough for Natalya and Calix and the like, I'm sure."

I absentmindedly stroked the leather of my book binding. Coralie's eyes dropped down to it.

"Would you like some help with that?"

I brightened, and then paused. "Are you sure? It'll be horribly boring for you."

She grinned. "I don't mind. It's not as if I have anything else pressing to do."

As the days ticked by, the weather growing colder and colder, both my reading and my understanding of composition improved. Things I had seen or heard began to make sense to me —like why a longer composition was a source of shame—or at least a marker of limited skill in the particular discipline. In composition class, the first year trainees wrote long passages for even the most simple of compositions. It ensured their workings took the exact shape they intended.

But as they grew in skill and control, they would learn to make them shorter and shorter, channeling the power with more precision. Trainees loved to tell stories about great mages of the past, some of them rumored to be so strong and so skilled, they could control a composition with a single word.

The story I heard repeated most often was that of the great general who won a decisive battle against Kallorway. He had been injured, near death, lying on the ground, his store of compositions exhausted, when he had composed a working great enough to win the day by scratching a single word into the dirt.

But that had been long ago in a different war, and I had to wonder how much the story had grown as it was passed down through the years. Still, such tales always made me uncomfortable. The more I learned, the more I understood why my one semi-successful working had so discomposed the mages who heard of it. There were far too many things about it that should have been impossible—especially for someone like me.

To my ongoing surprise, I received no more unexpected testing visits, and no mages appeared to hound, prod, or observe me. Either my unintended explosion had given them all pause, or Lorcan was somehow keeping them away. Why I didn't know.

In composition class, Redmond pretended I didn't exist, and I had no desire to seek his help anyway. But I needed help. Every evening I dragged my battered body up the endless steps, my mind almost equally exhausted by composition class and reading practice, only to sit in my room and attempt to shape power with my words.

Despite the rain which often soaked us now, my skill with the staff had finally begun to grow. And I rarely needed Coralie's assistance with the longer words in my books anymore. But neither of those skills would make me into a mage. Neither would teach me control. And while no obvious threat hung above my head, I hadn't forgotten the look on General Thaddeus's face during my testing. I was isolated from the rest of the kingdom here in the Academy, tucked away inside a bubble. If a sword was going to fall on my defenseless neck, it might well come with no warning.

And so I struggled alone, attempting to unlock my ability. And yet every night I slipped into bed, my head aching, feeling like a fool. It didn't matter how many words I spoke, they remained like the other words I spoke all day—flat and empty of any sort of power.

I might have grown sick of Jocasta's remorseless tutelage in the weeks I spent with her in that horrible room, but eventually I found myself back at the library. This wasn't something I could ask of Coralie, and I had nowhere else to turn. I just hoped Jocasta would be willing to help me, and that she had somewhere else for us to study. I couldn't imagine either of us had any desire to be closed up in that room together ever again. Even if it had been restored to its previous state by the creator mage.

But it wasn't Jocasta behind the desk when I arrived. Instead a middle-aged man with a cheerful face smiled a greeting at me. I had seen him before, although we had never spoken. Walden—the head of the Academy library, Jocasta's senior, and an Ellington. He had usually been busy when I saw him in the past, often helping older trainees.

Looking around now, I saw trainees scattered all over the library. I should have noticed them previously and wondered at their numbers. This must be where they studied their chosen disciplines before the evening meal.

"Ah, Elena," said Walden with a broad smile. "I was wondering when you would find your way back here. I've been looking forward to meeting you."

"You have?" I stared at him before realizing how rude that sounded and rushing to recover. "I mean, of course, I've been—"

He smiled again and waved away my stumbling words. "Of course I've wanted to meet you. I know all the other students, you see. And you've spent so much time here. I like to know those who frequent my domain." He gave me a mock stern look, and I found myself smiling back.

"Now, please, tell me—what can I help you with?"

"Well…" I bit my lip. "I do need help, but I'm afraid it isn't something I'm likely to find in a book."

Walden turned to survey the seemingly endless shelves of books behind him with raised brows before turning back to me. "Now you've intrigued me, do explain."

"I was thinking maybe Jocasta would be available to…" My words faltered when I felt the weight of someone else's gaze. Out of the corner of my eye, I saw an all-too-familiar figure standing a short distance away, the dark hair and bright eyes distinctive without my needing to turn to see him fully.

What was Lucas doing here? I tried to regain my train of thought, but I hated to outline my problem with the cold prince watching on.

If Walden noticed my discomfort, he didn't let on. "There's no need to bother Jocasta. I'd be more than happy to help you myself. Especially now that you've intrigued me so. You'll have trouble convincing a librarian there's a problem that can't be solved by a book. It's just a matter of finding the right one."

I swallowed and tried to ignore the green eyes that bored into me. If only Lucas would leave. I couldn't have hoped for a more welcoming reception than I was receiving from Walden, and I was starting to think it great good luck that I happened to come at a time when Jocasta was away from the desk.

"If you have a book on spoken magic, then by all means, direct me to it," I said at last, attempting to mirror Walden's own smile. "I would settle for even the hint of such a thing—although step-by-step instructions would be a great deal better." I broadened my smile to show I meant the words in jest.

"Ah! Spoken magic." Walden rubbed his hands together. "I had an account from Jocasta, you know, who was there at your testing. Remarkable. Truly remarkable. And a puzzle worthy of even my time." He winked at me, and my smile grew more genuine.

"Perhaps you would care to step into my office to discuss it further?"

I nodded eagerly, conscious that Lucas's eyes still hadn't left me. Did he approve or disapprove of my attempting to explore my power? Wasn't that what they all wanted? For me to unlock the secrets of this new ability? But when I risked a full glance at him, just as I moved to follow Walden, I couldn't see any happiness on his face.

Something about the situation had unsettled him, and I could feel the pressure of his eyes long after Walden's office wall stood between us.

Walden listened with great interest to my account of the confrontation in front of my parents' store. I almost suggested he compose the same working as Lorcan and Jessamine to see it for himself, but I managed to swallow the words just in time. Lorcan and Jessamine were both members of the Mage Council—two of the ten most powerful mages in the kingdom. I didn't want to embarrass Walden if he didn't possess the skill for such a composition.

"So you have no idea what unleashed the power?" he asked when I finished recounting every relevant point I could think of. "None at all? And you never felt even a stirring before that?"

I shook my head. "I have no explanation for it. And I have tried and tried to reproduce it since my arrival here, but it's been a rather useless exercise since I have no idea where to start."

"A most interesting conundrum." Walden ran his hand along his chin, his eyes distant. "You've tried speaking the binding words that begin a normal composition, I suppose."

I nodded. "I borrowed a book on standard compositions only last week and tried reading out every one of them."

I flushed slightly at the admission, but Walden just nodded thoughtfully as if it had been a reasonable attempt. He leaned back in his chair and steepled his fingers.

"I must ponder this further. And scour the library. There may yet be some useful hint to be gleaned from some ancient record." His eyes focused on me. "Do not despair, Elena! We will find the key to your control, I feel certain of it. There can be no greater quest than the search for new knowledge."

I smiled gratefully at him, and he came around his desk to clap me on the shoulder.

"Return in two days, and we will see what I have managed to uncover. Take heart. Success is just around the corner. I feel sure of it."

Although I shared none of his excessive enthusiasm, it still felt as if a weight had been lifted from my shoulders as I hurried from the library. Surely the head librarian of the Royal Academy of the Written Word would have more success in unearthing some clue to my power than I had yet managed.

"Elena." The low voice pulled me up just short of the library doors. Looking around, I spotted Lucas's tall shape between two shelves.

He beckoned me over, and I looked around reflexively to see if someone else might be standing behind me. Then I remembered he had called my name and flushed, feeling foolish and off-balance.

But I had nothing to be ashamed of. I had been admitted to the Academy with the express purpose of learning control—no one could blame me for attempting to do just that. I straightened my back and marched over to him.

"Lucas."

Something flickered in his eyes when I spoke his name, and I knew I had sounded unnecessarily belligerent. But I refused to back down. I crossed my arms over my chest and waited in silence for him to speak.

"You should be careful," he said at last.

I lowered my brows. "I'm not about to start attempting to write again, so you needn't be concerned for the Academy. I won't be bringing down any more walls."

Impatience filled his eyes. "You have no idea of your power, Elena."

"No," I said, exasperation loosening my tongue. "I don't. No thanks to any of you. I'm here because I did something new. I understand that. But this is supposed to be an Academy, isn't it? I might be forgiven in thinking some instruction would be forthcoming. Well, I'm sick of waiting around. If no one else wants to work out how to unlock my ability, I'm going to work it out for myself. And if you have a problem with that, you can…you can take it up with your father."

I somehow maintained my glare despite instantly regretting my words. What was I saying? The last thing I wanted was for Lucas to talk to his father about me on any topic whatsoever.

But as I watched, amusement joined the impatience on his face, and anger welled up in me again. With a ridiculous and undignified, "Humph," I turned on my heel and walked away from him. I wasn't one of his courtiers, and I refused to put up with his needling.

Of course, it was only later, when my emotions had cooled, that I admitted I probably had far more need than one of his courtiers to refrain from offending a member of the royal family. If only the sight of him didn't rile me so. But I knew that was no excuse really. My safety and that of my family should weigh more with me than one pair of infuriating eyes.

CHAPTER 13

Two days later Walden assured me he had only begun to trawl the vast resources of the library. I tried to hide my disappointment and asked if he had some reading material for me to assist in the search. But instead he reminded me that the next day was a rest day. When he asked how long it had been since I took some time out, I found I couldn't resist the allure of an entire day off.

And I didn't have to think for more than a second to know what I wanted to do with it. Which is how I ended up standing in the front courtyard of the Academy staring at the great gates that gave access to the rest of Corrin.

Coralie had offered to accompany me, but this was one trip I needed to do on my own. I wasn't going far.

Shaking my head at my own foolish hesitation, I pushed open the gates and slipped out. Noises and smells instantly surrounded me, making me wonder if the creators who crafted the Academy walls had built noise protections into their compositions.

I glanced back at the tall, sleek marble that surrounded the Academy grounds. I could almost feel the prestige rolling off the stone. But still it couldn't hold my gaze for long. Instead my eyes were drawn to my left, to the towering palace that dominated the city.

By using the same white marble, the Academy felt like an extension of the magnificent building. But there was no question which was the main attraction. The palace soared so high above me that its walls did little to block the effect. An untold number of people must live in such a vast place.

I tore my eyes away and looked across the top portion of South Road. Sitting directly opposite the Academy stood another apparent extension of the palace. Except this tall marble wall hid the Royal University. The current home of my brother, Jasper.

It seemed incomprehensible that we had been residing so close for all these weeks without seeing each other. But then perhaps Jasper had as little opportunity to leave the University as I had so far had to leave the Academy. Another thought struck me. Perhaps he didn't even know of my presence here at all.

Coralie had assured me that visitors were welcome at the University, and that in fact their extensive library was open for use by the public. She hadn't even seen the irony of her words, and I had refrained from pointing it out, conscious of how much I owed to her kindness.

But the words lingered with me now, as I darted across the street and approached the gates which matched those of the Academy. How many common folk had ever crossed this threshold except in the capacity of servant? Certainly none had ever come to use the library.

These gates included a smaller section that could be opened without pushing wide the whole thing, and I slipped gratefully through it. Pride for Jasper welled as I did so. I was here by a still-unexplained accident. But Jasper had earned his place among the elite. He had worked hard all his life to hone his natural gift, until his mind had the capacity to hold everything it would need to succeed in a world of the written word. Once he graduated he might lead a merchant company, competing with the mage merchants, or even get an official position of some sort.

The University had an even grander courtyard than the Academy with three fountains dotted across it, each burbling and splashing despite the cold weather. And unlike the Academy, which consisted of a single main building with only a few small outbuildings sheltering beside it, the University was made up of several large, imposing structures, joined with arched walkways.

I hesitated and looked between them all. Somehow I hadn't anticipated it being quite so big.

"Are you in need of assistance?" asked a friendly voice to my right.

I turned to see a tall young man who gave me a half-bow.

"We are always happy to be of help to fair visitors to our humble realm of learning."

A short girl beside him snorted. "With emphasis on the *fair* in your case, Edmond."

I flushed and resisted straightening my dress. I had put extra care into selecting my outfit and arranging my hair this morning, but I had done it for my brother, not to impress anyone else. I wanted him to see me in the fine clothes the Academy had provided and feel some measure of the pride in me that I felt in him. Of course, it would no doubt only last until I told him the mess I was in, but that hadn't prevented me making the attempt.

"You wound me," Edmond said to his friend, pressing a dramatic hand to his heart.

I halted just short of raising an eyebrow at him. He seemed more suited to a career as a Player than an academic. I glanced back over at the huge University.

"I could do with some assistance, actually," I said. "I'm looking for my brother who is a student here."

The third member of their group regarded me with narrowed eyes. "What's his name?"

His suspicious look and air of irritation reminded me that all three of them must be mages. When had I become so comfortable around their kind that I spoke to them without even thinking of their status?

When you bent power to your will with a spoken word, said a voice inside me. I straightened my back and gave him an equally cold look.

"His name is Jasper."

"Why am I not surprised?" The arrogant one turned away as if our conversation was finished as far as he was concerned.

I bit my lip in sudden concern. In all our pride in him, my family had never given much consideration to what poor Jasper's lot might be, surrounded by those who viewed him as inherently inferior. Did he have a Coralie to help him, or was he struggling through alone? I wished I could have found an opportunity to visit earlier.

Edmond's expression faltered only briefly, however.

"In that case, you want that door there." He pointed at a side door in the northern building. "All us humble junior students have our rooms there."

The girl snorted again. "Humble? You?"

Edmond pushed her lightly, and the two began to bicker good-humoredly.

Their unpleasant companion sighed. "Are we really still standing here?"

Edmond and the girl nodded at me in a way that was not exactly friendly, but neither was it rude, before ambling off in their friend's wake. As they reached the gate, I heard the girl whisper, "Wait a second, did she say she was Jasper's *sister?*"

She tried to peer back at me, but her friend pulled her out onto the street, and I didn't hear any more. I drew a deep breath and hurried for the indicated door, eager to find Jasper before I encountered any more mages. The door pushed open easily against my hand, letting me in to a long corridor lined with rooms.

I stopped a passing servant to ask for my brother, and after a moment's pause, the man directed me to a door part-way down the hall. I knocked on it and could barely contain myself while I waited for the familiar voice to call, "Come in."

I burst into the room and threw myself into his arms.

"Oof!" Jasper staggered backward before catching us both. "Elena?"

He pulled back to regard me with astonishment, and I surveyed his lean frame.

"Have you been eating enough?"

He laughed. "You sound like Mother. Why am I not surprised? Do I have to remind you again that I'm your *older* brother?"

I glanced around the room, surprised to see a number of luxurious touches. And no bed was in sight, although a door to one side seemed to open into another room. I knew Jasper had to pay board, but it didn't seem enough for a suite like this. The University provided for its students more lavishly than the Academy.

"This is nice," I said.

Jasper glanced around himself. "Yes, it's nice enough, I suppose. But you shouldn't be here. Come on, let's go to my room."

"Your room?" I followed him back into the corridor despite my confusion. "Isn't that your room? I asked a servant where to find you, and he directed me there. And there you were..."

Jasper opened a door some way further down the hall and ushered me into a small, single room. This one held a slim bed, a desk, and a single trunk for storage.

"Those are Gregory's rooms."

"Gregory? Who's he? And why were you in his rooms?" I crossed over to look out his single window. Being in a ground floor room, he didn't have the view I did back at the Academy, but he still had a pleasant outlook into a small courtyard with several trees and yet another fountain. That was something at least.

"He's one of the other non-blood students."

I turned to face him. The term sounded strange on my brother's lips where I had never heard it before.

"There are only three of us in the whole University currently. Gregory, Clara, and me. Clara is on a scholarship like me." He shook his head. "She's utterly brilliant, so it's not surprising. But as you know, the scholarship only covers classes. So, like me, her family is scraping to cover her other expenses." He gestured around him. "Thus the simple room. Gregory on the other hand…" He shook his head.

"A rich non-blood?" I asked. One of the kind who could afford to purchase compositions from mages, I supposed. The kind I had only been dimly aware existed before I encountered the larger world outside Kingslee.

"Exactly." Jasper shook his head. "Poor fellow."

"Poor?" I eyed him. "Weren't you just saying the opposite?"

"Well, not monetarily poor. At least not by our standards. But he doesn't really have the mind to be here. It's a constant struggle for him. His family is looking to make their way up in the world, though, so they weren't content for a mere apprenticeship for him—even in the family's prosperous shipping business. So here he is."

"Oh." I considered that. "I'm still not sure why you were in his rooms."

Jasper shrugged. "His family give him an allowance, but he knew he was never going to be able to keep up in classes. So instead of hiring servants—the University ones only do the most basic tasks, so most of the students hire extra services—he's spending the money on tutors."

"Tutors?" I tried to imagine a mage willing to tutor a non-blood.

Jasper laughed. "I would have been as skeptical as you before I arrived. But it seems there are always hierarchies. How do you think some of the less wealthy mages from minor families afford the services of servants themselves?"

I thought of Coralie and her talk of selling compositions. Tutoring might be considered less degrading for the poorer students.

"Gregory can't remember everything from the lectures like Clara and I can. So his tutors read aloud to him from the assigned texts. He's a good sort, so he lets Clara and me join the tutoring sessions in exchange for acting as his missing servants."

He laughed at my pained look. "I can assure you I've done stupider things in my time than run errands and act as a footman." He made a face. "Poor Clara has to clean his rooms until they shine, so it could be worse."

I raised an eyebrow at him, about to unleash a lecture on gentlemanly behavior, but he quickly cut me off.

"Oh, don't worry, she assures me she prefers it to running hither and thither around the University and city."

I considered Jasper's handsome laughing face. That might well be the case, of course. It was also possible, however, that it was pleasing my brother that Clara preferred. And I found myself hoping it might be the latter. Jasper needed someone who could keep up with him mentally, and there had never been any hope of that with anyone in Kingslee.

I only hoped my parents wouldn't be disappointed if he ended up liking her back. Perhaps they had been secretly hoping he would make a match with a girl from a family like Gregory's.

I looked around the room again before fixing my eyes back on my brother.

"You don't seem surprised to see me."

"Of course I'm surprised. And delighted—that much goes

without saying." He grinned at me, but I continued to watch him with narrowed eyes.

"Oh, you're surprised enough to see me on this particular morning, but you're not nearly as surprised as you could be."

A shadow passed across his face, and he sat on his bed, patting the spot beside him. When I sat as well, he angled himself to face me, concern in his eyes.

"I knew you were at the Academy, if that's what you mean. I would have visited except I wasn't sure exactly how things stood, and I didn't want to make things worse for you…I was hoping you might make your way across here eventually."

I looked down at my lap, twisting my hands into my skirts. "So, you know about…what happened? About me? You heard?"

Jasper laughed but, unlike earlier, it sounded hard. "Are you joking? A non-blood works a composition with a spoken word, and her brother just happens to be one of only two non-bloods in the entire kingdom to be offered a University scholarship in the last five years? Both the Reds and the Grays were crawling all over me."

I looked up at him in sudden alarm, but he shook his head.

"Relax, they didn't find anything. Of course. You don't get to a position like mine without respecting the limitations. Whatever the temptation, I don't go near any of the books."

His face twisted, and I could only imagine how hard it must be in an environment like this, and with a mind like his. No doubt he could teach himself to read in a mere fraction of the time it had taken me.

"They already watch us non-blood students like hawks, anyway," he said.

"I'm surprised they let you here at all," I muttered.

He shrugged, his expression cynical. "Well, they have to make some allowances to the common folk, don't they? Demonstrate goodwill and all that."

"Do they?"

He laughed at my dark face and pulled at my hair like he used to do.

"Well, they let *you* into the Academy, didn't they? And if that's not making a concession…"

I rolled my eyes and threw his pillow at him, not feeling in the least repentant when it ricocheted off and landed in a particularly large patch of dust in the corner of the room.

His face dropped again, and he looked at me intently.

"But in all seriousness, El, I hope you're watching your step."

I nodded but looked down to hide a flush. I'd been trying to watch my step, at least. I just couldn't always seem to control my tongue.

He dipped his own head to meet my eyes. "I mean it, Elena. This isn't like Kingslee where you could say what you liked."

I grimaced. He knew me too well.

"Or do what you liked, for that matter. You're rubbing shoulders with powerful people and—unlike at the University—there's no precedent for your presence." He hesitated. "I heard about the explosion."

My head jerked up. "You did?"

He nodded, still focused on my face. "That surprises you?" He paused again. "I don't know what it's like over there at the Academy, but Elena…" He stood abruptly and walked to the window, gazing out for a moment before turning back to me.

I waited, my brow creased. I wasn't used to this serious, concerned Jasper.

He crossed back over to the bed and sat down again, taking my hand in both of his. "Elena, lots of eyes are on you. Powerful eyes. What you did…it isn't just unusual, it's unprecedented. Unheard of. Almost undreamed of. There are…lots of opinions on it."

I frowned. "What's that supposed to mean?"

He bit his lip. "Just that you should watch your step, like I said. And your mouth." He bent a stern look on me.

I sighed. "I'm trying, truly I am. Believe me, I'm well aware of how *impossible* I am. But Jasper, it all feels so pointless when I can't even get it to work."

"Tell me," he said, and I had soon poured out all my struggles, relieved to finally have a friendly and familiar pair of ears. Ones belonging to someone I had loved and trusted before I even trusted myself.

Yet for all his keen mind, Jasper had no suggestions to help me when at last I finished.

"I'll keep my ears open," he promised, "but in all honesty, you're already ahead of me if you can read." The jealous gleam in his eye made me instantly ashamed for doing nothing but complain.

"Jasper, I wish—"

"Don't say it. There are some things that can never be. And your explosion only proves that. Impossible miracles are in limited supply."

I gave him an impulsive hug, and then sat back. My stomach rumbled, reminding me of how much time had passed. A distant bell sounded somewhere, and Jasper stood.

"Sorry I don't have any food to offer you, little sis. But we're not allowed to bring guests to the dining hall. And I'm afraid I have to get going anyway. We always have a tutor in the afternoon on rest day."

I stood as well. "Don't worry about me, I'm just glad to have seen you. And I'll come back when I can." I bit my lip. "I just don't know when that will be."

"You watch out for yourself and don't be worrying about me," he said, giving me a quick hug. "Do you know your way back out?"

I gave him an amused look. "We might not all be geniuses, Jasper, but it wasn't exactly complicated."

He grinned at me easily, before ushering me out of his room and heading off down the corridor in the opposite direction from the door I had used to enter the building. I watched him go until he disappeared before sighing and turning for the exit.

It had been good to see him, but I hadn't liked the expression on his face when he warned me to be careful. And only now that he was gone did I realize that I never pushed him to explain himself. Just what I needed—more nebulous threats to worry about.

Hurrying out into the courtyard, I pulled my thick cloak closed around me, trying to shut out the sharp wind that had sprung up. Keeping my head down, I hurried toward the gate.

"Elena?" The surprised exclamation made me pull up and look around me. Who else here could know my name?

But the tall figure who leaned against a nearby wall didn't belong at the University at all. When I stood frozen, staring at him, Lucas's eyes flicked to one side. I heard a number of voices, hidden before by the sound of the wind, and turned to follow his gaze.

But he pushed instantly off the wall and strode forward. Gripping my arm, he pulled me back to where he had been standing under the curved cover of a walkway. I stumbled after him, too surprised by the burn of his hand through my sleeve to struggle or protest. Was he as aware as I was that we had never touched before, not even in combat? The prince of Ardann didn't pair with the non-blood.

Twisting himself back into his previous position against the wall, he tugged me against him so that we stood face to face, my body just short of being pressed up against his. I struggled to breathe as I tried desperately to remind myself who he was and not to think about his broad chest or strong arms.

I looked up into his eyes, to find them looking down at me with an arrested expression. But just as I opened my mouth to demand an explanation, his gaze once again flicked to the side.

When I tried to twist to see the courtyard behind me, his grip on my arms tightened. I sighed, but Jasper's warnings still rang in my ears, and I refrained from pulling myself free.

Instead I listened, picking up on snatches of conversation between gusts of wind. It wasn't enough to follow what was being said, but I stopped trying when a name floated across to me. My mouth fell open in surprise, and I suddenly felt glad to be hidden away.

CHAPTER 14

*E*ven after the voices moved on and the clear sound of the gates opening and closing echoed across the courtyard, Lucas still held me in place. Except now his gaze had moved from over my shoulder to my mouth. I quickly snapped it closed.

For a moment we remained there, held in our strange position, just short of an embrace. My heart pounded although I couldn't seem to think clearly enough to work out why. Should I be afraid of something? Other than the message that I could never quite catch in Lucas's bright eyes, that was?

"Did someone say…was that…General Griffith?" I managed to choke out. Just his name was synonymous with the front lines and everything I had grown up most fearing.

Lucas nodded, his eyes shifting away from my face as he pushed me back. He kept a light grip on one arm, though, as if he was afraid I'd take off sprinting after the general.

"But, I thought he was at the front lines?"

"He was." Lucas's eyes still flicked around the courtyard, although a quick glance told me it was now empty, the various University inhabitants no doubt having hurried off to the dining hall like my brother.

"But what's he doing here?"

Lucas shrugged. "Consulting with Jessamine, I imagine. Or even visiting Julian."

When I looked confused, he made an impatient sound in his throat. "The general's older son. The twins' brother. He's doing a brief stint here at the University."

"Oh." I tried not to glare at him or say anything my brother would disapprove of, despite my rising resentment. Why should I know who Julian was?

Lucas shook his head. "You're like a child, you don't know anything. Whose bright idea was it to let you out of the Academy?"

I drew myself up, wrenching my arm from his grip.

"What are you doing over here, anyway?" He frowned at me. "This is almost the last place you should be."

"I was told access to the University was open to the public," I said coldly, struggling to hold on to my resolution to mind my tongue.

Lucas barked a laugh. "You're hardly the public, Elena."

I hissed in a breath, reminded all too forcibly of Coralie's thoughtless words. Did these mages truly think they were the only ones to exist in the world? *No—just that they're the only ones who matter.*

"No one *let me out* of the Academy," I snapped, "I'm just taking my rest day, the same as everyone else. And for your information, I was visiting my brother. Although I didn't realize I needed to give an accounting of my movements to you."

Lucas rubbed a hand across his face. "That's right, I'd forgotten about your brother."

I paused, my heart pattering, fear mingling with my anger. Lucas knew about Jasper? My brother's words pounded round my head. *Lots of eyes are on you, Elena. Powerful eyes.*

And for some reason, the prince had pulled me out of General

Griffith's path. He had wanted to keep me from one set of those powerful eyes.

I felt a new sting from his earlier words. I really did know nothing about the world I now inhabited. I had been foolish to forget that the bubble of the Academy floated in a much larger pool, and that at any moment, that bubble could burst, and the flood waters could come rushing in.

I opened my mouth, but Lucas's frustrated gaze ripped away my words. Which was probably for the best since I had been gone from my brother for only a few minutes, and I had already managed to let my tongue run free.

Whirling, I hurried across the courtyard and out through the gates. And this time no voice called my name, and no hand reached out to restrain me.

I kept my head down in classes after that, trying to remember my brother's warning. It didn't help that every time I saw Lucas, I could feel his hands gripping my arms, and remember his face as it had looked a mere breath away from mine. Was I right that he had been protecting me? And, if so, why?

I caught his eyes on me even more than usual, but he made no attempt to speak to me or to reference our encounter at the University. With no further uncontrolled outbursts, the other students had gradually drifted back to their usual seats, only Natalya and Lavinia stubbornly remaining as far from me as they could get.

Although I had ceased seeking out reading material from Jocasta, she had already assigned me enough texts on composition, that I no longer felt lost in class. And the day finally came when Redmond asked a question and, without thinking, my mouth opened, and I answered it.

He paused for a long, weighted breath, his eyes narrowed, but he could obviously find no flaw in my response.

"Indeed," he said flatly, and continued with his lesson.

Coralie grinned at me triumphantly, but I was already wishing I hadn't spoken up and resolving not to do so again. The last thing I needed was to draw Redmond's ire.

But then I caught Lucas staring at me from the next desk. And he looked most displeased. I glared back at him, my posture straight and unyielding. After that, I made an effort to try to answer one question in every class. Apparently the prince needed reminding that he had intelligent subjects among the common folk.

Every few days I stopped by the library to consult with Walden. Each time he came up with some new strategy for me to try and would coach me through it in his office, but my words always fell dull and lifeless from my lips.

Somehow the head librarian's enthusiasm didn't wane, as if the greater the challenge, the more he delighted in it. The one time I came earlier than he was expecting, I found him wandering up and down the shelves, muttering to himself, his bright eyes skipping from book to book.

I ran into Jocasta that time, too, and her disapproving eyes followed me. I didn't come early again after that. My reading had improved enough that I didn't need her exercises, and Walden was a much more pleasant tutor than she had ever been.

In combat, there were rumors we were soon to graduate to actual blades, so I could only be thankful that day hadn't yet come. I was finally beginning to feel comfortable with a staff, and given my failure with my ability, it was nice not to feel totally inept in one part of my life.

One particularly cold day, not long before Midwinter, Coralie headed straight for Acacia's rooms after breakfast instead of combat.

"I'll be good as new once she's seen to me," she promised through her streaming eyes and nose.

I saw her off with a sympathetic look, unsure how she'd even dragged herself out of bed. How different the winter flu season was with a healer on hand to step in before the illness peaked. I wondered often how Clementine was doing at home, and how many times she had been ill during the cold months so far. Were my parents surviving without me there to help nurse her?

We had only expected there to be one winter between my anticipated departure for the war and Jasper's graduation. And after that, my family would move to the capital to join him, where we could access the clinics that the healers discipline ran. Once we had saved up the hefty fee, of course.

Thoughts of my younger sister distracted me all the way to the training yard before it dawned on me that Coralie's absence meant I was short a sparring partner. A quick glance around the group suggested that she wasn't the only one struck down by illness. There was no sign of quiet Saffron, although her cousin was cracking jokes at the unresponsive Thornton.

When he called for us to pair up, I expected an awkward shuffle as everyone tried to avoid me, but Finnian strolled cheerfully in my direction.

I nodded at him awkwardly and adjusted my grip on my staff before deciding that I should make more of an effort to reciprocate his friendliness.

"Coralie's with Acacia," I said. "Saffron too? It's this awful weather."

Finnian nodded. "She has a harder time adjusting than me, I'm afraid. We don't get the biting cold weather like this up home."

"Where do you come from?"

"Torcos. It's way up north, on the North Road, just below the northern forests."

I bit my lip on a sharp retort. I could tell he was trying to be friendly rather than making a statement about my implied lack of schooling in geography.

Thornton called the first set of exercises, and we fell silent as we settled into a steady pattern of blocks and strikes. When he called for free sparring, I sweated slightly, my hands spasming against the staff.

But to my surprise, I held my own, even managing a few knocks of my own despite Finnian's skill. And when the class finally came to an end, Finnian grinned and actually clapped me on the back.

"Good bout," he said.

I stared at him, robbed of words by my shock at having a trainee other than Coralie voluntarily touch me. Then I remembered that one other trainee had touched me. Once.

My eyes slid sideways to Lucas. He had several sparring partners, rotating between them from class to class, but only Weston and Dariela ever succeeded in landing a blow against him. Usually he sparred with intense focus, easily the best trained and strongest in the class.

To my surprise, I found his eyes on me, however. I quickly whisked my own gaze away, but not before I saw his eyes narrow at Finnian's next words.

"Don't worry," the northerner said, with a wink. "I generally have that effect."

"What?" I gaped at him, trying to straighten my thoughts.

"Only that you needn't be embarrassed. I generally render the ladies speechless."

He struck an absurd pose, and I couldn't help laughing.

"I'll bear that in mind."

"Do." He fell into easy step beside me as I made my way back toward the Academy. "But, in all honesty, you've come a long way. You were truly terrible when you started." He laughed but there didn't seem to be any malice in it, especially after his earlier compliment.

And even I was surprised at how far I'd come. I had thought Coralie was still going easy on me, but after my session with Finnian, I wasn't so sure anymore.

"Some of the others grumble that old Thornton makes us work our way through the basics before he'll let us get to any of the fun stuff," Finnian continued, "but that's why."

"Oh?"

"My father says Thornton doesn't trust anyone's teaching but his own. And he's sworn that no trainee will graduate the Academy without sufficient skill in combat. So he insists on treating everyone like beginners and training them from the ground up."

I winced as I remembered the bruises I used to have after every combat class. And the lack of clear instruction from Thornton. All these mages might think he was starting at a beginner level, but I knew better.

"Was he here when your father came through the Academy, then?" I asked, unwilling to pick a fight with Finnian when he was actually voluntarily walking beside me and chatting as though I was just another trainee.

"Goodness no," said Finnian with a chuckle. "Thornton might be getting on the older side, but he's not that ancient. But my father tends to keep his mouth closed and his ears open. He's constantly assuring me you can learn a lot that way."

He grinned in my direction, inviting me to share his self-deprecating joke.

"He sounds a lot like my mother." I rolled my eyes, and Finnian laughed.

"To be fair, I imagine it helps when you're a duke and have access to all the council meetings," Finnian added, and my moment of fellow feeling evaporated.

"Your father is a duke?" The words sounded a little squeaky, so I cleared my throat.

"Duke Dashiell of Callinos, Head of the Healers," Finnian said, the pride clear in his voice despite his earlier joking.

I had known Finnian and Saffron were from the Callinos family, but somehow I had missed his father's status. I bit my lip, watching Calix who stalked ahead of us. Our year level might be unusually small, but it was also apparently illustrious.

Lots of eyes are on you, Elena. Powerful eyes.

I fell silent, although Finnian didn't seem to notice, keeping up a steady stream of one-sided conversation as we rounded the corner of the Academy and stepped inside the entryway.

"Elena!" An excited flurry of movement was my only warning before Coralie barreled into me, nearly knocking me over.

"Whoa there," said Finnian laughingly, reaching out to steady us both. "I know we're delightful, and you've no doubt been missing us, but we haven't been gone that long."

Coralie righted herself and ignored him, her feet dancing on the spot.

"What happened to you?" I asked.

"Acacia told me to take the morning off and rest. She said the healing needed time to work." She glanced at Finnian. "Saffron too. Which means we were the first to hear."

She grinned up at us both and waved a thick piece of parchment in our faces. Finnian snatched it out of her grip and quickly scanned it before passing it to me. He raised both eyebrows.

"Classy move. But then I guess we shouldn't have expected anything else. So everyone in the year got one?"

Coralie grinned and hugged herself. "Yes. Even you, Elena. They were pushed half under each of our doors during class, so I checked to make sure. But only us first years."

She sounded particularly triumphant at that, but I was only half listening as I slowly read the words on what appeared to be an invitation. I looked up at the other two.

"I'm not sure I understand."

"It's only an invitation to the Royal Midwinter Celebration." Coralie's dancing feet started up again.

When I still looked slightly confused, she sighed.

"The Royal Midsummer Celebration is the big one. Every mage in the kingdom is invited, although they don't all travel in for it every year, of course. But the Royal Midwinter Celebration is different. That one is exclusive. Getting an invite is an honor, a mark of royal favor. It's supposed to be the most elegant event, and this one should be even more extravagant than usual."

"Why?" I looked between her and the parchment in her hand. "And if it's such an honor, why did I get an invite?"

"Because of Lucas, of course." Coralie grinned and pulled her invitation back out of my hand. "His birthday is the day after Midwinter, so the royal family always celebrate it at this event. That's why it's smaller and more exclusive. And this year, he turns eighteen. I bet it's going to be magnificent! I can't wait to tell my family. My sister is going to be absolutely green."

"We've been invited because we're his year mates," Finnian explained, obviously picking up that I was still a little lost.

"Well, you'd probably have received an invitation anyway, Finnian," said Coralie. "But there was no way I would have been getting one otherwise."

Finnian shrugged. "These sorts of things are usually full of stuffy elders glowering disapprovingly at us young ones. And I always have to dance with Natalya." He grimaced, clearly trying to make Coralie laugh.

She obliged him easily, slipping her arm through mine and dragging me toward the dining hall, Finnian trailing behind.

"Yes, but this year we'll all be there," she said to him over her shoulder. "And I intend to have an absolutely wonderful time."

He shook his head, but he was grinning at her as he wandered past us to take his usual place at a further table. As Coralie and I sat, she suddenly blinked, looking rapidly between Finnian and me.

"Wait. Were you and Finnian actually talking when I arrived? Did you spar with him?"

Her words barely registered as I stared at her, a deep dread settling over me.

"Never mind that. I can't go to a celebration at the palace. *What would I wear?*"

CHAPTER 15

"I'm still not sure about this." I tugged at my long skirts and Coralie slapped at my hands.

"Stop that! You look perfect. Thanks to me." She looked smug, and when she put it like that I could hardly disagree.

And in truth, I did secretly agree—at least a little. She had lent me a green dress and somehow it brought out the green in my eyes that usually only shone through in moments of high excitement. And even the plain brown of my hair looked elegant in the tendrils she had left to fall softly around my face.

But that didn't mean I thought this was a good idea. I hadn't forgotten my one trip out of the Academy so far. Neither my brother's warnings nor my disastrous encounter with Lucas had faded from my memory.

The prince had told me that the University was almost the last place I should be, and my gut told me that the palace must surely be the one place worse. And yet even Lucas couldn't fault me for going this time. Not when his own family had issued the invitation.

The prince had been conspicuously absent in the week leading up to Midwinter, although classes had continued despite the week of festivities gripping the city. Apparently his royal duties trumped his studies on this occasion, at least.

But we had been given the actual day of Midwinter off, and I knew Coralie and I weren't the only ones to have spent most of it preparing for the evening's celebration. Although most of the other girls had whisked themselves off to their family's city houses for the day. Only Araminta, looking more anxious than I had ever seen her, waited in the entrance of the Academy with us.

The three of us weren't alone, of course. Thornton, Redmond, Walden, Jocasta, and Lorcan had all received invitations to the event, and Clarence also had nowhere else to spend the day, his family far away in whatever city they made their home.

I had hoped to slip out to see Jasper in the morning, but I had received a visit instead from a petite and charming-looking girl a few years older than me who identified herself as Clara.

"He was worried you'd try to come over and see him," she had said with a friendly smile. "Only we got a few extra days off class unexpectedly, and he decided to walk home to visit your family."

"Oh, how lovely." I tried to swallow my own disappointment at the thought of them all together without me. They would all be so delighted to see him, and at least now I knew they would have definite news of me.

Clara herself was on her way to spend the day with her own family, who resided in Corrin, but she gave me a small wrapped package from Jasper before she left. I didn't know how he had found the coin for the beautiful hair pin inside, but I wished I had thought of some way to scrape together a gift for him.

It might not be made of jewels, as no doubt the accessories of the other attendees would be, but I wore the pin in my hair proudly, glad to carry something of my family with me for my first visit to the palace.

And as the carriages pulled into the courtyard, I touched it, drawing strength from my brother's love. I had thought we would walk, but Coralie assured me we could not go traipsing through the streets in our finery. It turned out the palace was sending carriages to the Academy, and we would have seats along with the instructors.

I peered out the window on the ridiculously short drive. I had only ridden in a carriage once before, and memories of that occasion kept pushing unbidden into my mind. I rearranged my skirts around me, my elegant dancing slippers peeking out from beneath them, and shook my head.

I couldn't look more different from how I had on that previous journey. And yet, somehow, I felt almost as nervous. I tried to remind myself that I was on my way to a party, not a possible death sentence, but I couldn't make my rapidly beating heart believe it.

Powerful eyes are on you, Elena.

I had at least made Coralie tutor me on the important personages who would be present, almost exclusively members of the four great mage families. General Griffith of Devoras was still in the capital, and apparently Lucas no longer felt the need to hide me from him, since he would no doubt be in attendance with Natalya and Calix beside him, along with his other son, Julian.

Unfortunately General Thaddeus of Stantorn would also definitely be there, as a cousin of Queen Verena. And that was on top of his rank. I imagined that all the members of the Mage Council would be present.

Like Thaddeus, I had already met Duchess Jessamine of Callinos, University Head, Duke Lennox of Ellington, Head of Law Enforcement, and Duchess Phyllida of Callinos, Head of the Seekers. But I had to confess to some curiosity to see Duke Dashiell, also of Callinos—both Head of the Healers and Finnian's father.

Finnian continued to act as if we had always been on speaking terms, greeting me cheerily at class and meals, and occasionally sparring with me while Coralie partnered with Saffron. Natalya and Lavinia always glowered disapprovingly when he did so, but it seemed his status—thanks, I assumed, to the rank of his father —prevented any further change in their behavior toward him.

Instead they increased the snide comments they muttered in my hearing. But that I easily ignored, more than happy to take it in exchange for two other trainees willing to tolerate my presence—since it seemed that where Finnian led, his withdrawn cousin followed.

The heads of the growers, wind workers, and creators would also be at the celebration, and I wouldn't mind meeting Duke Magnus of Ellington, if it came to it. The Ellingtons were supposed to be the nice ones—more rich than politically powerful, according to my friends. And Acacia and Walden certainly seemed to support this assessment.

But then the haughty, withdrawn Dariela kept throwing me off. Would Duke Magnus be like her, or was she an aberration among her family?

I had no desire to encounter Duchess Annika of Devoras or Duke Casimir of Stantorn, however. I had met quite enough members of Devoras and Stantorn already.

And, of course, there was one other person waiting at the end of this journey. I tried not to let my mind dwell on Prince Lucas —no matter how many times it attempted to do so—but I couldn't quash the small curiosity at the back of my mind. Despite everything, part of me wanted to see the prince in his home environment, among the court. Although it seemed foolish to think that one night could make a difference in my ability to understand him—or rather, inability.

All too soon the carriage pulled up in front of a broad, sweeping set of marble stairs. I didn't have a fine enough cloak for such an event, but Coralie had assured me we wouldn't need them for such a short journey. It meant dashing up the stairs as fast as we could, though, eager to get out of the freezing night air.

Outside I received an impression of blazing lights, but it was nothing to the glow that greeted us inside the palace itself. An immense entryway was lit with more candles than I could count, reflecting off the pristine white marble. Stairs led upward, and an army of footmen directed us up them and through a wide door into an equally vast ballroom.

Inside the doors was a small platform where we paused for a moment to take it all in before descending four shallow steps to the ballroom floor. A red velvet runner on the stairs matched the color of the red drapes covering the walls. Impossible gold chandeliers—surely held in place by complex compositions—floated in the air, and everywhere I looked, gold touches winked in the light.

Red and gold. There could be no question this was a royal event. Without realizing I was doing so, I scanned the crowd until my eyes latched onto a figure at once familiar and strikingly different.

At the Academy, Prince Lucas stood out. Everything from the perfect dark locks of his hair to his bearing proclaimed his difference. But now…now he truly looked like a prince.

He wore what looked like a uniform, red with a gold sash across his chest, and tall black boots. A small gold circlet rested in his ordered hair, and the haughty, distant look I had seen on my first day—and so many days since—seemed magnified.

If I had never seen him before, I would never have dared approach him. In fact, though we might officially be year mates, I still didn't intend to approach him. I had no need of his condescension when I already felt so out of my element.

"Look!" whispered Coralie, tugging on my elbow.

I let her lead me to a far wall where a long table held endless delicacies. I marveled at an ice sculpture—a frozen swan about to take flight, perfect in all its details—but Coralie was still absorbed with whatever had first caught her attention.

"It's incredible," she said.

I pulled my eyes to the marvel that had her transfixed. A complex, many-tiered fountain of liquid chocolate.

"Um, yes please," she said, taking one of the tiny, delicate gold cups arranged around it and dipping it into the flow.

I hung back. Another thing clearly powered by some unknown mage. Somehow that made me less than enthusiastic to consume it. Was it only the royal family who entertained like this, or did all mages have energy and power to spare composing such useless workings?

"Welcome," said a voice behind us, and we both spun around.

So much for my plan not to approach anywhere near the prince. His entire demeanor suggested utter boredom, as if he were merely doing his duties as host, making his way round to greet each guest—even the ones he didn't like.

But when I finally met his eyes, they burned into me, and I almost fell back a step.

"You came," he said, his voice low, and his eyes disappointed.

"Of course." Coralie gave him a broad smile, apparently not receiving the same message from his face as me. "We were honored to be invited. Oh, and Happy Birthday!"

He gave a mechanical smile, still focused on me. When I stood there silently, Coralie kicked my foot.

"Ah, thank you for inviting me," I managed.

Lucas's eyes flashed. "I didn't."

I stiffened but was saved from an unwise response by a titter off to one side.

"Natalya. Lavinia." Coralie spoke through gritted teeth, giving the briefest head nod to our two year mates.

Neither of them bothered to return the greeting, although they stepped up to join us, their elaborate skirts twirling around their legs. Both wore expensive-looking jewels around their throats and wound through their hair, and gold embroidery flashed on their gowns.

"I knew it couldn't have been your idea, Lucas." Natalya rolled her eyes before fixing me with a condescending look. "No prince would choose to invite someone who would dress like that."

I puffed up and opened my mouth to give a response that was very far from wise indeed. It was one thing for them to constantly insult me, but the dress belonged to Coralie—the kindest person I had ever met.

But Lucas spoke before I could get any words out.

"On the contrary, you all look lovely. My celebration is graced by your presence." And he gave a half-bow, his gesture including all four of us.

Coralie, whose mouth had fallen open at Natalya's blatant insult, flushed with pleasure, so I swallowed my words. If she hadn't noticed the bored, court manners—so obviously insincere —then I wasn't going to point them out.

"If you'll excuse me…" With another half-bow, Lucas escaped, moving on to greet his next guest, no doubt, now that his responsibility to us was complete.

"Well, obviously he didn't mean *you*," Natalya said.

"He was just being polite." Lavinia pursed her lips and glared at me.

I just shook my head. "Are you two actually serious right now? I thought your families were supposed to be important or something. Isn't all this a little beneath you?"

Both of them swelled with anger at my mention of their families, but Calix strolled over at that moment, and looked down enquiringly at his sister.

"Nat? What are you doing slumming it over here?" His eyes raked disdainfully from my head to my toes.

"Following around royalty, of course, Calix," I said with a laugh. "Where she always is."

Calix raised an eyebrow. "The kitten has claws." He smiled. "Better watch out kitty, there are lions prowling tonight."

He gripped both girls by the elbows, drawing them with him as he sauntered away.

"Well," said Coralie after a moment of silence. "I don't know what's gotten into everyone tonight. Am I the only one who came here planning to actually enjoy myself?"

"I know what it is." I sighed. "It's me. They've gotten used to having me at the Academy, but it's another thing altogether seeing me at the palace." I gestured around us. "At this. Here I really don't belong."

Coralie looked at me uneasily, and I could tell she didn't want to agree but couldn't quite bring herself to disagree, either.

The orchestra had been playing since we arrived, couples circling the dance floor, and as we stood silently, a young man approached us. He gave a small bow to Coralie and held out an inviting hand.

"Dance with me?"

Coralie bit her lip and looked over at me.

"Go." I made a shooing motion with my hand. "You're here to enjoy yourself, remember?"

Her face still looked tentative, but when she turned it back to the other mage it transformed into a blinding smile.

"I would love to. I'm Coralie, by the way, a trainee at the Academy."

"Ah, that would explain why I haven't seen you around. I'm at the University."

He led her away, the two of them disappearing into the crowd. I glanced back at the table, considering taking a plate of food just so that I wouldn't feel so awkward.

But when my eyes fell on Dariela, standing not far away, I decided to approach her instead. It was a whim, really, since we didn't exactly talk at the Academy. But seeing her here in a different context—and standing alone—it suddenly struck me that she looked lonely.

And it occurred to me that she always looked a little alone, even when standing in the middle of a crowd. She might sit with the twins and their friends, but she was like Lucas—with them and yet also apart somehow.

I walked over with a smile and a greeting, complimenting her dress since it seemed like a safe place to start. She stared at me in silent surprise, and I began to regret the momentary fellow feeling that had propelled me over to her.

"Thank you," she said, after far too long a pause, before we both descended into silence again. I tried to think of something else to say but hadn't come up with anything when she gave me a single head nod and strode away. I winced and contemplated returning to the food, after all.

"Elena of Kingslee," said a gruff voice, before I could actually do so. "You've made quite a name for yourself, young lady."

Slowly I turned to face the speaker. The two men in front of me wore open robes displaying elaborate uniforms beneath. Only ten people present tonight were wearing robes, and I didn't need the gold and silver colors in front of me to tell me who these two were.

General Thaddeus I recognized, and the man beside him—the speaker—could only be General Griffith, Head of the Armed Forces of Ardann. I caught sight of Natalya and Calix half way across the ballroom, watching us. Lavinia had disappeared—dancing, perhaps—and a taller boy had joined them. He had Natalya's dark coloring and was no doubt their older brother, Julian.

I sighed. I should have known the twins weren't done with me yet. No doubt I had them to thank for sending these new arrivals in my direction. Belatedly I gave a head nod that might have been mistaken for a half-bow.

"Yes, sir, I'm Elena."

"Smaller than I pictured," he said, his measuring eyes weighing me and no doubt finding me wanting in greater ways than my height.

"I'm a sixteen-year-old girl, what were you expecting? A giant?"

He raised an eyebrow at my heated response, and I wished I

could take back the words. The specter of my class mates lurked on the other side of the room, but I needed to remember that this man was far more than just their father. He was one of the ten most powerful mages in the kingdom. Why couldn't I learn to control my tongue?

"I was unfortunately busy elsewhere and unable to witness the recreation of your composition for myself," General Griffith said. "Although Thaddeus here tells me there could be no mistaking it." His tone implied that his business had naturally been of far greater importance than anything going on here.

I stood tall, holding my mouth tightly closed, determined not to say another word unless asked a direct question.

"But I am naturally fascinated by such a new ability," the general continued. "Perhaps you could humor me with a small demonstration."

"W…What?" I stammered, instantly forgetting my resolution. "A demonstration? Here?"

He smiled broadly. "Why ever not? I am a busy man, you know, and here we find ourselves in the same place, at the same time. We must seize such moments as they are afforded to us."

I looked around wildly, but no help was forthcoming. I swallowed.

"Nothing *destructive*, of course," said Thaddeus, sharply, his cold eyes boring into me. "A small working should be sufficient. Something decorative, perhaps."

Still I hesitated, not having imagined such a scenario and unwilling to admit to the truth. Would I be instantly expelled from the Academy as a fraud? Did these two generals have that power? And what would happen to me—a commonborn able to read—if I was?

I glanced around hoping to spot Lorcan, but he was nowhere in sight. Instead my eyes fell on Lucas, his eyes somehow glued on us despite half a ballroom between us. Perhaps I had been wrong about who had sent General Griffith. Perhaps it had not been his children but Lucas, wanting to show me exactly why I shouldn't have come tonight, why I should have continued hiding away as he clearly wanted me to do, despite some protocol which must have dictated that I be given an invitation.

"Come, come," said the general, his voice sounding deceptively soft. Calix had mentioned lions, and his father reminded me all too forcibly of one preparing to pounce. "You've been studying at the Academy for a season and a half. Surely you can compose one small working without risking bringing the palace down around us?"

I licked my lips.

"Actually, I can't."

The general pulled back. "You can't?" Nothing about the surprise on his face looked genuine. "Tut-tut, I'll have to have a word with Lorcan. It seems he's slipping."

"Or so she says," muttered Thaddeus. "She had no problem bringing half the Academy down."

Hardly half. But I managed to swallow the words before they could emerge.

"Generals, a good evening to you both," said a cool voice.

Turning, I almost tripped in my stumbling efforts to curtsy to the newcomer. The queen—because it had to be Queen Verena— gave the smallest of nods in my direction. Rubies winked at her throat and from her crown, and although she was no taller than me, her golden dress took up three times as much space as mine. I took another step back.

A tall, elegant girl, several years my senior, stood at her shoulder. The tiara in her hair was more elaborate than the circlet Lucas wore, and there could be no mistaking her identity, either. I curtsied again, slightly more elegantly this time, to Lucas's older sister—Crown Princess Lucienne.

Both women had the same dark, almost black, hair as Lucas, but their matching eyes were brown flecked with gold. I looked around a little wildly, wondering if King Stellan was also about to descend on us. But when I spotted a towering golden crown, the man wearing it was some distance away, deep in conversation with Lorcan and Jessamine.

I drew a breath of relief, even as I wondered uneasily if they could be discussing me. But I tried to shake the thought away. One glance at this ballroom should be enough to remind me that nothing in this world revolved around me.

The king had sandy hair and his son's green eyes, although apparently both of his children had inherited his height. Unwillingly, my traitorous eyes flicked across to Lucas, noting the resemblance he had to both his parents. He still watched me.

I get it! I wanted to scream across the ballroom at him. *I get that I don't belong. Not here, and not at the Academy. You needn't send anyone else to convince me.*

The queen's voice dragged my gaze away from her son. "Is there to be a demonstration?"

"It seems not, Your Majesty." General Griffith bowed slightly. "Lorcan has been keeping her locked away for nothing, it would seem."

"Interesting." The queen's eyes transferred across to me, and I thrust my trembling hands out of sight among my skirts. She might not have the height of the rest of her family, but the queen carried herself with the same authority.

I tried to tell myself I only imagined the hardness in her face —a trick of perception perhaps, given her family resemblance to Thaddeus—but I couldn't be sure. The princess, at least, looked more open, regarding me with curiosity.

"You really cannot oblige us, girl? Not even for your queen?"

I curtsied again. "I assure you, I would if I could, Your Highness, Your Majesty."

"What a pity." The queen gave a soft sigh, managing to make even that sound elegant. "It is almost enough to make one wonder…" She turned abruptly to face the two generals. "A word, gentlemen?"

They both bowed to her, and the four of them moved away, the crowd parting before them as they approached the king and the other two heads. Only Thaddeus glanced back at me as they left, his eyes holding a warning.

I swallowed and looked around. Many more curious eyes now watched me, but no one else approached. I glanced back at the refreshment table but could no longer imagine keeping anything in my roiling stomach.

Darting along the edge of the room, I pushed my way through a partially dangling red curtain and out onto a wide, empty balcony. I breathed in the cold night air, leaning against the railing, and raising my face toward the stars.

Closing my eyes, I concentrated on my breaths.

I had tried and tried. I could not access my power. Perhaps Lorcan would let me return home.

But I didn't have to look around and remind myself where I stood—and among what company—to know that was an impossible dream. For all my efforts, I didn't belong here. But having now been at least partially admitted to this world neither could I return to my old life. They would never permit such a thing. And I had to admit I struggled to imagine it myself. My world had expanded too much to be constricted back into Kingslee again.

Slowly, slowly, my heartbeat returned to its normal pace, and my breathing evened. If I had allowed myself to become comfortable in my life at the Academy, it had always been an illusion. Nothing had really changed. My situation was no more uncertain now than it had been when I first arrived. And I had survived this long.

A soft sound made me startle, my eyes flying open. I wasn't alone out here after all.

CHAPTER 16

*L*ucas leaned sideways against the railing, facing toward me, his eyes on my face. How long had he been watching me?

I jerked back, only my hands remaining on the stone balustrade, my grip tightening convulsively.

"Come to tell me to leave?" I gestured around the deserted balcony. "I already got the message."

Lucas sighed. "Are you always so belligerent? Or is it just to me?"

"Are you always so rude? Or is it just to me?"

His eyes dropped from mine, and he ran a hand over his face.

"I shouldn't have come out here," he muttered.

"No, probably not." I forced myself to lean forward against the railing again and look out toward the stars. "Someone might see us and think you're fraternizing with me by choice."

He actually chuckled at that. "And I suppose they'd be right. At least, I don't think anyone forced me out here."

I spun to face him. "So why are you here then?"

For all my efforts, my nerves still thrummed from the confrontations inside, and I didn't have the energy to deal with another one. If only he would walk back inside and leave me alone.

But the intensity in his eyes captured me, the lines of his body looking suddenly tight and on edge, despite his relaxed pose.

"I don't exactly know." He paused. "I guess I wanted to know why *you're* here."

"Well, at the beginning of the evening, I would have said because you invited me. But now I know better."

I wanted to storm away from the balcony, but even with Lucas here, this haven seemed safer than the crowd that waited inside. And a small part of me wanted to hear his answer. To know what excuse—if any—he intended to give for his rudeness.

"No, I wouldn't have been so foolish." He finally broke my gaze and glanced out into the night. "I wish I knew who got in my mother's ear about it."

I bit my lip and examined his face while he looked carefully away. So it had been Queen Verena who invited me. Why? As a matter of protocol because I was officially part of Lucas's year level? Or had she been planning to request a demonstration all along? A demonstration I had failed to produce. But why not just visit the Academy herself in that case?

"Well, I'm sorry to have ruined your precious birthday celebration with my lowborn self and my inadequate gown."

His eyes flew back to mine before dropping down to take in my outfit. A faint tinge colored his cheeks, and he looked away again.

"I meant what I said earlier, Elena. You look lovely. You certainly don't embarrass me, if that's what you're thinking."

I rolled my eyes, trying to hide the fact that I was the embarrassed one. I knew I didn't measure up to him. Not tonight when he was every inch the prince.

"Your sincerity was oh so clear, Your Highness."

"Welcome to the world of court, Elena. Insincerity is a game we play, and there are plenty of eyes watching us play it tonight."

He looked at me steadily. "But what makes you think my insincerity was directed toward you?"

This time I looked away, unable to hold his gaze. What game was he playing now?

"Look there's really no need for you to be out here," I said. "I got your message loud and clear."

He frowned. "What message?"

"The generals. Your mother. I get it. I don't belong here. I can't compose, I have no control. I'm not one of you. You can be sure I won't be coming back to court."

He was still frowning, but at my last sentence, his face lightened. "Is that a promise?"

My hands tightened on the balustrade again, and I swallowed my instinctive response. He might make me want to retract my words in a fit of anger, but in this one instance I would hold my tongue—because I had no intention of returning here ever.

"It would certainly make things a lot easier for me," he said quietly when I made no response. "I don't suppose while you're in an agreeable mood, you could promise to limit yourself to the Academy entirely?"

I glared at him. "Are you trying to make me into a voluntary prisoner, Lucas? Because I can't say I'm inclined to play along."

"No." He made a quiet sound of frustration. "I'm trying to keep you..."

I waited, but he didn't go on.

"Keep me what? Under control? Out of sight? Locked away? What is it you're trying to do, Lucas?"

He closed his eyes. "I'm just trying to keep everyone safe. I don't know why you're so determined to thwart me."

I sucked in a breath. "Once. I only lost control once. And I've never picked up a pen again. I would *never*—"

He shook his head. "I didn't mean..."

Once again I waited, and once again he didn't go on.

"Look, if you can convince Lorcan to let me go, I'll return home in a heartbeat. Out of your way forever."

"What?" He started, and now it was his hands gripping tightly to the stone in front of us.

I watched the muscles in his arms bunch, his knuckles turning white, and tried to pretend that his presence here in the half-darkness had no effect on me. Whatever enchantment he had cast over me from the first moment I saw him still held me, despite his manner since then. I wished I could take the decorative sword from his waist and cut myself free of him.

"That is not…That would be disastrous." He stumbled over his words. "Elena, that is a terrible idea."

"Yes, somehow I thought you'd all feel that way." I sighed. "No one wants me here, and yet I can't leave either. It's a dilemma, wouldn't you say?"

He said nothing, and I mumbled to myself, "It's only for another year."

"A year?" He looked at me sharply. "What do you mean?"

I just shrugged. I felt no responsibility to explain to him the necessities of conscription. The fact that he didn't understand them was just another sign of the vast and uncrossable gulf between us. Between all of us common folk and mages.

"Elena." He pushed off the rail and stepped forward, gripping my shoulders. "You cannot leave the Academy."

His fingers burned through the thin material of my gown, his eyes just as fiery hot.

"I'm not going anywhere," I said. "For now."

He groaned. "Elena! Why can't you ever do what's best for yourself? Why can't you bite your tongue from time to time?"

Somehow a chuckle rose up inside me. "Now you sound like my mother."

He groaned again and stepped back. "Excellent." But as he watched me, a slight smile stole across his face. "I can only imagine what a trial you were to her."

I rolled my eyes and turned back to the stars. "It seems I was born to be a trial to everyone."

"No, apparently you were born to be something entirely unique."

I glanced sideways to find him watching me with a calculating, considering look.

"Go back inside, Lucas," I said softly. "Before someone notices you're gone and comes looking for you."

A shadow sped across his face, and then his court mask fell back into place. He gave me a half-bow.

"Very well. If you wish it."

He crossed over to the door but paused just off the balcony to look back at me, the curtain still in his hand.

"Elena—"

Whatever he had been about to say was drowned out by a loud rumble and a sharp crack. I got a glimpse of his startled face as a familiar sensation washed over me. And then the balcony bucked, the stone beneath my feet rippling, and the entire thing collapsed. I fell amid the chunks of marble.

CHAPTER 17

As I fell, my thoughts flew uselessly to a shielding composition we had been studying in class for the last week. I knew each of my year mates now carried a rolled parchment somewhere on their person, ready for such an emergency. Only I remained weak and helpless.

I slammed against a block as I fell, and words ripped desperately from my throat.

"Shield me!"

Power rushed around me and everything slowed. The cold night air disappeared, and I floated toward the ground, cocooned in warmth. A couple of marble chunks bounced away from me, and then the crashing sound finished. With the last of the balcony already resting on the ground, I landed gently on the top of the pile.

My feet faltered and slipped, my knees unable to brace me, and I fell hard onto all fours. Instead of jagged stone, I fell against a soft warmth. But as I knelt there, panting, it faded away. Broken marble bit into my hands and knees.

I clambered to my feet and balanced shakily on a large block. *Lucas!* The sudden thought nearly sent me staggering off the pile as I looked quickly around. Had he been far enough off the balcony to avoid the accident?

Looking upward, I saw the red curtain flapping free, the doorway it shielded now opening onto nothingness. Leaning out of the gaping hole was the prince, his distant face transformed by shock.

"Elena!"

"I…I'm fine." I gave him a feeble wave before letting my arm drop foolishly.

A commotion sounded from inside the ballroom, but the prince didn't turn toward it. Instead, he pulled out a rolled length of parchment. Tearing it, he stuffed the two halves back into his jacket and stepped into the open air.

My half scream of protest died when, instead of plummeting to the ground, he remained upright as if his feet rested on an invisible balcony. As I watched, he slowly descended to the ground, lowered on a platform of air.

Now that my initial panic had subsided, I could sense the power of his composition, centered beneath his boots. The sensation reminded me of the one I had felt as the balcony first began to give way. It was the same awareness of controlled power that filled the composition classroom whenever my classmates released a working.

The composition I had felt as the balcony collapsed had been subtle and full of far more finesse than the prince's working, but it had been unmistakable. Had he felt it? Had he composed it?

But when his feet touched down, just outside the ring of rubble, he clambered straight up to me, reaching out a steadying hand to grip my elbow. The shock and fear on his face were enough to instantly drive away the thought.

I managed a shaky smile. "You didn't learn that one in composition class."

"I am a prince, remember." He didn't smile back, instead

looking me over as if examining me for signs of injury. "How did you...?"

His words trailed away as we stared at each other with equally wide eyes. We both knew how I had survived. A dark look crossed his face.

"You just composed a shield. Verbally. You did a working, Elena." He took a sharp breath. "Have you been holding out—"

"What? No! Of course not." I pulled my elbow out of his grip and clambered down the pile of broken marble to firmer ground. He followed me, and I spun to face him.

"I guess emergencies bring it out. You all should have been dropping me from windows back at the Academy."

He ran a hand through his hair. "Sorry. The shock..."

I raised an eyebrow. "Did you just *apologize* to me? Talk about shocks!"

A reluctant smile curled his mouth, but shouts from above drew his attention.

"Your Highness!"

"Lucas!"

"What happened?"

He waved but didn't attempt to call back to them, and only seconds later yet more people came pouring out of a nearby ground level door. The red and gold uniforms of the Royal Guard swarmed us, and their general wasn't far behind.

"What happened here?" barked Thaddeus, surveying the destruction and both of us. His eyes narrowed and several of the guards moved toward me, but Lucas moved as well. It was only a single step in my direction, a subtle movement, but it aligned us together. The guards halted, glancing between the prince and their general.

King Stellan appeared beside Thaddeus, and the guards all stood to attention while I dropped into a hasty curtsy.

"Lucas! What is this?" The king's attention remained focused on his son.

Lucas's back straightened slightly. "The balcony collapsed, Father. We can be thankful there weren't more people on it at the time."

Something passed between their eyes, and the king nodded. "I felt your use of power."

Was the king alluding to the other power? The one that had brought the balcony down? If he had felt that working as well, he seemed willing to pretend he hadn't and accept Lucas's public explanation of a simple collapse—at least for now and in front of so many witnesses.

"A fortunate thing you were on hand to soften the fall, Your Highness," said Thaddeus. "Or we might have had a tragedy." His eyes dwelled on me in a way that made me think he wouldn't have found it too tragic as long as I had been the only victim.

"It would have been more fortunate if my son had not been required to draw on his personal store of compositions." The coldness in the king's voice made the general stiffen. "It would have been more fortunate if your guards had done their job."

Thaddeus bowed to the king. "Certainly, Sire. I shall review the situation myself. And I shall dispatch teams immediately to examine the remaining balconies for any signs of instability or weakness."

I opened my mouth to blurt out that it had not been an accidental collapse, but Lucas's hand shot out and gripped my arm so hard that I shut it again in surprise. By the time anyone's attention had returned to us, his hand had disappeared back to his side. But I kept silent all the same.

"It seems to me," said Lucas, his voice steady and calm, "that a thorough examination of the entire palace might be in order. Preferably with the assistance of a team of creators. After all, it has been generations now since the creators first constructed this place."

"An excellent suggestion," said the king. "See to it, Thaddeus."

The general bowed again and turned to bark orders at the

guards, whose numbers had swelled with the arrival of the king. Many of them took off in different directions, and only when the majority had disappeared did he turn back to us.

"Naturally Prince Lucas will wish to return to his birthday celebration," Thaddeus said. "But I imagine the young lady is in some shock. I can have my men escort—"

Lucas frowned, but at which part of the speech I couldn't be sure. And before he or anyone else could respond, a new arrival cut in.

"I assure you that won't be necessary, Thaddeus." Lorcan had joined us, flanked by Jocasta and Walden. My relief at the sight of their familiar faces surprised me.

"Elena is our student, and we will naturally see her back to the calm and safety of the Academy."

Thaddeus narrowed his eyes but gave a brisk nod. "Very well. In that case, I have important matters to attend to."

He strode away, and Lorcan gestured me to his side before bowing to the king and Lucas. "Your Majesty. Your Highness. I hope you will excuse our hasty departure from your delightful celebration."

King Stellan inclined his head toward all three instructors. "No, indeed. You must accept our apology on behalf of your student for the unfortunate accident. Naturally we will ensure such a thing does not happen again."

I sucked in a breath. Was he serious? I was the one on the balcony when it collapsed, and I was standing right here. Was he really directing his apology at the senior mage who hadn't even been present at the so-called accident?

But of course he was. I didn't know why I was surprised.

I caught Lucas giving me an uneasy sideways look and narrowed my eyes at him. I might have trouble keeping from snapping at him, but even I knew better than to lose control in front of the king.

Coralie appeared from nowhere as soon as the king and Lucas

had swept away, and it was only with some difficulty that I convinced her to stay at the celebration.

"I'm fine, truly I am," I assured her. "Please stay and enjoy yourself enough for both of us."

"She is in good hands," Lorcan told her with a look of half amusement and half exasperation.

"Go!" I gave her a gentle shove, and she reluctantly disappeared back toward the ballroom.

"Now, Elena, if you please." Lorcan gestured for me to follow him, and the other two instructors fell in around us.

I couldn't help the feeling that they were shielding me as they hurried me out of the palace grounds and down the short stretch of road to the Academy. We didn't bother to wait for a carriage, and I hugged myself in a useless attempt to keep out the cold.

None of us spoke, and I was glad for it, my mind racing too fast to form coherent words. Far too many intense things had happened in the last hour for normal processing.

I let them lead me into Lorcan's study without protesting, sinking into the nearest chair. For a moment the warmth now enveloping me made me close my eyes. I tried to ready myself for the barrage of questions that was no doubt incoming, but the first comment didn't seem directed to me.

"Did either of you feel something?"

My eyes shot open to find Lorcan regarding the other two instructors.

"Not either of the prince's two workings," he clarified, "but before that. When the balcony collapsed."

Jocasta and Walden exchanged a look, and Walden shrugged while Jocasta shifted uneasily.

"Maybe? It's hard to say. There were too many compositions being used at the celebration to be sure."

Lorcan rubbed his chin. "Yes, that's what I was afraid of." He stalked over and collapsed into the chair behind his desk. "Oh,

Thaddeus will investigate, no doubt, but I can't imagine he'll find anything. Not anything conclusive, anyway."

I blinked and looked between the three of them. Only Jocasta glanced my way, a frown between her eyes, but she made no effort to address me directly. Apparently the presence of an eyewitness was not of interest to them. Not when the eyewitness was me, at any rate.

I stood abruptly. Walden started and hurried over to grasp my hand.

"And are you truly unharmed, my dear? What a terrifying experience! Thank goodness Lucas was on hand."

His warmth softened his assumption that Lucas must have saved me—an assumption they all seemed to share—and I managed a smile. I could hardly blame him when he'd been working so hard to help me unlock my powers without success. I even felt a little guilty for not immediately telling him the truth about what had happened when the balcony collapsed.

"Indeed," said Lorcan thoughtfully. "We must speak with the prince as soon as he returns to the Academy. He may have sensed something given his presence at the scene."

I narrowed my eyes. I had no such compunction about concealing the truth from Lorcan, and certainly felt no inclination to be open with him now.

"I'm going to bed," I said, instead.

His eyes swung to me. "Indeed. A wise choice, I'm sure. And I think in future, it might be best if you confined yourself to Academy grounds."

I raised both eyebrows. "Is that an order? Am I forbidden to leave the Academy?"

Lorcan drummed his fingers on the desk. "Students are not prisoners. Such a thing would be unprecedented, and we are trying..." He frowned. "Let us say that I strongly recommend—"

"I'll take it under advisement," I said, my voice flat.

Lorcan's eyes narrowed, but he didn't actually protest, waving a dismissal instead. I left his office and climbed the stairs with my head in a whirl, my feet finding the familiar way while my head was somewhere else entirely.

I had felt power swelling over the balcony as it cracked, I was sure of it. Although apparently the composition had been too subtle—and too lost in a sea of other compositions—for anyone else to be sure of its origin or even existence.

I had also saved myself with a spoken composition. I was sure of that, too, although I had no clear idea of how exactly I had achieved it. And my second working must have had a little more control than my first since everyone seemed to be attributing my use of power to Lucas.

All I wanted to do now was try again. Perhaps the near catastrophe had unlocked something. I certainly hoped so, since if my power could only be accessed in moments of extreme stress, that was far from ideal.

But caution held me back from attempting anything further tonight, the collapse of the balcony having refreshed the memory of the crushing stones in the library. Better to wait until I could ask for Walden's help. He could set up some sort of shield before I started experimenting.

Surely now that we had two instances to draw on, we could find some shared aspect between the two that might unlock my ability.

Despite my statement to Lorcan about heading for bed, when I actually reached my room, I couldn't bring myself to lie down. Even my room felt too constricted, and I soon ended up pacing the deserted corridor, with no one to disturb me since all of the other first years remained at the Midwinter celebration.

I kept my steps to the left section of corridor, not wanting to intrude on the domain of the second years on the other side of the stairs. Many of them were no doubt celebrating Midwinter with their families, but I didn't want to risk running into anyone right now. At the first sign of returning first years, I would dash back to my room. I suspected Coralie would come knocking, but I intended to feign sleep. I wasn't ready to talk about what had happened with anyone. Not until I worked out if I could finally unlock my abilities properly.

It ticked over midnight—Midwinter no longer—but I didn't expect anyone back that early. No doubt the festivities would continue long into the night. And I knew my year mates had been looking forward to them too much to want to come home early.

Home. The thought stopped me. When had the Academy become home in my mind? I shook myself. This wasn't my home, and I couldn't forget that. My thoughts flew to my true home, and I wished I could have seen the look on Clemmy's face when Jasper turned up to surprise them. How happy they must all be now. How happy I would be if I was only there with them.

I let my mind wander from the mysteries of my ability and the strangeness of the court to dwell in Kingslee instead. It had only been a season and a half, and yet it scared me how much the memories of my home were fading.

A soft sound behind me made me swing around. Had I missed my opportunity to escape before the other students returned?

But the figure that stepped out of the shadows caught me completely by surprise.

"Lucas? What are you doing here?"

He took another step forward, and I took one back.

"Don't you have a suite with the fourth years? What are you doing all the way up here?"

"Looking for you." He took another step forward, and I took another one back.

"You shouldn't be here, you should be at your birthday celebrations."

He just shrugged and stepped again. This time my back hit the wall, just to one side of the tall window at the end of the corridor. Moonlight bathed us both as he finally closed the distance between us.

"I came looking for you," he repeated.

"Why?" I asked, my voice coming out more shakily than I had intended. This was the second time tonight I had found myself standing in the moonlight, far too close to the prince.

"Elena." His voice wound around my name in a way I had never imagined but I knew would now haunt my dreams. "You were standing on a balcony that collapsed. And you saved yourself with your words. Do you have any idea how incredible…" He shook his head. "Clearly you don't."

I stiffened, but when his eyes dropped to my lips, for once words deserted me. If only he would step back, perhaps I might be able to think again. Think about something other than how unutterably handsome and commanding he looked, still in his party finery, at any rate. And how much I hated him for looking like that when I disliked him so much.

"You felt it, right?" I forced myself to form the words.

He pulled his gaze up to my eyes, a frown pulling his brow down.

"Your working? Yes, of course."

"No, before that. When the balcony started to collapse."

"Oh. That." He braced himself on the wall behind me with one arm, looking downward to examine my face. "You felt that too?"

"Yes, I felt it." Somehow the words came out even though I wasn't sure I remembered how to breathe. I reminded myself he only had one hand up. I wasn't trapped. I could leave whenever I wanted to. Just as soon as my legs began working again.

"Non-mages can't feel power, you know."

"Wait? Really?" That shocked me enough to break through my stupor. How had I not known that before? *Because naturally mages don't write books about common folk and their experiences.*

So I couldn't write safely, but I could feel power. One count for, one count against. I wished I'd known the significance of that all those times I'd doubted myself.

"You are a mystery, Elena."

He regarded me with such a look of fascination, I put both hands against his chest and pushed. Hard. I wasn't a puzzle for the entertainment of a prince.

He gave way, dropping his arm and moving back a step.

"The real mystery is who collapsed that balcony." I gave him a hard look. "And whether they meant for you to still be on it or not."

His face didn't change, and I knew he'd already thought this through. But he didn't reply, and I sighed.

"You didn't say anything. To Thaddeus. About it not being an accident. About me."

"Thaddeus is…"

"Your cousin?"

"A Stantorn."

"What does that mean?"

He shrugged as if lost for words.

I sighed and moved to step around him. "Go to bed, Lucas. Or back to your party. I don't need or want you here."

His hand closed around my arm, halting my progress. His eyes found mine.

"It didn't harm you? That fall? Not at all?"

"As you see." I made a sweeping gesture down my body, but instantly regretted it when his eyes followed my motion. I still wore the green Midwinter dress, and I wished for my normal sturdy outfit and a thick cloak. This prince brought up far too many emotions in me, and I wished I could hide away from him and never have to untangle them all.

"Do you think you could do it again?"

"What—fall?"

But my sarcastic reply somehow didn't seem like enough. I considered. "Honestly? I don't know."

His lips parted slightly, but he only nodded thoughtfully. I pulled away before he could ask me to keep him updated or something. I owed him nothing.

But as I reached my own door, my steps faltered. I remembered the way he had moved toward me back at the palace, aligning himself with me, halting the approach of the guards. I looked back at him over my shoulder.

"Happy Birthday, Lucas," I said softly.

The moonlight clearly illuminated the surprise on his face, and I gestured at the dark sky outside the window.

"It's after midnight. Today is your birthday, right?"

He nodded slowly, and I gave him the smallest of smiles.

"So Happy Birthday, Prince."

I heard his sigh as I closed my door behind me.

CHAPTER 18

The trainees had all been given the day after Midwinter off. Many had spent the night with their families, making us a small group over breakfast. Lucas didn't appear. Had he returned to the palace and the celebration after our conversation?

I was tempted to ask Coralie, but instead reminded myself I didn't care what he had done. My friend had danced into the small hours and barely made it down in time to grab a plate of food before it was cleared away.

Her exhaustion saved me from an endless string of questions —all of which would no doubt be coming soon enough. But I used her distraction with the food to slip away as soon as possible. I had plans for my free day.

When I pushed open the double doors, I discovered I was the only student to rush to the library on my day off. Which was perfect for my plans. As long as the library head hadn't also taken the day off.

But when I knocked on Walden's office door, a bleary, "Come in," sounded.

"Ah, Elena, I should have known it would be you." He gestured for me to take a seat across from his desk. "And how are you feeling this morning? Fully recovered?"

I ignored his questions, too on edge for small talk. I leaned forward in my chair, my hands bouncing against my knees.

"Lucas didn't save me, Walden."

He blinked and frowned. "I'm sorry, I don't quite..."

"Last night. When the balcony collapsed. Lucas didn't save me. I saved myself." I didn't mention the power I had felt as it collapsed. They already seemed to have some inkling of that, and right now I was too focused on my own ability to want to be delayed talking about it.

"You..." Walden blinked again and then leaned forward across his desk. "You saved yourself? With a composition. Verbal?"

I just gave him an exasperated look. "No, with a written one I had stashed on my person. Of course verbal!"

None of the other instructors would have appreciated my sarcasm, but he just chuckled.

"But Elena, that is incredible news. Why didn't you tell us last night?"

"None of you asked." I slid back slightly in my chair and tried not to look like a sulky schoolchild.

Walden shook his head. "That we did not. Our mistake, it seems. But tell me everything. Everything."

And so I did.

"I want to try again," I said at the end. "But I want you to set up a shield first."

Walden smiled. "A wise idea." He spent a moment rummaging in his desk before emerging with a small piece of parchment which he quickly ripped in half. A whoosh of power swept around us, settling in a circle with my chair in the center.

"That should do us," he said.

But ten minutes later I slumped into my chair. "I'm sorry for making you waste one of your compositions. This is no different from all those other attempts."

"Don't give up yet," he said, tapping his lips. "Go over it again. Every thought, every word, every motion."

"Well, I was plummeting through the air with a bunch of giant stone shards. So I don't remember everything that precisely."

He smiled. "Do your best."

I repeated it all again, this time considering exactly what had gone through my mind as the floor fell away.

"So you thought about the standard shielding composition. And then you spoke your own composing. But it wasn't the same words..." He muttered to himself as he considered it from every angle.

I sat up straight. "Wait. You're right. I thought of the words I'd seen written out for the composition. I was watching Coralie write it only two days ago. I could see the words in my mind. And then I spoke them."

He frowned across at me. "But you said you only spoke two words."

"Yes." I chewed on my lip as I considered it. "I didn't speak all the words. But I spoke two that I saw."

"But what about the other time? Back in your village. We're looking for similarities, and you couldn't even read then."

"No, I couldn't..." I narrowed my eyes. "But I did see something. Something printed that a mage had dropped. A...a dispatch or something? I'm not sure what you would call it. Does that sound familiar at all?"

"A dispatch?" Walden gave me a curious look. "It sounds more like it would have been one of the news sheets some of the disciplines insist on circulating when they become worked up over some issue or other."

"Are there many of them? Would I be able to find the old ones somewhere?"

"We keep copies of all of them here at the library for record-keeping purposes."

I sat up straight. "Do you know which ones a mage might have been carrying at the start of autumn?"

Walden slowly rose to his feet, his face confused but curious. "Wait here."

He was gone for several minutes, and when he returned, he had only three pieces of parchment in his hands. I snatched them from him before he could even hold them out and scanned down the single sheets.

The first one I let fall to the ground, but the second I gripped in a shaking hand.

"Look at this." I thrust it into Walden's face.

He gripped my wrist, steadying me enough that he could examine the paper more closely.

"It looks like a standard anti-Kallorway sheet to me. Every now and then the Armed Forces feel that enthusiasm for the conflict is waning and have such things dispersed. What does it have to do with you?"

"I couldn't read then. I can't be sure. But look at what the first line says." I stabbed at it with my hand before realizing that I must not make any sense. I forced myself to take a deep breath and speak more slowly.

"You might remember that the men who attacked my family's store were worked up because they believed the mages had left writing behind them. Well, it's true. They had. One of these. It was found by a small child and could have brought disaster to the whole village. But thankfully someone older stumbled on the child before any harm was done." I looked up at him.

"And I was there too. We burned it, of course, immediately. But I did get a brief look at it first. Since I couldn't read then, it didn't mean much to me, but I think it must have been this one. It looks similar to my memory. And more importantly, look at the first line."

I held it out again.

STOP the Kallorwegian Aggression!

The bold title instantly caught the eye now as it had done then, when I couldn't understand it.

"I saw them," I said. "I saw the letters in my mind before I commanded the men to stop. And look what it says!"

Walden rocked back on his heels, his eyes wide. "And last night you pictured your friend's composition and spoke two of its words. But this is remarkable. I never imagined...When you couldn't read..."

"We have to try it." I stood and checked that I could still feel the slight pressure of his shield around me.

"Shall I write something for you? What shall I write?" Walden almost buzzed with excitement, as he crossed back behind his desk.

I didn't need him to write me something, though. I could easily visualize something simple without a written prompt. So as soon as he left the circle of the shield, I took a single step forward, the cocoon of his power following me and enveloping a half-empty cup of tea resting on my side of his desk. Staring at it, I called up the image of a single word in my mind.

"Boil!" I had to resist the urge to point dramatically at the cup.

A surge of power filled the air around me, poking into every corner of the space enclosed by the shield. When it reached the cup, the entire thing shattered with a resounding crack, boiling tea splattering up onto the ceiling and splashing back against me.

I gasped, relieved that the drops had landed only on my arms where my long sleeves protected me from scalding. I looked up guiltily at the liquid dripping from the ceiling, and then down at the shards of the cup.

But I couldn't prevent a smile spreading across my face. "I did it. I actually did it. I've worked out how to control my ability."

Walden gave a small cough. "Control might be something we need to work on."

But when I looked quickly up at him, he was smiling.

"Well done, Elena. Very well done, indeed."

Of course then the real work started.

"You obviously have an innate level of control," Walden said as he located another half-full old tea cup on a side table and moved it into the middle of the floor. "Otherwise that attempt would have ended in disaster when everything liquid inside my shield boiled." He looked up to fix me with a stern stare. "Including your blood."

I gulped as he went on.

"But that's what we've already seen in your two previous workings. Normally, control like that without training would indicate a very powerful mage indeed. But in your case we have no way of knowing if it's simply a byproduct of the way your ability manifests. Of course with a sample size of one, we hardly have the capacity to run any meaningful tests on the subject…"

His voice trailed away into indecipherable murmurings as it sometimes did when he got distracted by some technical train of thought. I cleared my throat, and he looked up, startled.

"Ah yes." He grinned. "To our test."

We kept at it all day. It turned out that despite his mutterings about greater levels of control, my compositions worked much the same as those of my year mates. If I wanted to direct the power properly, I needed to be specific. And to be specific, I needed to first master a set of binding words that would hold the power in place until I had spoken the entire composition.

Except it turned out to be a lot more difficult to properly envision the words before speaking them when I was trying to speak sentences, let alone whole passages. By the end of the day I was utterly wrung out and hadn't managed anything more complicated than successfully boiling the leftover tea in my sixth cup.

"Everyone speaks as if verbal compositions are the key to everything," I said, staring grumpily at the steam rising from the liquid. "But it doesn't seem very practical to me. A normal mage can release a stored composition in the space of a second. But how am I supposed to do that when I have to get off sentence after sentence? And I'll have to think of them on the spot, too. I can hardly pre-store them! A lot of good this ability is going to do me next time someone decides to drop me off a building."

Walden looked up at me sharply, but then shook his head. "Give it time, my dear. You've made excellent progress for one day."

I tried a smile but knew it came out lopsided. I wanted to recapture my excitement from the beginning of the day, but exhaustion weighed me down. My head felt fuzzy, and a sharp tension headache behind one temple was growing rapidly.

I had hoped to be further along. Because while I knew I had succeeded twice now with hastily constructed compositions, understanding the dangers changed everything. I didn't think I would dare try composing with a single word again. And lurking in the back of my mind was the knowledge that someone had just tried to kill me. Or possibly Lucas. But that was only slightly more reassuring since I lived and studied with him every day. And if he was the target, whoever it was clearly hadn't been worried about taking me down with him.

I had thought if I could unlock my powers, I would be safe. But it turned out to be a lot more complicated than that.

"What a surprise," I muttered to myself, "I should have known."

When the dinner bell rang, I stumbled blearily from Walden's office. I paused at the door to thank him for his efforts—he'd given up his whole day for me, after all—and he clapped me lightly on the shoulder.

"Elena…" He paused and then just shook his head. "Get some rest. You deserve it."

Rest sounded like a good idea, but my stomach had other priorities.

"There you are!" Coralie pounced on me as soon as my feet led me mindlessly into the dining hall. "I've been looking for you everywhere." She seemed to have recovered from her earlier exhaustion.

"I was with Walden." He had ordered our lunch brought to his office, so I hadn't seen Coralie since breakfast.

She rolled her eyes. "All day? It's a holiday, Elena. You're not supposed to spend it studying."

I just shrugged and filled my plate. She regarded me with narrowed eyes, so I quickly asked a question, hoping to head her off.

"How was the rest of the party last night?"

She clasped her hands together, her eyes glowing.

"Utterly, utterly incredible. I danced and danced and ate and ate. And walked out in the gardens with the nicest of my dance partners. He's a student at the University." She giggled. "And I might have let him steal a kiss."

I suppressed a groan. Hopefully this wasn't the start of a new crush like some of the girls back in Kingslee used to have. Ones which required their friends to listen to endless enumerations of the crush's virtues along with equally endless wondering as to the level of interest on his side.

"His name was Edmond," she added.

The name brushed against my memory. "Wait. I might actually have met him. Was he tall and seemed more like an apprentice Player than an academic?"

"That's him!" Coralie clutched at my arm. "Does your brother know him? Next time you see Jasper, could you ask for me? Whether Edmond has said anything, I mean."

"My brother's in Kingslee, remember?"

"But when he gets back?"

Reluctantly I nodded. I doubted this Edmond would still be talking about a dance partner from the Midwinter celebrations by the time my brother got back—if they were even friends to begin with, which I wasn't so sure about. And I didn't like the idea of being the bearer of bad tidings. But neither could I refuse such earnest pleading.

Coralie took several bites, seemingly satisfied with my unenthusiastic response, until she suddenly rounded on me, fork stabbing the air accusingly.

"Don't think you can distract me! You were standing on a balcony that collapsed! I want to hear everything." She lowered her voice, glancing around us at the tables that were considerably more full than they had been at breakfast. "Everyone was talking about how old the palace is, and how fortunate that the prince was on hand to prevent disaster. But don't think it escaped certain people's notice that you must have been out on that balcony alone with Lucas." She gave me a significant look, and my thoughts flew immediately to the two generals towering over me, the queen and princess at their sides.

But Coralie's eyes flicked meaningfully toward the table where Lucas sat with the twins, the Stantorn cousins, Lavinia and Weston, and the brilliant but aloof Dariela. My heart rate slowed to its usual pace. If that's who she meant, they could think what they liked, as far as I was concerned.

Especially since neither Lucas nor I made any effort to hide our disdain for each other. I couldn't imagine any of the people sitting at that table would harbor any concerns about me and the prince for long. Not when every one of them clearly thought I was unworthy of their precious Academy or of interacting with their important mage selves.

I had far more dangerous people to worry about. And not just people. After my breakthrough, my mind had been consumed by an entirely new worry. After a full day of composing and forcing myself to visualize my words, I kept seeing letters dancing in front of my eyes. A hazardous phenomenon that I needed to find a way to rein in before I ended up unintentionally speaking one of the words and destroying half the Academy by accident.

I could only be glad now that I had never been given the opportunity to learn to read as a child. My illiteracy had no doubt saved my life many times over.

"At midnight they cut this enormous cake, and the king gave a speech about his son." Coralie was chattering on about the night before. "And then Lucas gave a speech thanking everyone. And then he disappeared."

She gave me an excited and intrigued look, as if expecting me to dive into speculation with her. None of which was helping with my ongoing quest not to think about Lucas. Or look at him. Or talk to him. Or talk about him.

I said nothing.

"So, where do you think he went?" Coralie waited expectantly, but when I still said nothing, she hurried on. "I overheard Natalya talking to Lavinia. She was not happy. Lucas didn't dance with any of us from the Academy except Dariela. And I think Natalya was convinced he was just waiting until after midnight to ask her. You should have heard the cutting things she said about poor Dariela."

I couldn't resist a quick glance at their table. Dariela looked entirely unconcerned—as she always did—and an amiable peace seemed to exist between all parties.

"I don't know that I would describe Dariela as poor anything," I said. "Aren't the Ellingtons all excessively rich? She's also tall and beautiful and beyond brilliant. I bet she'll end up head of whatever discipline she ends up choosing."

Coralie shrugged. "Most of them are rich, but everyone has some poor cousins somewhere. You're right about Dariela, though. She's no poor cousin." She grinned. "And that's what makes it so excellent. Natalya doesn't want to alienate her, but she's by far her biggest competition. I think that's why she's so particularly nasty to you—you're her only safe outlet."

I rolled my eyes. "I'm pretty sure I inspire the nastiness all on my own. I'm commonborn, remember? And I'm also entirely useless and unable to compose a single..."

My words faltered as I suddenly remembered that was no longer true. A tiny spark of my earlier exhilaration fought its way up through my exhaustion.

Coralie stared at me.

"Wait," she whispered, leaning forward. "What is that look for?" Her eyes widened. "You said you were with Walden all day...Don't tell me you did it!"

I hesitated only for a moment, biting my lip, before the whispered words burst from me in a rush.

"Yes, I did it. I can verbally compose now. I actually did it!"

"Eeee!" Coralie dropped her voice guiltily when I glared at her.

Several of the other trainees looked over at us with idle curiosity—but one gaze bit into me. Lucas's eyes were sharp, his expression assessing. I quickly looked away, shaking my head at Coralie.

"Please don't say anything to anyone. I'm not ready to share it yet. I want to work on my control before I start getting asked for demonstrations." I scrunched up my nose.

"Demonstrations?"

I filled my friend in on the happenings of the night before the balcony collapse.

"Oh wow! Both the generals *and* the queen *and* Princess Lucienne? I'm glad I'd already left, I would have been quaking in my slippers."

"Thanks."

"Oh." She grinned. "Of course I actually mean I would have been standing loyally at your side, the picture of dignity, strength, and support."

I shook my head with a smile and cleaned up the rest of the food on my plate. "I just can't believe how tired I am now. One day of composing, and I feel like I could sleep for a week."

"A day? What do you mean?" Coralie took several more huge bites, rushing to finish her own plate.

I described my day of exercises.

"Wait, what?" Her voice sounded muffled around her mouthful of food. She paused to quickly chew and swallow. "You worked it out straight after breakfast. And then you were training *all day*?"

I nodded, my brow creasing as I stared at her in confusion.

"Yes? So what?"

"So what?! Elena, composing is exhausting. That's one of the reasons we have to spend so long at the Academy training. We have to build up our stamina as well as our skill and control. Why do you think mages dislike wasting their stored compositions? Of course the effort for us comes when we compose them and not when we work them, but still…It's incredibly draining. Don't you remember how I was when we first started actually composing in class?"

I shook my head. "I was with Jocasta then, remember? For weeks." I considered it. "And it was just after I arrived, I didn't have anything previous to compare it to. I guess everyone seemed tired in general, but I don't remember noting it in particular."

"Elena." Coralie dropped her voice even lower. "Lucas is by far the most advanced in our year level at composition—although Dariela is catching him fast. I'm fairly sure he's been having private tutoring ever since he turned sixteen. It's generally frowned on, even for those students who turn sixteen well before the autumn intake, but I guess the rules don't apply to royalty. But even he couldn't spend an *entire day* composing non-stop and still walk afterward—let alone carry on a coherent conversation."

I shifted uncomfortably in my seat. "I guess verbal composing works differently."

"Maybe…" Coralie's wide-eyed gaze unnerved me.

"I am excessively tired. In fact, I think I'm going to head for bed now." I stood but paused before leaving. "Remember—don't mention it to anyone."

"I won't." Coralie gave me a quick smile. "But I can't wait for you to show the rest of them."

And I had to admit that thought occupied some of my own mind as I finally slipped into bed. At least until my head hit the pillow and sleep instantly claimed me.

I missed the breakfast bell and would have missed combat class as well if Coralie hadn't hammered at my door without pause until I stumbled out of bed and let her in.

"Elena! You're not even dressed!"

Her horrified face galvanized me into action, and I soon had my clothes and robe in place and was hurrying toward our usual training yard. It had been a long time since I missed breakfast, but the extra rest had no doubt been worth it. I felt rejuvenated and alive, everything in me buzzing to try composing again.

I was so full of energy, in fact, that I managed to knock Finnian entirely off his feet with my staff. Thornton, who had been passing us at the time, actually paused, a look of pain on his face.

"Well done," he managed to choke out before hurrying off.

I giggled as I helped Finnian back up. "Did you see how much it hurt him to say that?"

Finnian rubbed his rear and shook his head at me. "Someone's in a good mood today."

Even sitting through composition was less painful than usual, and I volunteered the answer to not one but three questions, which put Redmond in a foul mood. I carefully listened to everything he said, considering how I might apply it to my own ability. Not that I intended to do any practice here in class with him. But I already had ideas for what to try next with Walden.

Only the prince's narrowed eyes—all too often focused on me—managed to somewhat depress my good mood. What was going on inside his head? Had he told anyone about my working at the palace? And did he suspect I had finally managed to unlock my ability?

But as soon as class was dismissed, I put him out of my mind, hurrying off to the library, a whispered encouragement from Coralie trailing behind me. She had wanted to come with me, to see my compositions in action, but I had convinced her to wait until I had things under better control.

Later at dinner she gave me a sympathetic grimace in response to my new downcast air. "It didn't go well?"

I considered her question. "No, it went fine."

When she looked at me disbelievingly, I sighed.

"I'm just being an idiot. I was hoping I would improve faster, but I know I need to put in the work. I'm sure I'll get there." I was trying to convince myself as much as her.

She just shook her head and went back to her food. "You only think like this because you don't know how this stuff normally works. You're already making unbelievable progress, Elena. Seriously. Unbelievable."

Walden still hadn't mentioned my apparent stamina, so I suspected Coralie had exaggerated there, but I knew she was right about my progress. After a season and a half of no progress at all, I was now flying along. I just needed a little more patience.

But it was hard to have patience when I wanted to finally catch up with the rest of my year. I couldn't wait to unveil my new ability in class.

As more days passed, however, I realized that even with so much dedicated help from Walden, it was going to take weeks before I reached that point. In fact, I doubted it would happen before spring.

And so I kept my progress to myself.

But I was making progress. I had far fewer failures now, as I slowly acquired the knack of picturing the words at the right speed and detail to allow me to speak them. I could even complete quite long and detailed workings.

But I needed to have them memorized in advance, of course—at least if I didn't want to end up getting muddled and leaving out something important. So a lot of my time went to memorizing the words I would need.

Except with all the time I spent practicing, I could hardly think without words springing into my mind's eye. So still more time went to suppressing the words when I wasn't composing so that they didn't appear at unplanned and dangerous moments.

This risk was Walden's biggest concern, and he kept me to a slow pace until I was sure I wouldn't accidentally unleash any uncontrolled power outside of his office.

I never lingered in the main library now, always hurrying straight for his door. But one day, on the way out, Jocasta stopped me.

"I haven't seen you here in a while." She frowned at me.

I stared at her blankly. "What do you mean? I'm here every day."

"No, here in the library, I mean."

"Oh." I looked around for some kind of escape, not wanting to have this conversation. "Well, I guess I don't have any classes in here yet, and..."

She just watched me.

"I really appreciated your help, though. All the reading you gave me..." I'd been wondering for a while if she was offended that I'd abandoned her tutelage in favor of working with Walden. But then, she'd never seemed to like the assignment, anyway.

I shifted awkwardly from foot to foot.

Jocasta sighed. "It's your life, Elena. I guess I'm just a bit surprised."

I stared at her.

"When I started teaching you, you were so excited to learn. Something about unlocking mysteries. I even heard you muttering to yourself once about the words calling to you."

I managed a weak smile, embarrassed she'd heard that. I used to think they called to everyone, but now I wondered if it was actually my suppressed ability that had created the effect.

Jocasta shrugged. "You seem to be making great progress now, but I guess…"

I frowned. None of the other instructors had mentioned anything, so I hadn't been sure if Walden had been keeping any of them updated. He knew I wanted to catch up before spreading the word around, but then I guess it wasn't surprising that the assistant head of the library would know what was going on in her own library.

"I guess I thought you had a greater interest in reading than just unlocking your power," she finished. When I just stood there, she gestured at the library behind her. "I gave you books on composition because I knew you needed to catch up in class, but this library holds a lot more than that. And it's always open to students."

I bit the inside of my cheek, suddenly unable to meet her eye. She was right. I had become obsessed with controlling my power and catching up with my year mates. So much so that I had forgotten that early excitement at being able to unlock all the secrets of this vast place.

"The dinner bell's already sounded," I said, mumbling a quick farewell and fleeing the room. Jocasta had always been impatient with me, so there was no need to let her poor opinion affect me so much now.

I should be more than used to it. With the exception of Walden, Coralie, Finnian, and possibly Saffron, everyone here had fairly low opinions of me. Well, maybe not Damon or Acacia, but I saw them so little they hardly counted.

But her disappointed expression still haunted me, which is perhaps why I didn't notice any warning signs before something hard hit me in the back of the head, sending me sprawling forward across the corridor floor.

CHAPTER 19

"Really?" drawled an unimpressed voice. It was a girl, but with the ringing in my ears, I struggled to recognize it. "Is this what we've come to?"

I twisted around, scuttling backward to get away from the threat. Five figures loomed over me.

"It's been half a year, Dariela," said Weston, sounding almost as bored as the previous speaker but a great deal more vindictive. "So apparently this *is* what we've come to. Expected to share class time with a commonborn girl with no control whatsoever. I thought we could safely leave it to our elders to get rid of her, but they seem unable to act for some reason. And since she didn't seem to get my message in combat on her first day, I'd say it's past time we showed her she's not welcome here."

I was too focused on his face to see the movement to my right. Calix's foot caught me in my middle, driving me back against the stone wall with a crack.

I groaned, barely able to get the sound out before he kicked me again. Pain lanced up my side to join the throbbing in my head. I tried to push myself upright, drawing on my months of combat training, but a new foot kicked me back down. Four of them circled me now, keeping me pinned against the wall. My vision had started to blur, but it wasn't hard to make out the twins and the Stantorn cousins. Apparently I had been wrong when I deemed them harmless compared to my other worries.

"I don't have time for this nonsense," said Dariela. "I'm here to learn. You all want to distract yourselves, go ahead. But I'm out." She took off down the corridor toward the dining hall.

But she hadn't yet disappeared from sight when a new figure appeared. A brief surge of hope that it might be an instructor or one of my own friends was dashed when I recognized the silhouette.

"Lucas knows we're right," Lavinia said with a nod to the new arrival, but her voice lacked confidence. I should have taken more note of Coralie's warning. Apparently my year mates' distaste at seeing me invade even more of their world had led to a more violent response than I had anticipated.

I looked past Lucas, hoping he wasn't alone, but no one else was in sight. I was later for the meal than I'd realized. My eyes returned to him, my silent plea cut off by another foot to the ribs that caused my head to crack back against the stone of the wall. I whimpered—the only sound I could manage—and curled up with one hand around my middle and the other attempting to cover my head.

"I can assure you I am not in the habit of beating my unarmed year mates," said the prince's voice.

Calix just snorted in reply. "Princes don't get their hands dirty, Lavinia. That's what they have us for. Not that we're using our hands." He smirked as he drew his foot back to strike again.

When the attacks had been nothing but words, the two boys had been happy to sit back and leave it to their sister and cousin. But just like on my first day with Weston, when it came to physicality, the boys apparently had no hesitation wading in.

Despite knowing better, my eyes flew instinctively to Lucas. A dark look had come into his eyes, and he stepped toward us, his hands balling into fists. I had the fleeting impression he meant to attack—but me or Calix? As always he only left me confused.

Anger surged through me and with it a sensation of power. The initial shock and pain had driven any thought of defense from my mind, but I now remembered that I wasn't the helpless common girl they thought me.

Unbidden, the binding words rose up in front of my eyes, and I spoke them, almost tripping over the words in my haste. Calix paused, casting a confused glance at Weston.

His hesitation gave me the extra moments I needed to complete my composition. "Shield my body from blows, and repel—" at the last moment, I realized I needed a tighter focus on the working and forced new words to form in front of my eyes. "...my four attackers without causing serious injury. End binding."

As I spoke the final word, power blossomed around me, wrapping me in a bubble. At the same time, four tendrils of it burst outward, thrusting Calix, Natalya, Lavinia, and Weston away from me. They all hit the far wall hard, Lucas just dodging out of their way in time to avoid getting swept up.

For a panting breath, I stayed curled in place, pain still radiating through me, my eyes locked on his. He didn't turn to check on his friends, and I couldn't read the expression in his eyes. Because it couldn't possibly be elation.

Then he broke my gaze, striding off down the corridor without a backward glance for the others who all now slumped against the far wall groaning.

I watched him go. At least I had retained enough sense to modify my working at the last moment. For all my rage against him, it would be unwise to magically attack a prince.

Just like it would have been unwise to leave my composition open enough that I might have caused serious damage to a trainee from an influential mage family. If I'd had more time, I could have shaped it not to harm them at all, but the blinding pain in my middle and head made it hard to regret the lack of direction.

I managed to push myself to my feet, although both hands now clutched my middle and I couldn't quite stand straight. Wobbling slightly, I glared at my four slumped opponents.

"I may be commonborn, but I do have control. So I recommend you all leave me alone."

All four of them stared at me, apparently struck dumb with shock.

I shrugged, the movement making me wince, and shuffled off down the corridor. I had made it a short distance when racing feet sounded, and someone rushed to put their shoulder under one of my arms.

"You're on your feet and moving, that's a good sign," said Acacia's calm voice. "In that case, let's get you into my offices."

I let her guide me forward, groaning again when she lowered me into a chair.

"You look worse than the first time we met," she said, actually grinning as she selected a series of parchments from out of her robe and drawers.

"You're a monster." I groaned.

She ripped the first parchment, and her cool mist settled over me, bringing numbing relief.

"I take it all back," I said, "you're a credit to the Academy."

She just shook her head, still grinning, as she ripped another parchment, this one considerably longer than the ones I had seen her use in this office on my first day. I tried to ignore the grinding noise that preceded a sudden increased ability to breathe freely.

She ripped two more, and I focused on breathing deeply while the last of the mist settled over me. When the sensation disappeared, I gingerly pulled up the layers of my clothes and examined my side. The skin looked clear and unblemished, not so much as a bruise in sight.

"You know, you first years have been a quiet year." She bustled about, disposing of the torn pieces of parchment and closing her drawers. "I expected to have you at least in here more often."

"Thanks? I think." I hopped to my feet. "Although don't go forgetting my epic failure in the library."

"No, indeed. How could I forget? It took me weeks to replenish the compositions I had to use on you and Jocasta. Those were the big ones." She gave me a mock glare.

"Elena?" Coralie came bursting into the room. "There you are! I heard there was a fight. Thank goodness Acacia was on hand."

Acacia shook her head. "Looked more like a beating to me." She eyed me. "Are there other patients needing my attention then?"

I shook my head. I had no doubt that if any of the others had been sufficiently hurt to need her attentions, they would have barged in here on their own demanding she see to them first.

"Come on, you've completely missed dinner, but I've saved you some food." Coralie waved her hand for me to join her at the door.

I shuffled over with a murmured thank you to Acacia. It wasn't until I was long gone that it occurred to me to wonder how she had known to come running for me in the first place.

I don't know who talked—I couldn't imagine the others being eager to broadcast their attack and subsequent defeat—but somehow the word got out. Whispers and stares followed me as they had in my first couple of days and after the disaster in the library.

And when I arrived at combat the next morning, Thornton sent me straight back inside.

"You're wanted in Lorcan's office," he said as Natalya smirked at me.

I ignored her. She and the other three had all drawn back at the sight of me that morning, and two of them had visible bruises, so I could cope with a little smirking.

Lorcan's reaction worried me a great deal more. Had one of them reported the interaction to him? I could only imagine how they would have described it, if so, and I didn't imagine the narrative would have carried much similarity with the truth.

But when I knocked on the Academy Head's door, he greeted me with a broad smile.

"So, it seems you've been holding out on us, Elena." He gestured toward a chair, and I sank into it. "I take it your studies with Walden have finally borne fruit."

I swallowed and nodded, waiting for him to make mention of the altercation the evening before. He said nothing about it, however.

"Naturally I am fascinated by this development." He fixed me with a stern stare. "But I will need you and Walden to keep me apprised of your future progress."

I nodded, glad to hear Walden had indeed kept my trust.

"Now." Lorcan clapped his hands together. "A demonstration would be in order, I think."

He had me compose a working to lift several small objects from his desk and send them flying around the room. A glowering Redmond, who arrived soon after, had me set several pieces of parchment on fire. I half expected Lorcan to object to that suggestion, but he merely scribbled down a shield composition, tearing it as soon as he'd completed the last word.

Lorcan had barely thrown a jug of water over the burning pile when Jessamine, the University Head, came bursting into the room.

"She did it?" She looked around until her eyes latched on me. "I came as soon as I got your message."

"I imagined it might bring you running," said Lorcan, an amused gleam in his eye.

Jessamine eyed the sodden, blackened mass on the floor. "What have I missed?"

So then I had to repeat both demonstrations while the three of them watched with varying levels of fascination. And once the two heads got talking, the technical language flying, even Redmond unbent a little and joined in the discourse. Walden was summoned at some point and questioned on the progression of our efforts and training and the many unsuccessful methods we had attempted.

No one asked me anything, and I soon retreated to a chair on the edge of the room. I could only follow some of what they were saying, and after a while I gave up trying altogether until Jessamine suddenly rounded on me.

"You. Elena." She frowned at me. "Are you tired?"

"Yes," I said, well and truly tired of the whole thing.

She nodded as if she had expected as much and turned back to the conversation. Walden gave me an odd look, and I realized belatedly what she must actually have meant. Had those four little compositions exhausted me?

The answer to that should actually have been no. In fact, I felt a great deal less tired than I generally would at this time of the morning after a session of combat training. I didn't bother to correct her, though. They all thought me far too much of a curiosity already, and if there was any truth in what Coralie had told me that news would only exacerbate the situation.

If they want to know more detail, they could consider including me in the conversation.

The clang of the lunch bell jerked me out of a half-daze brought on by my period of inactivity. Lorcan looked up only long enough to dismiss me absentmindedly, before they all continued their conversation.

Walden smiled at me in a friendly way, but the other two didn't even appear to notice my departure as I slipped quietly from the room. When I entered the dining hall, however, my presence was definitely noted. A hiss of surprise sounded from the table usually occupied by the prince and his highborn companions.

"She's still here!" Natalya said in an audible whisper.

I slid into place beside Coralie who glared at the other table before turning to me.

"So? Did you get in trouble?"

I shook my head. "No one even mentioned it. They were all just excited because I've worked out how to unlock my ability. I had to give all these demonstrations, and then Jessamine arrived, and the conversation got too technical for me."

Coralie shook her head. "Someone really wants you to stay here. And it's driving that lot over there crazy." She grinned.

"I'm pretty sure I know exactly who it is. Lorcan and Jessamine—since they see me as a fascinating object of study."

Coralie ignored me, her eyes still on Lucas's table. "You know, it's kind of satisfying to see something that they can't order how they want. Let them have a taste of what it's like not to be born into one of the great families."

I raised an eyebrow. "Try being commonborn."

"No thanks," said Finnian, taking one of the seats across from us. "No offense, Elena." He grinned at me, and I couldn't help smiling back, although I rolled my eyes at him as well.

Finnian might be born into as powerful a family as anyone—other than Lucas—but it was somehow impossible not to like him.

Coralie also smiled at him, but she gave an apologetic look in my direction. "Sorry, Elena, I forget sometimes."

"Sometimes?" I tried not to let too much anger sound in my voice because I knew it wasn't really directed at her. But some of it still leaked through. "What about all the time? The whole lot of you. You really have no idea what it's like out there for the rest of us. Struggling to get by without any of the resources you take for granted. Without even the ability to write each other notes or keep records of any kind."

They both stared at me in shock while I ranted on.

"You all act as if we're idiots, but it seems to me, we're probably smarter than the lot of you. We have to be to get anywhere in life. Just imagine how much intelligence it would take to run a business without any written records or any help from compositions. And many of us *commonborn* do just that. We pass on our skills from generation to generation without any Academy or University to help us. And yet, do you know how often any of you mages talk directly to me? You'd rather ask another mage who wasn't even present for answers to your questions when I'm sitting right there with all the answers!"

I stopped for a breath.

"I talk to you," said Finnian, seeming unperturbed by my sudden attack, despite it being so far from his usual joking tone.

I instantly deflated. "I know you do. You and Coralie are my only friends." I ran a hand across my face. "I shouldn't have unloaded on you like that. You're not the problem—not really. The fact that you're sitting here with me proves that."

"Well, you're not wrong," he said, taking a calm bite.

"Really?" I eyed him warily, but he looked back at me with a serious face and clear eyes.

"Nothing you said is untrue. And we do forget it, all the time. Even my family."

"Even your family?" My brow crinkled in confusion.

"His father's the Head of the Healers, remember," said Coralie in a subdued voice. "They run clinics in all the major cities. Clinics that are open to anyone."

"Anyone who can pay," I muttered, before biting my tongue.

"Yes, they do charge a fee." Finnian sighed. "Otherwise they'd be overrun, and we wouldn't have the resources to continue." He made a face. "Mages don't work for free, you know, and we have a limited supply of energy. Especially with so many healers needed by the Armed Forces."

I opened my mouth, but he cut me off.

"And, yes, I know there aren't enough healers there either. And that too often soldiers succumb to their injuries before they can be taken to a healer. But it's better than having none, that's for sure."

Reluctantly I nodded. Far too many died anyway, and no doubt the healers' strength always went first to any injured officers—since officers were all mage members of the armed forces discipline. But at least the commonborn who served with the Armed Forces didn't need to pay a fee to access healers.

A boy from Kingslee had returned from his term of service only the year before with tales of having his arm almost entirely regrown. It had given my family hope that the healers could fix Clementine—once Jasper got a rich enough job that we could afford to pay their fees, of course.

"Other than the odd lone mage selling compositions, the healers are the only discipline actively available to the common folk," Coralie added. "That's why healers are often more understanding of non-bloods."

"We're not the only ones who help," Finnian said. "The creators and the growers and the wind workers all do work that benefits everyone—building roads, ensuring the crops grow, etc. But I'll admit they do it under royal direction or under order from the Mage Council. They won't work to help individuals."

"Commonborn individuals anyway," I said, giving him a significant look. "I'll bet if your family needed help with building some manor or saving some farm, they'd be willing to assist."

Finnian grimaced. "We wouldn't need to ask. There are plenty of Callinos mages in all of those disciplines who would help us in their spare time."

Coralie sighed. "The difference between the great families and the rest of us. We have to rely on who we have, and we don't always have the right skills." She looked over at me. "But at least we have some skills, I suppose."

I managed a smile for her sake. "I really am sorry to attack you like that, Coralie. You're clearly the most open person here." I sighed. "Which I guess is what depresses me sometimes."

"And yet, here I sit," said Finnian quietly.

I looked quickly over at him, and he met my gaze steadily.

"You bring change just by being here, Elena. And if the rumors I'm hearing about your recent activities are true, there's a lot more change coming." He raised an eyebrow, and I reluctantly nodded.

"Ah." He sat back in his chair, his eyes brightening with interest. "So you really truly can work verbal compositions?"

I nodded again, and he glanced over at Coralie. "I have this strange feeling that our whole world might look different by the time you graduate, Elena. Don't underestimate how much difference one person can make."

I wanted to let his words buoy me, but he obviously didn't know that there was no way I was going to graduate. I only had until I turned eighteen. And since spring had arrived—meaning my seventeenth birthday was fast approaching—that only left me one more year.

CHAPTER 20

Redmond continued to ignore me as much as possible in composition class, and I gratefully accepted the unexpected reprieve. It gave me an excuse to continue my private lessons with the much more friendly Walden.

I tried to limit them to the session after composition, though. My other free time I spent roaming the library or curled up in my room with a book. Reading had been difficult and labored for so long that it was hard to believe what a joy it was now. I should never have abandoned Jocasta's reading assignments to focus solely on my powers.

I didn't need to go to Jocasta for books anymore, though. Instead I relished the freedom to read anything I wanted to read. From history to politics to fairy stories. It had never occurred to me that someone would waste valuable writing resources on something so entirely unpractical. But as soon as I read one, I understood why. These must be to mage children what the village storytellers were to the rest of us—gateways to a magical land where anything was possible. A land that resembled reality just enough to stick in our hearts and minds.

Although less intensive, the main difference in my lessons

with Walden was that Lorcan or Jessamine were wont to appear at will, sometimes with academics from the University in tow, to observe my efforts. I tried my best to ignore them, but I always performed worse on a day when I was observed.

Apparently I didn't perform badly enough, however.

On the day of my seventeenth birthday, I was woken before breakfast by a knock on my door. Rolling sleepily out of bed, I pulled it open and nearly fell backward in surprise. Instead I tipped myself forward and into my brother's arms.

"Happy Birthday," he said, ruffling my hair and briefly squeezing me back. When I showed no signs of letting go, he shoved me back into my room and entered, looking curiously around.

"Nice view." He crossed over to stare out the window.

I mumbled an agreement, still half asleep, and commanded him to remain in place while I got dressed. I was soon in my normal outfit, robe in place, and sitting on the bed while he took the chair.

"How did you get up here?" I asked.

"I ran into someone called Damon? Once I managed to convince him I really was your brother, and also dropped the information it was your birthday, he showed me which room you were in."

"How was Midwinter?" I asked eagerly. "How was Clemmy? Not sick, I hope! And Mother and Father? Were they all utterly surprised?"

He smiled. "There were all the tears and exclamations you could ask for." His face dropped a little. "We just wished you could be there, too."

I nodded, speaking quickly because I didn't want to dwell on it. "But at least you could give them news of me. And I got your present. I even wore it to..." I halted, not wanting to talk about the celebration at the palace either.

"Yes, I heard about that," said Jasper grimly, all his previous good humor wiped away. "Well, not about your accessories, but…"

I regarded him uneasily. "You're not here to give me birthday wishes, are you?" I whispered.

He grimaced. "Not *just* here for birthday wishes." He paused, but when I said nothing, rushed on.

"I didn't get back until two days after Midwinter, but they were still talking about it. You wouldn't believe some of the theories that were flying around. I didn't hear all of them, since everyone knows you're my sister, but I made Clara tell me."

"I can probably guess." I sighed. "How many people think I must have somehow collapsed the balcony in an attempt on the life of the prince?" Thankfully no one with any real authority seemed to have seriously considered such a thing—most likely because they doubted my competence to pull it off—but I could just imagine the sort of rumors that would fly around a place like the University.

"Not the majority, thankfully," said Jasper.

"I hope they haven't been giving you a hard time because of me."

He shrugged. "No more than usual."

I winced, but he reached over and tugged at my hair.

"Don't worry about me, little sister. I'm plenty tough enough."

"So what do the majority think, then?" I asked.

"That you got lucky, and the prince rescued you. Or at least that's what they did think. But there are new rumors circulating now. Ones that make me question whether that's really what happened."

He fixed me with a sharp look, but I couldn't meet his gaze, my own dropping into my lap.

"So it's true?" He sat back with a low whistle. "My sister—a mage!"

"Sort of."

He leaned forward. "You mean you can't control it?"

"No, I can control it. And I'm getting better at it all the time. I'll catch up to my class soon, although I have different limitations from them. That doesn't mean they see me as one of them, though."

"No." His face turned hard. "And that's why I had to come. I'm sorry it's so early, but I had to get over here before classes started."

He stopped and ran a hand through his hair before getting up and sitting beside me on the bed.

"You need to be more careful, Elena."

"What do you mean?"

"I mean that there's nothing that scares these people more than someone else having powers they don't have. And—even worse—someone commonborn. Someone who shouldn't have powers at all."

"Maybe it will do them good to have a taste of what life is like for the rest of us," I said defiantly.

But he leaned forward and grasped my shoulder.

"This isn't a game, Elena." His voice was low and urgent. "This is your life—and maybe the rest of our lives, too. I'm telling you that you make powerful people uncomfortable. And that the stronger you get, the more uncomfortable they become."

I swallowed. I was being watched. I was always being watched. How many times would I have to hear that message before it sank in? I kept telling myself nothing had changed since I first arrived, that caution was still needed, and then I turned straight back around and forgot my caution all over again. I would never have guessed when I arrived that it would be so easy to fall into a false sense of security here.

I remembered my recent outburst in the dining hall—at the son of one of the council members, no less—and covered my face with a groan.

"What do you want me to do?" I asked, my voice muffled by my hands. "They know about my power. I can't just stop using it."

"No." He sighed. "But you can control how strong you appear. I heard…" He paused before continuing. "I heard a less commonly discussed rumor. Did you by any chance use a verbal composition to fend off a whole gang of other trainees? Trainees from the great families?"

I groaned again. "That made it to the University?"

He shook his head at me, his eyes wide. "So that's true too? I wasn't sure…"

"They attacked me! I had to defend myself."

"I suppose so." He shook his head, his concerned expression holding a tinge of amusement. "Is it possible for you to not make enemies, Elena?"

I raised both eyebrows at him. "How have you gone with that at the University, Jasper?"

He gave a reluctant chuckle. "Fair enough, I suppose." He leaned back and gave me a look. "What a pair we make. Why couldn't we have been ordinary and stayed in Kingslee and taken over the store? Like everyone else."

I sighed, but an insidious thought crept into the back of my mind. Despite all the danger—and not just to me—did I truly wish for that? Now that I knew a world of reading. A world of power. Now that I could thrust away four attackers with a spoken word…Could I really wish myself back in an ordinary life?

But I could never admit that to Jasper. Honest, loyal, dependable Jasper, who had never done anything but work for the good of the family. None of us had ever asked him if he wanted to leave his entire life to go to the University where he would likely be ridiculed and ostracized. And he had never complained, not once.

I had no doubt that he would give it all up in a heartbeat if it turned out the good of the family required him to walk away, after all. I might speak when I should hold my tongue, but Jasper never did so. Despite how many times he must have been exasperated by the relative stupidity of those around him.

A wave of love washed over me, and I leaned forward to give him a hug.

"I don't deserve you, Jasper."

He extricated himself and gave me a confused look. "I'm pretty sure it's your birthday, not mine. I should be the one complimenting you."

I shrugged. "You deserve praise more than me."

He frowned and looked me directly in the eye. "I said you needed to hide your strength, not that you actually are weak, Elena. You are incredible, and unique, and possibly the most amazing thing that has ever happened in Ardann. I am honored to be your brother. Don't doubt it. Don't doubt yourself. Just tread warily. Stay safe."

I sniffed and wiped away a tear. "See? My point is proven."

He shook his head and rolled his eyes before thrusting his hand into his robe.

"Oh, I nearly forgot. I have this for you." He held out a small package wrapped in plain material.

I took it slowly. "You already gave me a Midwinter present. And I haven't given you anything. How are you affording this?"

He smiled. "It isn't just from me. It's from the whole family. I've been holding on to it since I got back."

I gently unwrapped it, letting it fall away to reveal a small wooden box covered in intricate carvings. I gasped.

"It's beautiful." I ran my hands over the wood. "You carved it yourself, didn't you?"

He just continued smiling. "Open it."

I turned the small key in the tiny lock. Inside I found a small paperweight—a colorful and glossy stone, polished until it shone.

"Father thought you might have need of something like that. Now that you can read."

Beside the stone sat a bag. I didn't need to open it to identify its contents.

"Yes! Midwinter cookies!"

Jasper grinned. "I know it's well past Midwinter now, but I also knew you wouldn't mind."

"Definitely not. I missed these. No one here makes them."

Our mother made the best Midwinter cookies in Kingslee. Hard, indestructible things that lasted for months—unless you dipped them into tea at which point they turned soft and utterly delicious. My hand brushed against the bag, my mouth already watering, and something small and soft poked out from underneath. I drew out a small woolen doll. The kind I used to make for Clemmy when she was small.

Each one was only as tall as one of my fingers, but I had made the details as intricate as possible. She had wanted a family of them—one for each of us—and had kept them, despite being mostly past the age of dolls. I drew in a shaky breath.

It was Clementine herself. She had sent me the doll I had made to represent her.

"She misses you," said Jasper softly.

"I miss her too," I said through tears.

The bell for breakfast sounded, and Jasper sat up abruptly.

"I have to go!"

I wiped at my eyes, nodding as I put the lid back down and turned the key before removing it and placing it safely inside my dress.

"Me too."

We both stood and gave each other a final hug before hurrying out of the room and down the stairs. Jasper received several curious looks, but no one questioned his presence, and he had soon barreled straight out the front doors and back toward the University.

I barely made it into the dining hall before Coralie attacked.

"Elena!" She gave me a slight shake and then a hug. "Why didn't you tell me?"

"Ummm…" I stared at her. "Tell you what?"

"That it's your birthday!" She glared at me. "That's not the sort of information you hide from your friends. I'm hurt."

"Oh. That." I examined her face. "I'm sorry, I didn't mean—"

She burst out laughing. "Just joking. It's your birthday! You can't get in trouble today."

"Did you tell that to Redmond? Or Thornton?"

She scrunched up her nose. "Wasn't that your brother I just saw leaving? I assume he came to wish you happy birthday. Shouldn't you be in a better mood?"

The tiny key weighed down my pocket and sent my thoughts upstairs to the pieces of my family that now lived in my room.

"You're right."

"I am?" Coralie looked so shocked I had to laugh.

"Now you're making me feel bad. I'm sure you're often right."

"Am I?" But she looked distracted, shoving me into my normal chair and gesturing to someone I couldn't see.

Finnian appeared and sat across from me, Saffron sliding into the seat next to him. She had never sat with us before.

"Happy Birthday," she said quietly, and Finnian repeated the good wishes more heartily.

"Thank you." I grinned at them both. "Now tell me I'm being excused from both combat and composition, and it will really be a good birthday."

Finnian grimaced dramatically. "Such feats are beyond me— even for your fair birthday self."

"But we've got the next best thing," said Coralie, bouncing on the spot.

A servant appeared next to me carrying an elaborate cake, covered in dripping chocolate. He placed it in front of me with murmured birthday wishes.

I turned wide eyes on Coralie. "I thought you only just found out about my birthday. From Damon, I assume."

"I did." She beamed. "But we're mages, remember?"

I drew back without thinking, and Finnian laughed. "We didn't compose it, don't worry."

Coralie rolled her eyes, and I took a relieved breath. It looked delicious, but only the most skilled mages could compose edible food from nothing, and as much as I loved Coralie…

"Of course not! I just meant we have money, you idiot. A little in some cases, a lot in others." She directed a significant look at Finnian. "We sent a servant to the bakers as fast as he could run."

"It looks incredible." I examined it closely. "Too good to eat."

"Don't be ridiculous. No cake is too good to eat." Coralie sat, almost drooling as she eyed the delicacy in front of me.

"But it's first thing in the morning," I said.

"But it's your birthday," she countered. "And on birthdays, there is no inappropriate time for cake."

"Just promise me you're not going to sing." I fixed her with a stern look.

"Actually…" Finnian opened his mouth and took a deep breath, and I almost lunged across the table at him.

Coralie pulled me back before I ended up with a front full of cake.

"Relax, Elena. He's only teasing you."

"He likes to do that," said Saffron, glaring at her cousin.

"What can I say?" Finnian spread his arms wide. "I can't help myself." He certainly didn't look in the least repentant.

The cake turned out to be one of the most delicious things I had ever eaten, despite the early hour of the day, and I insisted we share a piece with Clarence and Araminta at the next table. Clarence looked surprised—he had been reading while he ate and seemed to have missed the appearance of the cake—but he accepted a slice willingly enough. And Araminta followed his lead, although she looked slightly terrified and cast a single quick glance at the only other occupied table, further down the row.

"Oh, never mind them," said Coralie cheerfully. "For once they're all envying us."

And I did catch Lavinia, at least, casting a longing glance at the chocolaty tower in front of me. But Natalya pulled her hurriedly past our laughing group when they left the hall shortly afterward, the others following in their wake.

"You can't be late on your birthday," Coralie said, pushing me to my feet. "You go ahead while I get these leftovers taken care of."

Finnian gave her a mock stern look, and she giggled. "I don't mean eat them. There's still plenty left. The servants can save it for our lunch."

She shoved me away again, so I started slowly toward the door, only to discover that one at least of Natalya's crowd had yet to leave the room. As I reached the doorway, I almost brushed against Lucas's shoulder, pulling back at the last minute when I recognized him.

He stepped through, and after a moment's hesitation, I followed. But outside the room he paused and glanced back at me.

"Happy Birthday," he said softly.

I just stared at him. It was the first time we had spoken since the attack in the corridor.

He shrugged and gave a smile that seemed almost pained. "You wished it to me, so…"

His words reminded me of the doubt I'd had that night as we stood alone in the moonlight. The creeping thoughts that perhaps he wasn't as bad as I had first imagined. But his subsequent behavior had set things straight.

I stared through him, and swept past, hurrying toward the front door and combat class.

"Elena," he called softly after me, his voice easily catching my ears despite the low volume.

I faltered. But I never found out what he had been going to say. Instead an official herald thrust open the front doors and entered the entrance hall, a royal guard flanking him on either side.

I glanced back at Lucas, thinking they must be here for him, but I detected confusion behind his usual confident expression. When I looked back at the newcomers, I found them all staring at me.

I stared back.

"Elena of Kingslee?" asked the herald.

"Yes, that's me."

"You are hereby summoned to court to appear before the Mage Council. We will escort you there immediately."

 gasp behind me told me Coralie had reached the door of the dining hall in time to hear the herald's words. I didn't look back though. How long had I been expecting something like this? Too long.

I stepped forward, proud of myself for not faltering or hesitating. I did thrust my trembling hands into my robe to hide them, however.

The herald nodded and turned to leave, but the two guards stepped forward, clearly intending to flank me now instead of the messenger. I felt a presence move forward to stand beside me, however, and the two men paused. After a shared glance, they resumed their previous places.

Coralie wouldn't have that effect. I looked sideways and saw that Lucas kept pace with me, his narrowed eyes haughtily daring the guards to question or approach him.

"What are you doing?" I whispered aggressively, but he just directed his cool look at me, one eyebrow raised.

"I didn't realize I answered to you, Elena."

I bit back my retort when one of the guards looked back over his shoulder at us, and instead stalked forward, keeping my gaze firmly in front of me. Even a tiny sound—almost like a chuckle—from beside me didn't make me turn back to the prince.

The herald gestured me into a waiting carriage—had they been expecting me to struggle and didn't want to have to walk me even the short distance? The gold robes of the guards marked them as officers—mages—so perhaps they had. None of the three of them made any move to follow me inside. The prince, on the other hand, climbed easily in behind me.

I sat back against the seat and glared at him. When he merely looked back at me with a level gaze, I transferred my attention out the window. We had nearly reached the palace—the drive ludicrously short—when words burst out of me.

"Did you know about this?"

"No." He sounded serious, and almost…worried.

My brother's words echoed around my head. I truly had meant to heed them, but I hadn't had time to do so. And now I might never get the chance. I just hoped whatever was about to happen wouldn't rebound on my family. No matter what, this time I needed to hold my tongue.

"You should say as little as possible," said Lucas suddenly.

I instantly felt a rebellious desire to ignore his advice, but I firmly squashed it down. This was too important to let such petty feelings overset me. I slipped my hand into my pocket to clutch at the key hidden there. I could do this. For my family.

My second arrival at the palace couldn't have been more dissimilar from my first. No lights burned to welcome us, despite the day being overcast. And no line of footmen waited to usher us inside. Instead another six guards appeared, these ones common folk who looked to the two mage officers for direction.

When the prince emerged from the carriage and resumed his place at my side, they fell in behind their superiors, trailing us in two columns. The herald had disappeared, and Lucas guided our steps now.

My anxiety overwhelmed most of my curiosity, but I did

absorb that the red and gold theme of the celebration matched the regular decor of the palace—red velvet and gilding offsetting the white marble everywhere I looked.

We didn't mount the stairs this time, instead taking a side door down a long corridor. We passed enormous elaborate doors that I could only imagine led into the throne room, but Lucas's stride never faltered. I breathed a sigh of relief for that at least.

Instead he led us to a regular-sized door nearly at the end of the corridor. Only the gilt pattern around the handle and door-frame declared the room inside anything special.

Lucas paused for a moment, glancing down at me, and I got the distinct impression he wanted to ask me if I was ready. But either I was wrong, or he realized the foolishness of such a question, because he turned the handle without speaking and entered the room ahead of me.

"Lucas." If King Stellan was surprised at the appearance of his son, he hid it well.

"Father." The prince nodded to the king and then to the others in the room before striding down the long table to take a seat just behind his father's chair. An oval table—the king at its head in a carved wooden chair with a towering back and substantial arm rests—took up most of the room. Five chairs in a less elaborate style lined each curving side, and another towering one sat at the foot of the table, the elegant folds of the queen's skirts almost overflowing it, despite the generous size.

All ten of the remaining seats—obviously for the ten members of the Mage Council—were filled. Lorcan made no attempt to meet my gaze, although I knew he had marked my entrance.

I looked around at them all. Both generals regarded me steadily—Thaddeus with open hostility and Griffith with wary interest. But, like Lorcan, Jessamine made no move to look at me. She was apparently too familiar with my appearance for curiosity now.

I cast my eyes over the remaining six, trying to place them all.

Phyllida of the seekers—relative, however distant, of Lorcan and Jessamine—wore her sleek brown hair pulled back just as tightly as I remembered. The other Callinos—Duke Dashiell of the healers—was easy to pick although I hadn't seen him at the Midwinter celebrations in the end. He looked too much like his son to mistake. I wondered if the likeness made me imagine the greater look of kindness he seemed to wear.

The only other woman—wearing the green robe of the growers—must be Duchess Annika of Devoras. She looked enough like General Griffith to make me wonder if they were first cousins, or even siblings. She sat beside the red-robed Duke Lennox, Head of Law Enforcement and another face I recognized. He had seemed to soften toward me by the end of my testing, but I saw none of that softness now. It was hard to believe he was a relative of the open and friendly Walden.

Which left only two. One wore a blue robe and must be Duke Magnus of the wind workers—another Ellington like Lennox, although I could see no family resemblance. He regarded me quizzically, a look of uncertainty in his eyes, that made me hope he at least hadn't made up his mind.

The peach-toned robe of the remaining duke—the same color as the creator who had repaired the library after my destructive loss of control—looked out of place on a man with such stern lines to his face. No surprise whatsoever that Duke Casimir was a Stantorn. Whatever sides were being drawn—if indeed there were sides—I had no doubt he would be against me.

The king cleared his throat, and my eyes flew to him.

"Please take a seat, Elena of Kingslee."

I didn't move, unsure where he wanted me to go, until one of the guards gestured for me to take one of the chairs lining one wall of the room. The two gold-robed officers sat near me, the only other witnesses of this meeting.

"You called this meeting, General Thaddeus." The king sounded official, but also slightly bored. As if he didn't want to be there. Given the gleam in his eye, I could only assume it was a calculated affectation. "I hand the floor over to you."

Thaddeus gave a slow nod and looked around the table. "As you know, it has taken some time for the full council to gather, but some among us felt this matter could not be settled with any less than our full numbers."

The direction of his narrowed gaze made it clear that Lorcan bore the brunt of his displeasure. The Academy Head merely stared coolly back.

The general continued. "It has come to my attention that the first year trainee going by the name of Elena of Kingslee—"

I had to refrain from snorting despite the seriousness of the situation. *Going by the name of?* Was he serious?

"—has manifested new abilities of unknown strength and has used these abilities in a violent manner in the presence of a member of the royal family."

I straightened, any desire to find humor in the situation instantly erased. I glanced over at Lucas. He looked impassive, but I had caught him giving a slight twitch at the general's words. He was surprised. Whoever had told the Head of the Royal Guard about the altercation back at the Academy, it hadn't been him.

Why did that give me the tiniest feeling of relief?

Lorcan made a disgusted noise in the back of his throat. "Oh for goodness sake, Thaddeus, we aren't at an official court hearing. Is all this formality really necessary? Or are you just trying to cover the fact that the trainee in question did not direct any violence toward a member of the royal family?"

Thank goodness I had retained a tiny grain of sense in the middle of my beating, or I might not have had even that defense.

"The violence may not have been toward the prince," General Griffith bowed slightly in Lucas's direction, "but as the father of two of the victims, that affords me only the slightest measure of relief."

Ah. Of course. That was where Thaddeus had heard of it, no

doubt. Why could I not remember that my year mates were not just sixteen-year-olds like me, mere fellow students? With a slight start, I remembered that I wasn't sixteen anymore. Not as of today. Happy birthday me.

"If I remember rightly," said Phyllida, in the calm voice I had heard her use previously, "altercations among trainees is not exactly unheard of at the Academy." She sent a knowing look at Duke Lennox across from her, and for a moment he looked as if he was trying to suppress a smile. Had they been year mates?

"Between normal trainees, perhaps so," said Thaddeus. "But this girl is no normal trainee. Her strength is unknown—as is her control."

Jessamine rolled her eyes. "Really Thaddeus? The girl has been at the Academy for how many months now? Can you really claim to be concerned about her control?"

Thaddeus glared at her. "I am well aware that you and Lorcan would like to keep the subject of your studies in easy reach, Jessamine. Which is perhaps why you failed to report to me her loss of control—which resulted in significant damage to the Academy and one of its instructors—or her recent attack on her fellow students."

"Attack is such a strong word, Thaddeus." Jessamine frowned with distaste.

"What would you call it then?" He continued to glare a challenge at her.

"And why would I report either of those incidents to you, Thaddeus?" asked Lorcan. "I certainly can't imagine why *Jessamine* would do so. May I remind you that we all agreed that as a trainee, Elena falls under my responsibility."

"Not all of us were happy with that decision," the general shot back.

"And not all of us were present for it," added General Griffith. "Look Lorcan, it was all very well when the girl showed no great proclivity for composition. Or even ability to compose at all. If you wanted to keep her there learning how to beat people with staffs, you were welcome to do so, as far as I was concerned. But it seems the situation has changed…"

He shifted slightly in his seat to look at me, the first of them to do so, and I tried to look as harmless as possible. Despite my desire to snap that I had a name and wasn't *the girl*.

"Indeed it has," said Thaddeus. "Even the incident at the Midwinter celebrations could now be called into question. And once again, the prince came all too close to harm on that occasion."

"Don't get carried away, Thaddeus." Dashiell's deep voice sounded for the first time since I had entered the room. "Many of us were present that night. And whatever this girl may or may not be, she's still a first year. There is no way she brought down that balcony without any of us sensing it. She can't possibly have acquired the subtlety required for such an act."

My eyes flew to Lucas, and I found him looking back at me. *Someone* had brought down that balcony, and for some reason it sounded like the council didn't know it. Were the prince and I the only ones who had been close enough to feel it with any certainty?

Dashiell looked down the table at Lorcan, and I remembered he was Callinos, like the Academy Head. "I am correct, am I not, Lorcan? This girl does not exhibit such advanced skills?"

"Certainly not. She is, if anything, behind her peers at the Academy. There are…limitations to her verbal direction of the compositions. We are still working—in conjunction with our colleagues at the University, of course, to develop workarounds and streamline—"

"Very well, Lorcan, we'll take your word for it," interjected the king. "No need to get into one of your technical speeches."

I bit the inside of my cheek. *They* were working on developing ways to properly utilize my ability? I could have sworn it was Walden and me doing the work…I shifted slightly in my seat but remained silent.

"This is exactly the problem, Your Majesty," said Duke Casimir, backing up his fellow Stantorn. "We all know what Lorcan and Jessamine are like when a new and difficult problem presents itself for study. It's what led them to be selected for their positions in the first place. But can they really be trusted to assess the threat in front of us clearly?"

He gazed up and down the table at the other heads. "I will admit I was intrigued when I first heard of the situation. Excited, even, when I considered all the potential ramifications. But it has become increasingly obvious that this new manifestation is no more powerful than our current abilities. Instead it is a great deal less controlled." His cold eyes turned to me, and it took everything in me not to tremble at the look in them.

"It is far too early in her training to determine the potential extent of her power." Jessamine sighed. "And this talk of control again. We have been closely monitoring—"

"I do not just speak of control in the traditional sense," said Casimir. "We must also consider what it means that the girl in question is commonborn. Raised among the common folk." He paused significantly and no one else spoke. "Unfamiliar with our ways or way of life."

It took everything in me to bite my tongue as most of the heads in the room turned to examine me as if I were an interesting animal who had wandered by accident into their midst. I understood the meaning behind his words as well as any of them did.

I was commonborn, and therefore I wasn't on their side. I might resent them. I might have reason to turn my power and ability against them. I couldn't be trusted.

This was what concerned them. And what had I done? Exactly what they most feared.

"Precisely," jumped in Thaddeus. "And, indeed, her only use of power outside the strict confines of the classroom illustrates the point precisely. She is not one of us, and it is far too dangerous for her to be allowed any further training. Jessamine said it herself—who knows what the extent of her powers might be if we allow this farce to continue?"

Jessamine exchanged a quick glance with Lorcan, and I winced inside. She had only fed him more ammunition against me—and he had seized it eagerly.

"I don't know, General," said Lucas's calm voice.

The entire table turned to look at him. From the expressions on their faces, I suspected a few of them at least had forgotten about his presence altogether.

"You say the fight is evidence she's not one of us," he continued. "But it doesn't seem that way to me. After all, she was hardly the instigator." He glanced significantly over at General Griffith. "And I believe that starting in second year we will even be actively encouraged to attack each other with whatever power we can muster. Is that not so?"

He looked to Lorcan, his face open as if genuinely asking the question.

"Indeed, Your Highness," Lorcan replied.

"So it sounds to me like she was behaving exactly like one of us." He looked around at them all. "Just a thought I had."

"What is this nonsense about not being the instigator?" asked Griffith, coming just short of actually glaring at a member of the royal family. "I assure you—"

"Don't forget that I was present on the occasion, General, as your esteemed colleague reminded us upon our arrival at this meeting. And as an impartial observer, I can assure you that the mageborn trainees were the instigators of the violence. They also received far less physical injury than their victim."

Several eyes turned back to me, and I could feel the impact of the word victim settling through the room, along with an image of me battered and bruised. It was an image of weakness. And it was exactly what I needed.

Duke Magnus frowned, his blue robe rippling as he shifted in his seat. "It sounds increasingly as if we have all been summoned here frivolously, and some of us from important work—it is planting season you know." He exchanged a look with the green-robed Annika. "It almost sounds as if we have been summoned here to discuss a squabble among trainees. Hardly a matter for the full Mage Council." He directed a disapproving look at Lorcan.

"I insisted you all be present," Lorcan said smoothly, "precisely *because* the matter is a squabble among Academy trainees. It is unprecedented that even a partial council should attempt to inject themselves into such a minor internal matter within one of our areas of authority." His gaze stayed steady on Magnus. "I cannot imagine you would welcome such a change in council practice."

Magnus leaned back in his seat, his expression thoughtful.

"I recognize your concern, Lorcan." He looked across the table at Thaddeus before glancing at Lucas. "I suppose the presence of the prince among the first years has introduced an element of confusion for Thaddeus here. Head of the Royal Guard and all that."

"Members of the royal family have always studied at the Academy." Lorcan's eyes narrowed. "And no previous head has been expected to bear such insults."

"Insults?" Magnus raised an eyebrow.

"The suggestion that the Academy is not adequately equipped to protect any royal person studying there."

"Oh, calm down, Lorcan," said Lennox. "No one is suggesting you're inadequate at your job."

"Aren't they?" Lorcan raised both eyebrows. "It seems to me that is exactly what is being suggested."

"Enough," said the king, who had been quietly following the

conversation. His eyes briefly met those of the queen, who had been equally silent, but whatever he saw there didn't give him pause. "I am satisfied by my son's assurance that he was never in any danger, nor was there any threat or aggression made toward him."

His eyes moved to me, and I went completely still, forgetting even to breathe.

"As for the matter of the commonborn trainee...She cannot be released without further training in the necessary control. So it seems to me that the matter before us is whether she is to continue as a trainee, or whether she is to be treated as a criminal, locked away as we would a rogue mage."

Lennox cleared his throat. "That would not be a simple undertaking, Sire. For the usual mage prisoner, removing all stored compositions and all methods of composing is fairly easily achieved. But if compositions can be verbal..."

"So we are talking of execution, then?" The queen raised a single eyebrow.

I went cold all over. I had never read a word until they granted me permission to learn. They couldn't execute me now. Could they?

My eyes traveled frantically up and down the table, trying to count the numbers and read their expressions. When my gaze fastened on Lucas, I found him once again looking at me, something powerful and unsettling burning in his eyes.

"I am inclined to see things as Lorcan does," said the king, giving me hope. But his next words dispelled it. "This is a matter of management within your disciplines and not the safety of the kingdom. I will therefore leave it to your own vote. Although naturally I will retain the deciding vote in the case of a tie. The vote before us is whether the council will interfere in Lorcan's running of the Academy, namely his authority to permit the attendance of a commonborn student, who appears to be a new breed of mage. A vote for the council to refrain from interfering in the matter will result in the girl, Elena of Kingslee, remaining at the Academy for further study by Lorcan and Jessamine. A vote to forbid the taking of commonborn students under any circumstances will result in the necessary execution of the girl in question."

"Naturally I vote that the council refrain from meddling in the running of the Academy," said Lorcan quickly. "As they have always done in the past."

"As do I," said Jessamine.

"And I," said Phyllida.

"And I," added Dashiell, after a slightly longer pause.

So all the Callinos heads had voted together. No great surprise there.

"As much as I respect my colleague," said Thaddeus, the qualification sounding as if it hurt him, "I cannot, in good conscience, vote to allow any potential threat to the royal family to remain. I vote to forbid the presence of a commonborn student at the Academy."

"As do I," said Casimir, backing up his Stantorn family member even more swiftly than the four Callinos heads had done.

General Griffith took a deep breath and then nodded. "As do I. The kingdom cannot face threats from within while we are so occupied fending off threats from without."

He looked across at Annika, and she nodded once.

"I agree."

So Stantorn and Devoras had stuck together. No surprise there, either. I looked at Lucas, too tense to look at the council members themselves, and saw his gaze crossing between Lennox and Magnus of Ellington. Everything came down to them now.

CHAPTER 22

*L*ennox looked down at the table, ignoring the intense gazes of his fellow council members. After a moment, he glanced up at Magnus, and something unspoken passed between them.

I held my breath, dizziness nearly overwhelming me as the moment drew out.

"The laws of our kingdom have been entrusted to me," he said at last. "And I cannot condone an execution where no laws have been broken. Just as I cannot condone a change to how we manage our separate disciplines. Of course, if the girl Elena were to break one of our laws, I would not hesitate to act. As I am sure Lorcan would not hesitate to hand her over to me."

He nodded at Lorcan, and Lorcan nodded back. Then his eyes took in the rest of the table.

"And I can assure you all that in such a circumstance, my discipline would be more than capable of discharging our duties, whatever abilities this girl has amassed in the meantime."

A brief smile flitted across Lorcan's face. The Academy Head had cleverly framed the issue as a challenge to his authority and his ability to fill his role. His opponents hadn't seen that their doubt cast question not only on Lorcan, but also on Lennox and his ability to enforce the law if I were to turn rogue.

Magnus nodded slowly.

"I vote with my kinsman. And I hope it will not be necessary to recall me to the capital again before the completion of my usual spring tour of the kingdom."

He heaved himself to his feet, bowed to the king and then the queen, and strode from the room.

I slumped back in my chair, my head reeling, and my breath coming short and fast. All of that and nothing was to change. I would continue at the Academy.

And thank goodness for that—given the alternative, my mind whispered.

Lucas left the room immediately after that with both his parents, not faltering as he swept past me, although I felt the burn of his eyes. Lorcan gestured for me to accompany him from the room, and we returned to the Academy in near silence.

"It's my birthday today," I said, as we stepped through the main doors into the Academy entrance hall.

I had no idea what had prompted me to speak.

Lorcan paused and looked back at me, a startled look in his eyes.

"Oh." For a minute we just looked at each other. "Happy Birthday."

"Thank you."

He cleared his throat. "Sorry about that…" He waved in the direction of the palace. "On your birthday."

I shrugged. "It could have been worse."

For another moment we simply regarded each other, both very much aware of what it could have been. I considered thanking him for his efforts to save me but found I had no desire to do so. He had done it for himself, not for me.

He cleared his throat again, nodded once, and disappeared toward his office.

~

Spring continued to warm the air, and greenery sprung up around the Academy. The dreaded day arrived when we exchanged our staffs for dull practice swords, and I once again returned to bottom of the class. Only this time I had company there. Neither Clarence nor Araminta appeared to have ever wielded a blade before, and Coralie and Saffron had only the slightest familiarity with them.

It was easier to take because I had finally caught up in composition. My extra lessons with Walden ended, and I now practiced alongside my year mates, producing verbal compositions in class. Redmond provided little in the way of assistance, so I had to work out how to modify the methods he taught without his help.

I had my revenge, however, because Lorcan and the University academics now came to our class to monitor and observe my development. They often made suggestions—and not just to me. Many of them had all sorts of ideas about how the class could better be run, and Redmond spent much of the season stalking around the Academy in a foul mood.

I was glad for the extra effort that modifying our lessons required because I would have been bored otherwise. In class we moved at a snail's pace compared to the speed Walden and I had progressed at. After a while I realized that most of the students found the level of composing we did exhausting, and that our slow pace was designed to gradually build their capacity. Only Lucas and Dariela rarely looked tired, and I sometimes caught the visiting academics observing them with interest.

Impatience, not exhaustion, filled me during our classes, but I remembered Jasper's words and hid it. I soon fell into the rhythm of doing no more than the basic compositions asked for, always ensuring that nothing I did made me stand out from the rest. I certainly never mentioned that the few compositions we completed left me with plenty of energy to spare.

On the occasions when Jessamine attended in person, she watched me with calculating eyes, but she never actually questioned me or suggested I was holding back. And the only other person who watched me with suspicion almost never spoke to me at all. Lucas and I had never spoken of the council meeting where my fate had been decided, so I hardly expected him to start a conversation about my progress in class.

Checking out book after book from the library kept my mind alert and engaged, although Coralie thought I was mad to invite extra work. But then she had been reading since she was a child and considered the sort of topics I studied a bore. I didn't bother to try to explain it to her.

After our conversation with Finnian in the dining hall, she had made a noticeable effort to be more sensitive about the lives of us commonborn, but she still didn't really understand. How could she?

But I felt as if my world was expanding—growing wider with each book I read. The kingdom of Kallorway, the brief mentions of the mysterious Sekali Empire, the history of our conflicts, the history of our royal family, the history of mages and their ability to compose—all of it fascinated me. The structure of the great mage families and the mage disciplines themselves, our economy, even our geography, held me captivated. How much more I could get from maps when they were labeled with words.

Now that I had started, I couldn't stop. My appetite for more knowledge was insatiable, and my advancements in verbal composition faltered as a result of my inattention to them.

But then one warm spring day, sick of reading cooped up in my room, I wandered through the library after composition class ended, a book tucked under my arm. The sight of all the older trainees studying caught my attention. Some of them sat alone, but many huddled in small groups. The largest group had gathered in a side room—similar to the one Jocasta and I had used while I was learning to read.

The memories of that time made me halt, a shiver running up my spine, but curiosity compelled me forward. The door had been left wide open, and I stood just outside, listening to Jocasta speak to the trainees.

"The human body has limits that even a healer cannot circumvent. Energy levels are the most basic of these, and it is why a patient will need rest after a significant healing. It is also why a mage cannot push themselves past their own limits while composing and then simply compose themselves back to full health."

Her eyes flickered to me, but her expression didn't change, and she didn't halt in her lecture.

"I would like an essay by next week on how the limits of the human body affect the work of healers. Beginner level students, your essays should explore the limits in our understanding of energy levels and why we have been unable to find a way to replenish them through the use of power. Advanced students, you will discuss the various stages of illness and injury from which a healer cannot effect a patient's recovery. Include a summary of how the skill of the healer affects these thresholds."

As she outlined the assignments, the students all made notes on pieces of parchment in front of them.

"You may hand them in one week from today when we will reconvene for a guest lecture from Duke Dashiell."

Several of the students exchanged excited looks at that piece of news. I took it that the Head of the Healers didn't often address the students studying the healing discipline.

Jocasta dismissed them, and they filed from the room, talking quietly among themselves. Those who noticed me ignored me, until Jocasta herself exited.

"There's no need to lurk at the door, Elena," she said. "Class is always open."

"But I'm only a first year. I don't do discipline studies."

She shrugged. "Discipline study is across year levels. It has to be when so many students choose to change their disciplines of study from year to year. We simply assign different tasks to the beginning and advanced students. And much of the study is done independently, anyway."

She chuckled. "If it wasn't, Walden and I could never keep up with the load between us. As it is, we rely on guest speakers from the disciplines themselves. Although not usually from the actual heads."

She gave me a meaningful look. "And we could never have taken the time out to individually tutor you, as we have both done now."

I pressed my lips together and refrained from pointing out that it had not been my suggestion that she tutor me. Regardless of who had made the request, she had devoted many hours to teaching me—her only reward a near death experience at my hands. And apparently my transferring my tutelage to Walden had only increased her workload in other ways since she must have picked up his load with the older students in order to free up his time.

Before I could reply, her eyes moved over my shoulder.

"You're a little late, Lucas."

I resisted the urge to spin around, but the prince stepped into my line of sight anyway.

"My apologies, I had court business to attend to. I heard Dashiell is to pay us a visit. And that there's an assignment?"

She nodded. "To be handed in one week from today. An essay on how the limits of the human body affect the work of healers. Specifically, the limits in our understanding of energy levels and why we have been unable to find a way to replenish them through the use of power."

Her eyes moved back to me. "Think on what I said, Elena." Then she nodded and strode away toward her desk at the front of the library.

Lucas didn't move. "So what are you meant to be thinking on, then?"

I eyed him, my brow crinkling. Did he think we were friends all of a sudden? I put my chin up.

"I'm going to join the class."

"First years don't do discipline studies."

"You're a first year."

Something like resignation flashed in his eyes. "Yes, I am."

How much did it chafe him to have been delayed in starting at the Academy? I narrowed my eyes. Did he think he was better than the rest of us because he was a year older? More capable?

"So then it seems first years can join. I guess I'll see you in class."

"I guess you will." His cool eyes didn't waver, so I spun on my heel and marched out of the library.

Only when I reached my room did I remember that if I really was joining the class, I should have gone looking for books on healing and energy levels. I sighed. The library had probably been nearly cleared out by now by the other students.

Reading, I enjoyed. But did I really want another class added to my load? I shook my head at myself. It didn't matter. I couldn't back down now that I had let Lucas bait me into declaring my intention to join.

But as I slipped into bed that night, I decided that I would have made the same choice regardless. The rest of the students had time before them. They all had three full years of discipline study before graduation. But I had less than a year now until my eighteenth birthday. If I waited for next year, I would have only six months. And somehow I imagined the ability to compose healings would come in all too handy on the front lines.

CHAPTER 23

With the thought of my conscription spurring me on, I ended up joining the group studying the armed forces discipline as well, although the whole thing confused me. Why would any mage choose to join the Armed Forces and become an officer when it would almost certainly mean ending up on the front lines? Only ones who liked to blow things up, I supposed.

It was a strange juxtaposition, studying how to destroy one day and how to heal the next, but no doubt both skills would come in handy. And at least when the armed forces trainees gathered, I didn't have Lucas's eyes boring into me. His second discipline was law enforcement, apparently. Not that I had been paying attention, or anything.

I tried a few of the simplest healing compositions on myself in the privacy of my rooms, but I had nowhere to experiment with the type of compositions used by the Armed Forces. Even the less violent ones used for tracking enemy movements or disguising our own troops didn't lend themselves to use inside the Academy.

But Coralie assured me I would have plenty of chances to practice in second year.

"Combat class will be moving to the arena, remember." She shivered. "And then our bouts will include compositions as well as weapons. I'm already terrified of going up against Dariela or Weston. They'll rip me apart."

I noticed her obvious attempt not to look in my direction.

"I don't need reminding of what they'll do to me if they get the chance," I said. "All the more reason for me to be studying now. You could join me you know."

"It's actually a pretty smart idea," said Finnian from across the table.

I eyed him. "But let me guess—neither of you will be joining me."

He grinned. "You want us to try harder to understand you commonborn, well here's an insight into us mageborn. Avoiding as much work as possible is a time-honored Academy tradition. Trainees have been studying and perfecting the techniques for years." He winked at me.

"Lucas is in the classes."

He waved a hand. "Oh, royalty aren't the same as the rest of us. Surely you've noticed that by now."

I chucked a bread roll at him and gave up trying to convince either of them to join me.

My studies so consumed my time that I hadn't ventured out of the Academy since I was dragged before the Mage Council. But one particularly warm day, right at the end of spring, the bright blue sky tempted me too much to sit and read.

Coralie had disappeared somewhere, having long since given up on the hope of my joining her for our rest day, so I ventured outside on my own. The taste of the coming summer reminded me that the Academy would adjourn for the year half way through the warmer months, and I would hopefully have the chance to return home to see my family. I could only imagine what Clemmy would say if I arrived home only to admit that I had seen nothing of the capital in nearly an entire year of residence.

I wished I had some coin so that I could buy my little sister something nice from one of the city markets, but I had no way to raise any funds. Even if I had been able to write a composition, trainees were forbidden from selling them until they had graduated and achieved full mage status. Few of them would actually choose to do so at that point, of course. And while I might wish to, the permission wouldn't do me much good. Not unless I could find someone who needed something done immediately rather than expecting to take possession of the composition and use it at their leisure.

I had no actual expectation of ever graduating, anyway, but I still found myself daydreaming about ways I might sell my services as I hurried past the mansions of the mage families that filled the streets near the Academy. Healing seemed the most obvious answer, and I resolved again not to leave the healing classes until necessity forced me away from the Academy.

I had already looked up the compositions that might heal Clemmy. Some of the simplest ones that would alleviate specific ailments were within my current skill level. But healing the underlying problem of her weak immune system would be far more complex. Most likely it would require an apprenticeship with the healers discipline before that sort of control and understanding of the human body was achieved.

I loved the idea of being able to speak and see her grow instantly well, but the specter of Duke Lennox reminded me that any such attempt—even the healing of a trifling cold—would be foolhardy. While the other trainees were permitted to practice their compositions under the supervision of their families, I highly doubted the same permission extended to me. None of the mages would want me composing anything away from the watchful eyes of the Academy. And I didn't intend to give the Stantorn and Devoras heads a reason to have me arrested.

When the railings that protected the mage mansions gave way to storefronts, I slowed my steps. These were far grander shops than I would ever frequent—even if I had some coin—but they still interested me.

I peered in through large panes of glass at beautiful silks, winking jewelry, and exotic spices and delicacies. One entire shop was filled with complex and intricate toys for children and another held every variety of writing equipment you could imagine.

My steps grew slowest as I passed a store filled with shelf after shelf of books. The store owner smiled invitingly at me through the glass, and I pulled back quickly, hurrying on before I remembered I wore my white robe. No wonder he had looked welcoming rather than threatening. He assumed I was mageborn.

He must be mageborn himself—from one of the minor families, perhaps—to be permitted to spend his days surrounded by words.

When the shops finished, the commonborn part of the city began, and my steps picked up. This was the area I wanted to visit. The area my family dreamed of one day inhabiting.

I entertained myself by trying to guess the function of the free-standing red sandstone buildings I passed. At least one looked to be a healing clinic, and one was marked as a law enforcement hub, using the symbol for law enforcement used by the common folk. A small park nearly lured me off the road, the grass full of running, laughing children, but my nose pulled me onward. I must be near a market.

As I searched it out, I relished the thought of my family living in such easy reach of all of these resources. How much more full their lives would be here in Corrin than trapped as they were now in the confines of Kingslee and the unending daily drudgery of their store.

The market square soon opened to one side, busy with hurrying people who wove among the dawdlers—those who were there to talk and browse through the stalls at leisure. My rumbling stomach made me wish I had begged a packed lunch from the Academy kitchen, but it was too late for that.

I dove into the crowd, ready to push my way through as I had always been forced to do during village gatherings, but to my surprise the crowd parted before me. No one paid me any great notice, but somehow, wherever I walked, open space appeared around me.

For a moment I felt unnerved, examining the crowd around me with confusion. And then a flash of white made me kick myself mentally. I had forgotten my robe again.

I wished I had left it behind at the Academy. I had thought to spend a few hours among my own kind, but I clearly looked out of place here. The lack of curiosity suggested that I wasn't the first trainee or University student to lack the coin for the upmarket mage stores, but that didn't mean I belonged either.

I wanted to call out, "I'm not a mage!" to the people I passed, but I bit my tongue.

My robe betrayed me, after all. I *was* a mage—even if the mages themselves couldn't accept me. And it struck me with blinding force what that meant. I had been looking forward to returning home soon, but I would now have no more place in my village than I had in this market. I had become some strange hybrid, on edge among the mages, constantly waiting for them to turn against me, but no longer at home among the common folk, either.

With no coin to buy anything, and no anonymity to enjoy, I soon wandered out of the market. Back on the street I blended in a bit more, lost in the traffic of horses, carts, carriages, and other pedestrians. When a fellow pedestrian dodged out of my way, I could at least pretend they had been moving to avoid a horse or a rough patch in the cobblestones.

The gray stone of the tall buildings in this part of the city seemed colorless, but it was offset by the window boxes everywhere. I remembered noting them when I first entered Corrin in the autumn. Now, however, they were alive with blooms and bright cheer.

I tried to focus on them, since they had no eyes to dart away from mine, but a strident voice pulled my attention back to those in the street.

"Leave me be, woman!"

A man in a red robe shoved at a commonborn woman who crowded too closely against him. Her face was tear-streaked and hysterical, and she didn't seem to be aware of the scene she was creating.

"I tell you, I need to report a crime."

"Do I look like a clerk? Let go of me."

"But he's getting away!"

The man glared down at the woman. "I. Don't. Care. The lot of you are always turning on each other. I've got more important things to worry about."

My steps faltered as I stared at him in shock. He was wearing a red robe and had clearly been descending the steps of a large sandstone building marked with the symbol of law enforcement. He had chosen his discipline; how could he be so callous about a reported crime?

Rage boiled through me. Clearly he only cared about crimes against mages.

I stepped forward, meaning to confront him, but he gave the woman a final push—this one hard enough to send her to the ground—and stormed away before I could reach them.

I continued to hurry forward anyway, meaning to help the woman to her feet, but a guard in a red uniform and a clerk—commonborn members of law enforcement—came rushing down the steps of the building to assist her. My feet still carried me toward them, my anger making it impossible to simply walk away, but a hard hand clamped down on my arm.

I jerked to a stop, turning to confront familiar green eyes.

"Let go of me!" My anger poured out onto the prince, but he didn't flinch or let go.

"She doesn't want help from you." His voice sounded softer than I expected, and it made me pause, blinking at him in confusion.

"What do you—"

He gestured at my white robe, and I bit back a frustrated snarl. How could I have forgotten again?

I wilted, relaxing in his grip, and he instantly let go and stepped back. When I looked toward the woman, I saw her disappearing into the building.

I trembled still, having been denied even the smallest of outlets for my anger and disgust. I wished there had been something I could have done to help her.

"What are you doing here?" I whirled back on Lucas. "Have you been following me?"

He raised both eyebrows, and I instantly felt foolish. Of course the prince of Ardann had not been following me all day.

"I had business in the city. I do on occasion, you know," he said, and I thought I detected a hint of amused condescension.

"Then I suppose you're used to sights like that," I snapped back. "And naturally you wouldn't consider stepping in and reminding that *man* what it is exactly that his job in law enforcement entails."

Lucas shook his head. "Your disdain for mages is a little too obvious, Elena. You might want to work on that."

"And you might want to work on your disdain for us common folk. We do make up the majority of your family's subjects after all."

"Perhaps." He didn't sound convinced. "But then I'm not the one whose life depends on it."

"No—theirs do!" I stared at him, chest heaving as my mind caught up with my mouth. "Wait. What do you mean my life depends on it?" Had something changed since the council voted to leave me be?

"You do remember that Mage Council, do you not?" He raised an incredulous eyebrow. "Some very important people have been working hard to keep you hidden away and safe—despite your apparent lack of interest in assisting them. You might at least pretend to make an effort to look a little less like a threat."

"Very important people? Who? You?"

When he just blinked at me, I flushed. Where had that come from?

"Lorcan comes to mind," he drawled at last. "Or haven't you noticed how little emphasis he put on your studies? How slowly he let them develop?" He chuckled. "It must have been killing him to rein in his curiosity, but he's always known how to play the long game. He looks like a distracted academic half the time, but he understands court intrigue better than most. I was astonished he held off that council meeting so long."

I shrugged, although his words made me uncomfortable. Suddenly I found myself rethinking all of my interactions with the Academy Head.

"Too bad he couldn't hold it off forever," I muttered.

"No, it was inevitable." Lucas looked at me with hard eyes. "But so much time had passed. Even those most opposed to your position at the Academy had grown somewhat used to the idea— whether they realized that or not."

"How do you know all this? Lorcan consulted with you, I suppose?" I loaded all the sarcasm into my voice that I could muster.

"No, of course not." He sighed. "But I know how he thinks. Members of the Mage Council can hold their positions for decades. You can be sure that understanding the inner workings of their minds is a matter of great interest to my family."

I fell silent, considering his words. I had learned so much in my months of study, but he made me feel young and foolish and naive. Some things couldn't be learned from books, and there were so many subtleties about this world of mages that I didn't understand.

I looked around with a start. I wasn't quite sure how he had done it—he certainly hadn't touched me again—but somehow Lucas had got us both moving as we talked. We were already well up South Road, heading north toward the Academy.

He was dressed the same as me, in our trainee robes, and I eyed him sideways, a sudden thought striking me.

"Where are your royal guards, Your Highness?"

When I started to speak, he looked over in my direction, but when I finished, his gaze shifted away. He made no answer.

I shook my head. "Don't tell me your business wasn't so official after all? Who's being reckless now?"

He narrowed his eyes but didn't have time to respond before a large arm reached out and yanked me into a side alley.

CHAPTER 24

$\mathcal{I}$ stumbled and almost fell as the iron grip pulled me away from the main road. Before I could get my bearings, or even see who had grabbed me, a second set of arms pulled me into a rough hold, dragging me sideways and through a door. The first man followed, slamming the door behind him.

The second attacker towered over me, his arms holding my back firmly pressed against his chest, my arms pinned at my sides. I finally screamed, the sound delayed by my shock, and the first man hit me hard across the head. My neck snapped to one side, and for a brief moment my vision blurred. Then three seasons of combat training kicked in, and I responded on instinct.

Slamming my head backward, I smashed my skull into my captor's neck. He wheezed, his arms loosening, and I stomped hard on his foot. He staggered slightly, and I pulled myself forward and free.

The man in front of me immediately stepped forward and grabbed at my arm. I moved to block him without needing to think about it, at the same time ducking under his raised arm and shoving him in the back.

He lurched forward and into the second man, but both quickly regained their balance. However, the second it took for them to do so gave me a chance for a quick look around. We stood inside a large, empty building, the details lost in the dim light. Surely a warehouse of some sort, though, currently without goods except for a few crates against the far wall.

I spun around, looking for the door, but as soon as I saw it, my heart sank. Two more men stood between me and the exit. And they were already advancing to help their companions.

I darted sideways, my steps echoing loudly. There must be another door somewhere. But the two new men began to run as well, angling to cut me off. I tried to put on a further burst of speed, but the taller of them caught me, bringing me crashing to the ground with a running leap.

I braced my fall, taking the impact on my arms, but he had acquired a firm grip around one of my ankles, and despite my kicking feet, held on.

"Don't let go," yelled a deep voice behind us. "I'm not losing the pay on this one no matter how hard she fights."

I continued to kick out wildly, trying to drag myself forward, but the man pulled himself up and pinned me to the ground.

"What about the other one?" asked a second voice, clearly more wary than the first.

"Sullivan and Matthews stayed to deal with anyone who tries to follow, remember."

I went limp against the floor, trying to lull my new captor into changing his position, so I could make another attempt at escape. But he didn't move, distracted by his companions' conversation.

"Yeah, but he might not be so weak, and no one ever said anything about a second—"

A splintering crash sounded through the large space as the door swung open and slammed against the wall. The man pinning me down jerked slightly, and I tried to push myself up onto my hands and knees, even as I reflexively looked to see what was happening.

Lucas stood in the open doorway, his white robe bright against the gloom. His eyes raced across the room before landing on me. I thought I saw a flicker of confusion cross his face as he watched me struggle, and then he shouted across the distance.

"Elena! What are you doing? COMPOSE!"

I went limp again as a spark raced through me. What had I been thinking? Had I really forgotten *again?*

Lucas reached inside his robe, clearly going for a composition of his own, but I didn't wait to see what it would do. Whispering the binding words, I called up the mental image of an armed forces composition I had never had the chance to test. The words tumbled out over themselves as fast as I could speak them.

"Incapacitate all attackers within this building. End binding."

Power pulsed out of me, sweeping across the empty space, stronger than anything I had felt before. Its connection to me lingered, and I could feel it reaching for anyone in its path.

The man on top of me screamed and went limp. I pushed myself upward, and he rolled to one side, thudding against the ground. I scrambled onto my knees in time to see the effect of my invisible force hit the others.

The tall man who had pulled me into the building bent double, groaning, before he collapsed to his knees and then pitched forward to lie prone. The other two had tried to run, heading deeper into the warehouse, but the power sought them out, sending them both silently crashing to the ground.

They were all unconscious now, but the power didn't fade away. I felt it reaching for one final victim, and my eyes locked on Lucas in horror. I had never meant for him to be included in my composition.

Whether he felt my power or was warned by some other instinct, he dropped two of the curls of parchment from his hand. With blinding speed, he ripped the third, and I felt my force crash into a barrier of his own power.

For a moment, the wave of my power crested over him. But an invisible bubble prevented it from reaching him, and gradually it softened and died.

I knelt where I was, panting and staring at him. He looked more shaken than I had ever seen him, but he quickly recovered, stooping to retrieve the two untouched compositions he had dropped. Shoving them into his robe, he strode toward me.

He held out a hand to help me to my feet, but I ignored it, pushing myself up unaided.

"Are they…dead?" I poked at the closest attacker with my foot.

Lucas knelt to examine him before moving to the next one.

"No, not dead. Just unconscious. And that one looks like he might have some broken bones." He nodded back at the one beside me.

I shook all over, despite my efforts to calm myself. I was glad they weren't dead, but I couldn't be sorry about the rest of it. Who knows what they had planned for me?

"What should we do with them?" I asked.

He looked up at me, and I shrugged defensively.

"You're the one studying law enforcement. I don't exactly know the protocols for this sort of situation."

"I'm the prince of Ardann, and you're the first Spoken Mage in history. I think we should get back to the Academy and leave the clean-up to the Reds."

Spoken Mage. I felt a new shiver up my spine. I looked around at the sprawled bodies. I had done this. I had done this with my words.

Lucas gripped my shoulder, feeling the tremors running through me. "That was a powerful working. It's no wonder you're feeling weak. Come on."

He pulled me toward the door, and I let him, dodging around the body of the large one without looking at it. When we emerged into the alley, we had to avoid two more bodies. Sullivan and Matthews, presumably. I didn't look at them closely.

"Thank you…for coming to help me," I said, rather belatedly.

Lucas gave me a strange look. "I wasn't really sure you would need me. But I thought if they had a mage with them…" His brow crinkled. "What happened?"

I shrugged, embarrassed to admit the truth. My combat training had come instinctively, my muscles responding to the long months of training. But my other ability had been entirely forgotten in the terror of the moment. Just as I had continuously forgotten my white robe during my day in the city.

"They were bold for thieves," he said, after a pause. "Especially to take on an Academy trainee."

I started as we emerged back onto the main road, almost stumbling over a loose flagstone. When I regained my step, I stared at him.

"Those weren't thieves."

He frowned at me, his eyes shadowed. "Of course they were. What else would they be?"

"They were after me, specifically."

He had long since dropped his grip on me, but at that he reached out again and patted my shoulder.

"It's natural to feel that way, especially while you're still so weak. But for all the efforts of the Reds, there is still crime in Corrin, you know. Some people will take advantage of anyone, if they think they can."

His eyes seemed to be communicating something more than his words, but the anger burning through me made me too impatient to try to understand it. My shaking stopped. It confirmed what I had already guessed—my physical reaction had been shock not weakness from my use of power. I felt weary and sore, but not excessively so, especially with the energy from the scare still coursing through my system.

I gestured at my robe. "Really? You think an Academy trainee seemed like a good target to a bunch of street criminals? Your opinion of the intelligence of common folk is even lower than I thought."

Lucas glared at me. "You're defending them now?"

"Of course not!" I glared back at him. "But someone had told them I was weak. They didn't expect me to be able to defend myself against them. They were definitely targeting me."

Two red-robed guards appeared at the street corner in front of us. Lucas increased his pace but gave me a warning look over his shoulder before he reached them.

"There are thieves everywhere, Elena. Don't let your imagination run away with you."

I swelled, too infuriated for words, as he hailed the guards and reported the attack, directing them where to find the so-called thieves. These men recognized their prince, even if the criminals hadn't, and they both stood to attention, not questioning his words.

One suggested he fetch an escort to accompany us back to the Academy, but Lucas rejected the offer.

"See those men are arrested and as quickly as possible. As you can see, I am well able to defend myself." He smiled, the gesture holding a veiled threat rather than any goodwill.

Both guards nodded briskly and took off in the direction he had indicated. Neither made any suggestion we should go with them.

As soon as the men had left, Lucas strode on toward the Academy, and I hurried to catch up with him.

"Do you really think this was some random attack?" I spat the words at him. "And I suppose you think that balcony just happened to collapse as well?" The disdain dripped from my words. "What are you? A fool?"

His steps slowed, and he gave me a piercing look. We had never properly spoken of the collapse or the subtle surge of power that preceded it. The one we must have both felt.

"I don't know what to think, Elena. And if you knew what was good for you, you would feel the same way. So, I repeat. It is unfortunate that thieves decided to target you. They must have been desperate or fool-hardy to attack a trainee. No doubt other such criminals will think twice before doing so in the future."

I blinked at him, my rage dying away. Embarrassment took its place as I realized I had once again failed to pick up on the subtle signals that made up this world I still knew so little about. So Lucas didn't necessarily believe it was thieves, he just thought it was the safest story to stick to until we had further information. And that we should make sure we told the same story.

A little of the anger returned. He couldn't speak plainly to me? No doubt he thought it beneath him to discuss the matter openly with someone commonborn.

The Academy came into view, startling me. Had we walked so far already? Lucas stepped sideways, so that he brushed against me as we walked, and then slipped his shoulder under my arm. I almost stumbled again at the unexpected interference, and he steadied me.

"That was a major working you composed back there," he said. "You must be exhausted. It's amazing you made it back to the Academy on your own two feet."

I looked up at him, and my heartbeat instantly sped up at the proximity of his eyes. I had to look away quickly before I could process the warning they held. After a moment, however, I nodded. I wasn't going to play the fool again. I understood his warning, even if he didn't want to properly articulate it.

"And you might not want to mention to our instructors just how much you condensed that composition." Now there was a hint of amusement in his voice.

I looked back up at him, this time able to resist the effect of his face so close to mine.

"I was kind of pressed for time, you know."

He shook his head. "I'm serious when I say you're lucky it

didn't burn you out. It was risky to go for uncontrolled, brute force like that."

I flushed a little and looked away. That hadn't been my intention. I had reacted out of fear, cutting out most of the limitations from the original composition. Remembering it, another image rose to mind.

"Are you going to tell anyone?"

"Tell them what?"

"That my composition attacked you, too." I bit my lip. "I still don't understand why it did that. It wasn't my intention, I swear."

"Elena." He sounded tired. "There's a reason we spend four years at the Academy learning finesse and control. And we don't just dash off the first words that come to mind. There are legitimate reasons why some of us feel that a Spoken Mage is dangerous."

I said nothing, as struck by the title now as I had been when he first used it back in the warehouse.

"You specified all attackers in your working," he said, apparently interpreting my silence as further confusion. "You failed to limit it to people attacking you. I was there to attack your captors —which made me an attacker."

"Oh." My voice sounded small, and I hated it. But he was right. I hadn't thought my words through, and if he hadn't been so fast with his shield composition…

"I'm sorry."

He gave the slightest start, discernible only because he was still pressed against me, helping me along.

"Did you just *apologize* to me?"

My eyes flew to his, and the laughter reflected in their depths made me lose my breath again. But I forced myself to grimace, acknowledging that I recognized my own words from Midwinter.

Before I could think of an appropriate response, however, he led us through the doors of the Academy. Several trainees were crossing the entrance hall.

"What happened to you?" Natalya sounded half-shocked, half-contemptuous, her eyes flying between Lucas and me.

I stared at her for a confused moment before glancing down at my once-white robe—now dirty, torn, and blood-stained from several long grazes on my arms.

Lucas stepped away from me quickly, and I swayed, the whole experience catching up with me, as someone in the distance called for Acacia.

By the time the healer arrived, Lucas had already disappeared.

CHAPTER 25

$\mathcal{E}$veryone at the Academy accepted Lucas's version of events—or at least pretended to do so—and I kept my mouth shut about it. Lucas had reminded me that, unlike him, I didn't understand how these people, or their complicated dynamics, worked. And I couldn't decide who would be safe to talk to.

Well, other than Coralie, but what could she do about it? Nothing but worry, and she was already worried enough. First year would end half way through the summer, but not before exams, and our instructors had already begun to talk of them—usually in dire and threatening terms.

I took none of it seriously—I had no need to win prestige among these people, or to curry favor in hopes of a better discipline placement after graduation. But finally Coralie's concern wore me down.

"Relax, Coralie. Please." I passed her an extra serving of dessert, figuring she needed it. "You're driving me crazy. I promise if by some unexpected catastrophe you fail, I will stay back and repeat first year with you."

"Repeat?" She stared at me blankly. "Is that what happens in common schools if you fail?"

I stared back at her. "Of course. What else could happen?"

She lowered her voice. "The Reds."

"The Reds? What does law enforcement care about a failed trainee?"

"There are few things more dangerous than a mage who can't learn control." She shook her head. "All mageborn must attend the Academy, and anyone who fails is locked away. For life. Without any further access to the written word."

I gaped at her, my mouth open. "Imprisoned? For failing at school?" I closed my mouth and swallowed, an image of Duke Lennox rising before me. What had he said at the Mage Council? That imprisoning me would not be a simple matter like imprisoning other mages. That execution would be the only safe option…

Coralie must have seen something of the terror on my face, because she quickly swallowed her mouthful and patted my hand reassuringly.

"But we won't fail. They make first year exams easy because they know we're still beginners. It's not like they want mages to fail."

But her own anxiety belied her words, and she didn't know of my recent experiences. It might be true that no one wanted *her* to fail, but I didn't believe for a second the same was true of me. Clearly someone wanted me to do far more than fail.

The thought haunted me over the next days, as a new interpretation of the attack occurred to me. When I entered the library to study for the latest healing essay, my mind was so full of the thought that my feet led me to the back of the library before I had made any firm decision on my destination.

A lone figure studied there at a single desk, as he always did at this time. Everyone else knew to respect the space of royalty. Everyone except me, apparently.

I plopped down into a seat on the other side of his desk and leaned forward, my elbows propped against the surface.

"What if it was a test?"

"Excuse me?" He narrowed his eyes at me, unused to interruptions.

I ignored his look but did lower my voice. "The attack. What if it was a test?"

"A test?" He frowned. "Of what?"

"My ability. My control." I took a deep breath. "The likelihood of my passing the exams."

I watched as understanding filled his eyes, followed by a thoughtful look. He didn't say anything, however.

"You heard them at that council. They don't believe I can be safely imprisoned. If I contravene any laws, I'll be executed. And I've just found out mages aren't allowed to fail at the Academy. What a simple way to be rid of me—as long as they could be sure I wasn't going to pass, of course."

"That sounds a little far-fetched, Elena."

"Would you say that if it was your life in question?"

"Considering I've nearly been caught in both of these apparent attacks on you…"

I wrinkled my nose. "*Nearly* is not the same as actually. And you have no reason to be worried. You'll never fail. But what if I do?"

He regarded me steadily. "So don't fail."

I gaped at him, but he merely returned to the book in front of him.

I spluttered. "Just—just like that?"

He shrugged and looked up, annoyance on his face now. "What exactly were you expecting me to say, Elena? You're worried what will happen if you fail. So don't fail."

I leaped to my feet. "Of all the obnoxious—"

He raised an eyebrow at me, and I spun around and stormed out of the library. Never mind execution, there was no way I was failing now. In fact, I had every intention of coming top of the class. That would show certain arrogant, uncaring, obnoxious…

~

I briefly considered dropping my voluntary discipline studies so I could focus on exam preparation instead. But Jocasta watched me with a look that said she expected me to abandon classes at any moment, and combined with the infuriating sight of Lucas—who showed up every day as he always did—I couldn't bring myself to do it.

So instead I found myself returning to the library late one evening, determined to fit in a little more study before bed. I had a common feeling with Jasper these days, having to work harder than everyone else since I couldn't take any notes. I had no idea how he did it when he couldn't read either.

Most of the lights in the library were off, and I wondered uneasily if trainees were supposed to be here at this hour. But a golden glow shone from the back of the room, so I made for it with soft steps. Surely they wouldn't leave any lights on if the library were closed. And the doors had been open.

A solitary trainee studied alone in the back of the room, in his usual spot. I stood for a moment, undecided and awkward, until Lucas looked up and gave me such a challenging stare, that I put my chin up and took the desk across from his.

He continued to regard me silently, but when I pulled out a book and began to read, I felt his eyes drop back to the parchment in front of him. We remained there in silence for the next two hours, until my eyes began to droop so badly I had to admit defeat and head for bed.

As soon as I did, Lucas closed his own book and followed me out of the library. He didn't say anything, though, and I soon left him behind as he headed for his suite on the fourth year floor.

The next night I found him there again. And the night after.

On that third night, we were interrupted by Walden, who was strolling the perimeter of the library, pushing in chairs and checking for abandoned books. He whistled cheerfully to himself, the sound breaking off when he looked up and saw the two of us.

"Well, well, well, exam prep, I suppose." He smiled at us. "You know, strictly speaking, the library isn't supposed to be open to students this late."

Lucas gave him a look of such royal superiority and expectation, that I shook my head and quickly began to pack up my books, determined to show the librarian that one of us, at least, respected his domain.

But he shook his head and held out a hand to stop me.

"No, no, I'm not so hard hearted as that. And I can't have my favorite trainee failing." He winked at me, and I resisted the urge to smirk at Lucas. Apparently not everyone was falling over themselves to curry royal favor.

After chatting for a few moments, and recommending several books to me along with broad hints that I might find them useful for Redmond's exam, Walden continued on his way.

Lucas watched his retreat.

"He's awfully friendly," he said, once the librarian had disappeared.

"Surprising, isn't it?" I said sweetly. "For a mage. But sometimes people do surprise you."

Lucas gave me a flat look. "And sometimes they don't."

I looked down at my book, not wanting him to see how his words stung. It didn't matter how hard I tried, it would never be enough for people like him.

"You seem extremely concerned about the exams," Lucas said, surprising me into looking up again. Apparently Walden's visit had loosened his tongue.

"I should think the reasons would be obvious," I replied.

"It just strikes me that if your little theory is right, then you have more to worry about than just passing the exams."

"What's that supposed to mean?" He had my full attention now.

"Only that if the attack was a test, I can only assume you passed. In which case your mystery enemy will not be reassured at all. Assuming they do, indeed, want you dead, that is."

"Plenty of people want me dead. You know that."

He shrugged. "It's not personal, Elena. It's politics. And in politics things change all the time. Just because that's what they wanted a month ago doesn't mean that's what they want now."

I closed my book, forgetting to mark my page. "Ugh. How can you stand it?"

A slight crease appeared between his eyes. "I don't have a choice. Just like you. We neither of us chose our life."

I pushed my book away, pulling another toward me blindly, merely because my hands wanted something to do. His words gave me the same uncomfortable feeling from months ago when I learned how his family had designated him the disposable one. I reminded myself that I was nothing like this prince—not really.

"It has some advantages for you, though, doesn't it?" I stared across the desks at him. "Like when you wanted to report a crime, no one brushed you aside."

He sighed and rubbed the side of his head, as if I wearied him. I maintained my stare.

"Responsibility and privilege go hand in hand. It's always been like that."

I shook my head. "Power, you mean. Power and privilege go hand in hand. Responsibility is what those in power are *supposed* to have. You know, like making sure that the law treats everyone equally."

"Equal?" He laughed. "Grow up, Elena. Nothing in life is equal. We are all of us products of our birth, ability, and choices. And not necessarily in that order."

I almost snarled at him. "You think I don't know that? I'm commonborn, remember? I've had to watch my sister cough and burn and grow weak every time the smallest ailment passes through the village, knowing I can do nothing to help her. Because no healer would deign to visit a town like ours—where no one is rich enough to pay their fees. I've watched families turn against each other in the hardest decision anyone could have to make—which of them they should offer up as a sacrifice to conscription. I've seen the mothers cry once their boys have left." I paused as a rock settled in my gut. "Of course, it's not always the boys." My voice dropped low. "I know all about not being equal. And maybe that's why I believe it's the duty of those in power to strive for equality."

Lucas stared at me, his face twisted, and for a moment I thought I had gotten through to him. Then he spoke.

"Conscription? You could hardly have picked a worse example to make your case. Ardann are not the aggressors in this war. We fight Kallorway for our survival. If we lost, the whole kingdom would suffer."

"Easy to say when you're not the one forced to fight."

He stared at me incredulously. "How long have you been here, Elena? How many hours have you spent in this library? How can you still know so little of our ways?"

I straightened, drawing an angry breath, but he pushed on.

"Why do you think we spend half our day on combat training? You're upset because you common folk must sacrifice one from every family? Look around! Every mageborn in the kingdom attends this Academy, and yet there are so few of us. One from every commonborn family must go to fight, it is true. But every single mageborn must go. We wouldn't have a chance of holding back Kallorway otherwise."

The angry retort on my lips froze. "Wait...what?"

He shook his head. "Four years at the Academy. Two at the front lines. And then entry to the University or training within a discipline. Our lives have less choice and more structure than most of yours."

"Most of *ours*? The other day I was the Spoken Mage—one of you. Now I'm one of them. Which is it, Prince?"

He gave a long sigh, his face growing suddenly weary. "I don't know. Tell me when you decide."

My eyes dropped from his face, my mind still reeling from his revelation. How had I missed something that important? I thought back over many conversations at the Academy, searching for the clues I'd missed. Had I really been that self-absorbed?

"That doesn't absolve you of responsibility for the rest of the kingdom," I muttered, unwilling for him to carry the point entirely.

"Absolution?" His laugh was grim. "No, I don't suppose any of us have that."

Neither of us spoke again for the rest of the evening.

The days grew unbearably warm, but not even Coralie attempted to lure us out of the stuffy building. She, Finnian, and Saffron had taken to joining me in the library in the empty session after composition to study for exams. As well as a long written exam, they would also be expected to demonstrate three different compositions—both composing and working them in front of the examiners.

Redmond had commanded me to stay back after class one day and had informed me that I would need to complete the same set of questions in a different room. I would read the exam questions and then answer verbally for a panel of examiners. I would also demonstrate my compositions to that same panel once the verbal exam was completed.

I didn't bother to ask why a panel was necessary. From the interest shown in my progress so far, I could only imagine the spots had been highly sought after. How many of them would be there hoping to see me fail? Ready to influence the exam in that direction, perhaps?

Redmond's face made it clear he highly disapproved of treating any trainee differently. Making an exception for me, in particular, seemed to almost cause him physical pain. But since I could hardly complete a written exam while forbidden from writing, I wasn't sure what option he would have preferred. Other than my being failed outright without ever being given a chance, perhaps. He was the only Stantorn instructor, so that probably would have been his choice. No doubt Lorcan had stepped in on my behalf.

The twins and the Stantorn cousins largely ignored me now, too distracted by their own study to have time and energy even for their usual snide comments. As Lucas and I progressed in our studies, Dariela—although she gave no other sign of caring about her position as head of the class—appeared at our evening study session in the library. Her presence made no difference since Lucas and I hadn't had a proper conversation since our argument the night Walden found us. It just meant that now three of us sat and studied in silence.

Pale, academic Clarence continued to keep to himself, although I saw him occasionally staggering in and out of the library with enormous piles of books. Personally, I thought he would do better spending his extra time on combat practice.

The lack of jabs from the twins and their friends wasn't the only sign of the equalizing effect of exams. Poor, terrified Araminta overcame her apparent fear of associating with me to join our afternoon study sessions. When I saw how her hand shook as she copied out notes, and how she stumbled when we verbally quizzed each other, I wished I could take a swipe at whoever had decided on such an unrelenting and punishing system.

Araminta might struggle to keep up with the rest of us, but I had never seen her lose control of a composition. She didn't try anything adventurous enough for that. I could no more imagine her causing anyone harm than I could imagine Clemmy doing so.

Clementine. The thought of my sister always buoyed me up, providing an extra shot of energy. As soon as the exams were completed, we would all be released for the rest of the summer. Which meant home and my family. After nearly a year away, I was so close to seeing them all again.

Jasper would remain at the University for the summer break, studying and using his extra time for odd jobs in the city to help fund his next year's room and board. But perhaps he would be able to slip away for Midsummer as he had done for Midwinter.

Somehow the weeks passed. My head always hurt by the time I fell into bed—stuffed far too full with questions, answers and memorized compositions—and I dreamed about exam questions every night. I had finally acquired enough familiarity with the sword that I wasn't in any danger of lopping off my own arm by accident, but I still trailed most of the class.

Finnian had agreed to give Saffron, Coralie, and me extra coaching, so we all met for an hour before breakfast. None of us had slept enough for weeks, but all the moaning about being tired didn't stop any of us from attending the extra practice session every day. It seemed that the trainees' legendary ability to avoid all extra work didn't extend to exam preparation.

And then the big day dawned.

We would complete our combat exam in the morning and the composition one in the afternoon, just like our normal class session. And while we were all highly strung and anxious, we could be grateful at least that we wouldn't have to physically exert ourselves all morning. Instead we would each engage in a single free bout with one other student, observed by Lorcan and Thornton. And the Academy had taken pity on us first years and given us the first slot of the morning before the older trainees completed their own combat exams.

"Just don't chop me up too badly," Coralie said to me glumly as we all traipsed out to the dusty training yard after attempting to choke down breakfast with varying degrees of success.

I snorted. Coralie had come a long way since we'd started training with swords and was better than me.

"Not much chance of that. You're the one who should be promising to have mercy on me."

"Relax. You'll both do fine." Finnian looked calm and unaffected, the only one of us to have eaten breakfast as if it were any other day. But then he was the son of a duke and had been training with a sword for years. Only Lucas, Weston, Calix, or Dariela would have a chance of keeping pace with him.

Secretly I felt a little sorry for Saffron, being paired with her cousin. I was hoping that Coralie and I would look better by dint of being vaguely evenly matched, at least.

But after we reached the training yard and completed a short warm up with the rest of our year mates, we all received a shock.

Thornton, his face carefully blank, consulted a piece of parchment in his hand and announced, "The first randomly drawn bout will be between Lucas and Araminta."

CHAPTER 26

*A*raminta stood frozen, looking as if she were about to faint, while Coralie, Saffron and I exchanged horrified looks. Randomly selected? No one had mentioned that we wouldn't be sparring with our usual partners.

Lucas stepped forward, his face as impassive as Thornton, his dull practice sword gripped loosely in his hand. Araminta made no move to join him.

Thornton cleared his throat, his expression turning sour. "We don't have all day, Araminta. Please step forward for your exam."

The poor girl somehow managed to propel her legs into motion, but she looked back at the rest of our study group as she did so. I gave her the most encouraging look I could muster, attempting to mask my own terror as to who I might be paired with. It must have worked, because her grip tightened, and her back straightened.

It didn't help much, though, of course. Lucas might not have the vindictive streak of someone like Weston, but he was the most skilled swordsman in our year. And he made no effort to go easy on Araminta. She managed to block him twice and to attempt a single, rather weak, attack herself. Then his sword flashed, and while I couldn't see how it happened, her sword went flying, and his dull blade rested against her throat.

"Yield," he said, and she started to nod before remembering the sword at her throat and squeaking out, "Yield."

"Well that was just depressing," Coralie whispered in my ear. "Although if she manages to pass with that effort, then we should all be safe."

Thornton made several notes on his parchment and then called the next names without looking up. "Finnian and Dariela."

Lorcan smiled, no doubt anticipating a much more interesting bout, and I heard Calix murmur, "This should be good."

And it was, of course. The two of them were even more evenly matched than I had hoped to be with Coralie—only their skill was far greater. They parried and thrusted, ducking and weaving across the training yard for a full fifteen minutes before Dariela managed an expert feint that caught Finnian off guard and let her move in for the kill stroke.

With her sword tip resting against his heart, he grinned, barely out of breath, and called, "Yield."

Lorcan actually applauded, and Thornton gave a dry, "Excellent." Possibly the first time I had heard him give such high praise.

Knowing my luck, I'll be up next, I thought, but to my relief I didn't hear my name called.

Saffron and Clarence went next, and the northern girl looked beyond relieved when she heard her pairing.

Finnian clapped her on the back as he moved back to join us. "Run him through," he said cheerily, but she ignored him, her eyes losing focus in the way they did when she was preparing herself mentally for a bout.

Clarence lasted far longer than Araminta had done since Saffron was far less skilled than Lucas. But she still managed to sneak her blade past his defenses in the end, landing a sharp blow to his chest. The tall boy quickly yielded, mostly looking relieved to have it all over. From his face, he knew he had been lucky in the draw.

Both Coralie and I remained, but I didn't much like my chances of being paired with my friend. Not when all four of my least favorite year mates also remained. When the next two names called were Natalya and Coralie, my heart sank the rest of the way into my boots.

Coralie cast me a sympathetic grimace, aware that Natalya would be a far easier opponent than either Calix or Weston, who both still remained. But a moment later, when she stood facing the Devoras girl, her sole concentration was on her own bout. And she did better than I expected, lasting several minutes and even landing a glancing hit against Natalya's arm before being forced to yield to a sword tip at her throat.

Natalya looked pleased with herself as her brother and Lavinia congratulated her, but Coralie looked reasonably cheerful as well. Her face fell when Thornton announced the next bout, however. Calix and Lavinia.

"Ouch." She winced sympathetically at me, but my face seemed to have frozen, and I couldn't respond. There were only two of us left. Me and Weston.

I didn't even see Calix beat Lavinia as fear washed through me. I was going to fail. And then I was going to be executed.

But as Lavinia called, "Yield," and Thornton made yet more notes on his parchment, my eyes fell on Lucas. He looked between me and Weston, and then to Thornton. I couldn't read his expression, but he was certainly contemplating something.

And then sudden anger drove out my fear. Thornton, my disapproving Devoras instructor, had claimed the bouts were drawn randomly. But what were the chances that I would be drawn last? And with Weston as my partner. Just like that first class nearly a year ago when I was massacred. I had been expecting to be set up for failure, but my concentration had been on the composition class—the place where I was different. I had been looking in the wrong direction.

The rage racing through me was energizing, and I strode forward as soon as Lavinia and Calix rejoined the group, not even waiting for my name to be called. My hand gripped my sword hilt so hard, my knuckles turned white.

Weston sauntered behind me, a grin on his face. This would be nothing like Lucas and Araminta. The prince had shown no mercy for his opponent, but neither had he shown any cruelty. Weston, on the other hand, was clearly looking forward to cutting me to ribbons. Preferably with a generous serving of humiliation on the side.

I dropped into the correct stance and brought my weapon up in front of me. Weston took his time assuming his own position, but I didn't let my concentration waver. Whatever happened, I was going to hold my own for long enough to achieve a pass. If they meant to pass Araminta—and surely they did—they would be forced to pass me, too.

Weston began without warning, lunging forward in a fast feint. I pulled back just in time, using a clumsy block that only just deflected his blade. He grinned and launched forward again immediately. I skipped even further back, and the sounds from the rest of the group faded away.

My attention funneled in on Weston, and I found myself settling into a rhythm I had never experienced before. My muscles moved before I even directed them, producing each block as needed. The attacks came so fast, though, that I had no opportunity to return any of them. It was all I could do to stay out of reach of his blade and keep my own weapon in hand.

When he landed a blow—a hard whack to my left arm that was clearly designed to hurt rather than force a yield—I focused even more on keeping out of his reach. I danced my way around the training yard, retreating from him.

"This is supposed to be an exam in combat," he taunted, his voice too low to be heard by anyone else, "not in running away."

I didn't waste my breath replying. Everyone present knew Weston was a superior swordsman to me. If it was true they would all find themselves on the front lines, he would learn soon enough the value of retreat in the face of superior force. Or not. I wouldn't be weeping any tears for him either way.

I saw an opening and lunged forward. Too late, I realized it had been a trick. Unable to pull back, I instead reacted on instinct, as I had done when attacked in the city. Dropping my sword, I fell forward into a roll, spinning underneath his flashing blade and popping up behind him.

I drove my elbow back into his spine as hard as I could. He grunted and stumbled, dropping to one knee. Spinning, I leaned over and snatched my own weapon from the dust. Bringing it up as fast as I could, I lunged for his throat.

He swayed away from me, only just pulling his sword up in time for a weak block. I pressed forward with a stronger attack, but somehow he got his feet under him and blocked me again.

His eyes held an ugly look now, and he battered my sword away and drove forward. Clearly he had been holding back before, playing with me. Against his new fury, I held out for bare seconds, before his sword tip rested against my throat.

I tried to yield, but the pressure of his sword point increased, and I started to choke. Still he pressed harder.

"Weston." The quiet voice that cut across the training yard didn't belong to either of our instructors. But Weston instantly dropped his point, stepping back from me. He turned to look at Lucas with narrowed eyes, but the prince met his look coolly, not backing down. Authority and confidence radiated from the royal, and Weston's eyes dropped. He returned to the group.

I took a moment to breathe beautiful fresh air, coughing several times before stooping to retrieve my dropped sword.

"Well," said Thornton at last, "that was different."

I grinned at him. "My specialty."

Lorcan gave a cough that sounded suspiciously like a chuckle, and Finnian actually laughed out loud, clapping me on the back when I reached my friends.

"Good show."

"You did notice I lost, right?" I shook my head at him.

"Well, you were always going to lose," he said with unabated cheerfulness. "But at least you did it with style."

I rolled my eyes at Coralie who looked like she didn't know whether to join him in laughing or look horrified.

"Are you all right?" She gestured at my throat, and I winced.

"A little tender but, everything considered, I expected a lot worse."

"I think he did, too," said Finnian, his voice thoughtful.

"What?" Saffron's brow creased in confusion.

"I think you took Weston by surprise. He expected to have it more his own way."

"Him and Thornton both, no doubt," I muttered, and Finnian gave me a sharper look than I liked. His joking manner made it easy to forget the sharp mind hiding behind it.

"That was the last bout," I said quickly. "The exam's over, right? Let's go find some lunch."

"Wait, we have to hear our results first," said Coralie.

"What, right now?" I asked.

"Of course. It's not like they have to go and mark papers," she replied.

Lorcan and Thornton stood some way apart from us all, talking quietly, while we all hung around in varying states of suspense. I saw Thornton's eyes dwell on me before sliding to Araminta. His face twisted, and then he nodded once.

Lorcan turned to us all and clapped his hands loudly.

"Congratulations, first years. You have all passed."

A murmur passed through the group, and Araminta turned pink with pleasure.

"Your rankings are as follows." Thornton paused dramatically, but I didn't care about my ranking as long as I had passed.

"First: Dariela."

Natalya and Lavinia cheered and congratulated their friend, apparently pleased to have a girl leading combat.

"Second: Lucas."

They gave nearly as enthusiastic congratulations to the prince, who looked neither pleased nor displeased. I wondered if he was secretly disappointed not to lead the class. Unlike Dariela, his pairing had hardly given him the chance to showcase his skill.

Thornton read out the rest of the list without pausing. "Weston, Finnian, Calix, Natalya, Saffron, Lavinia, Coralie, Elena, Clarence, Araminta."

Weston stalked away immediately, his friends trailing behind him, several shooting glares at me as they passed.

But I was far too elated to care. I had passed. Even Araminta had passed. It seemed like a miracle.

"It looks like your tutelage paid off," I said to Finnian with a grin. "I hope you aren't disappointed in your own ranking. You came higher than a couple of those who actually won their bouts."

"You observe me full of elation." He grinned a little wryly.

"Thank goodness it's over, I say." Coralie actually sounded a little bit like her cheerful self. "Only one more to go."

CHAPTER 27

It turned out to be far too early for lunch, but Finnian forbade us all from doing any last-minute studying.

"You'll only confuse your brains," he assured us. "And increase your blood pressure."

Instead we all sat in the dining hall, and he made it his role to get us all laughing, despite the stress. Older students trickled in around us, some looking visibly relieved and others somewhat battered. By the time the servers arrived, the dining hall had acquired its usual hum.

Coralie had fallen silent, however, her eyes on a group of particularly bruised-looking second years.

"I've been so focused on passing, I haven't thought much about how it's all going to change next year." She turned back to face us, gesturing slightly at the group with her head. "But just look at them. Terrifying."

I swiveled to frown in the direction of the older students. "What do you mean?"

"Next year we start in the arena." Saffron shivered.

It took me a moment to remember the significance of that.

"Weapons and compositions." I whispered the words. "Combined. Great." I couldn't stop my eyes from flashing over to where Lucas sat. I had recently had some experience on combining combat and composing, and it had nearly ended in disaster. And that was with non-mage opponents.

At the Academy, my opponents would only have to rip a parchment while I had to somehow spout a whole list of restrictions and parameters. Or risk being hauled back before the Mage Council for destroying one of my fellow trainees.

"Don't look so pale, Elena," said Finnian. "It'll be fun."

"Easy for you to say," I muttered, but a platter of roast meat distracted me. Apparently the Academy put on something of a feast for the students on exam day.

"Dig in," said Finnian. "We're not done yet."

When we finished our meal and headed for our second exam, I found myself envying the rest of my friends. They got to move as a group, drawing strength from each other's presence, while I split off to approach a small classroom I had never entered before.

All of the year levels took the written portion of their exams together in the largest classroom. I had peeked in earlier and seen it lined with individual desks. Jocasta and Walden would supervise the written portion, and then each year level would take turns composing in front of Lorcan and Redmond. The first years would go first again, and the fourth years wouldn't be finished until just before the evening meal.

I wished I could complete my exam questions under the friendly gaze of Walden, but his supervision of the main group meant the only instructor I actually liked was guaranteed not to be on my panel. When I knocked on the door of the room where I was to be examined, a voice called for me to enter.

Inside I found a row of chairs, all already occupied. Lorcan had been joined by Jessamine, the University Head, with two other black-robed mages beside her. I recognized them from my never-ending stream of observers. The next panel member didn't surprise me—of course Redmond would want to be here to glare at me the entire time—but the two beside him did. Perhaps he had arranged for their presence, no doubt drawing moral support from the presence of his fellow Stantorn, Duke Casimir, Head of the Creators, and their ally Duchess Annika of Devoras, Head of the Growers. Both had voted in favor of my execution at that memorable council meeting.

I scanned the line up again. Lorcan, Jessamine, and her fellow academics had the superior numbers. Lorcan's doing, no doubt. I didn't know if my passing or failing could come down to a vote, but I could only hope their presence would be enough.

I stood in front of the examiners, no chair or desk provided for my use. Redmond stepped forward and handed me a parchment full of words.

"You will read each question aloud and then give your answer. You will be timed."

"Overall, or for each question?" I asked.

He narrowed his eyes at my apparent impertinence, and reluctantly replied, "Overall."

I nodded, and he sat back down. I should be able to take my time on any unexpected questions then. I wasn't going to let his hostility intimidate me into rushing and getting the answers wrong.

I cleared my throat and read out the first question. The list seemed endless, but once I started, I fell into a rhythm. At first, I looked only at Lorcan and Jessamine and the University observers, but as my confidence grew, I let my gaze roam over the other three as well.

All of my extra study seemed to have paid off, and I found an answer springing easily to mind for each question they asked. Some of them were more complicated than I had expected, though, given Coralie's assurances that they went easy on us first years. I spared a quick, concerned thought for Araminta.

In fact, there were so many questions that I felt a brief

moment of unease for all my friends. They only had an hour for the written portion of the exam, and I couldn't imagine how anyone could actually write out answers to all of these in that time. I actually had a small advantage being able to speak my answers at a faster pace.

As the questions continued, my voice grew hoarse, and one of the University mages brought me a glass of water. While I drank it down greedily, I saw the two of them exchanging a glance and observed a brief whispered exchange with Jessamine and Lorcan. The latter then directed a hard stare at Redmond, who carefully avoided catching his eye.

I frowned but pushed it all out of my mind. This wasn't the moment to be distracted. When I finally reached the end of the questions, only just within my allotted hour, I strode forward and returned the parchment to Redmond. I couldn't help giving him a satisfied smirk as I did so. I dared any of them to fail me after that performance.

Redmond took the parchment with an unpleasant look.

"Well?" I asked. "Did I pass?"

He cleared his throat and glanced at the duke and duchess beside him.

"Of course you did, Elena," said Lorcan from the other end of the lineup. "An excellent job. And that despite the mix up. Very well done, indeed."

"Mix up?" asked Duke Casimir coldly.

Lorcan nodded at him. "You've no doubt forgotten your own first year exams, Casimir, and naturally you would not be familiar with the questions for this year. But I had understood Elena was to receive the same questions as her year mates. However it seems that somehow both the first and second year questions ended up on her sheet. A strange occurrence, but clerical mix ups are an inevitability, I'm told. Of course, we generally try to avoid them at exam time, and I assure you I shall look into the mistake personally."

Redmond was still carefully not looking at his head, and I almost felt sorry for him. Almost.

Mostly I just felt relief that my friends had been facing a far shorter and simpler list of questions. And somewhere under all that was the stirrings of pride. Lorcan had just said that I passed a second year level exam.

"Unfortunate, indeed, although it doesn't seem to have discomposed her." Casimir eyed me coldly. "But while theory is all very well, it is useless on its own. We have all been sitting here for the last hour because the girl dare not write without blowing us all up. The real question is, can she compose?"

Lorcan nodded. "I propose we proceed immediately to the practical portion of the exam. Redmond and I will need to be leaving soon to supervise the performance of the rest of our students."

I straightened, the pride and elation draining away. I hadn't quite passed first year yet.

"Very well," said Casimir. "Let us proceed. I believe three of us were to each come up with an exercise for the girl."

Lorcan nodded. "We were pleased to allow our guests to participate in such a way."

I bit back a frown. No doubt the honor had gone to the visitors with the highest rank. Jessamine, Annika, and Casimir then. One friend and two foes. I eyed Jessamine's anticipatory expression and amended the thought. One non-foe and two foes. I would hardly count Jessamine as a friend.

She leaned forward toward me, gesturing at the man beside her without looking at him. He stood.

"I understand you have been conducting extra research on the healing discipline."

Annika and Casimir both frowned, and I suspected this was news to them. I struggled to keep my expression straight, half-expecting Lorcan to protest on my behalf—none of the other first years would be getting discipline specific composition assignments. But he looked almost as eager as Jessamine and made no move to override her words.

The man who had stood shook back his black sleeve, exposing a long gash still seeping red blood. I swallowed and took an involuntary step backward. Casimir made a disgusted noise.

"He has already been treated with a pain-relief composition," Jessamine said. "And something to slow the bleeding. But I would like to see you attempt to heal the injury itself."

I looked at her, fear biting at me as it had done when I realized who my combat partner was to be. My eyes flashed to Lorcan, but still he made no protest. This wasn't a first year level composition. I had thought Jessamine, at least, would wish me to succeed, but it seemed her curiosity had overridden everything else.

I took a steadying breath and briefly closed my eyes. It wasn't a first year composition, but I had struggled through an advanced assignment on cuts and similar wounds. It had seemed a relevant thing to study given my fast-approaching conscription.

I had even spent several nights memorizing a beginner level composition for healing basic cuts. It had struck me as a useful thing to know, especially after Lucas's reminder that I might well have bigger things to worry about than passing my exams. I called it into my mind's eye, a full half page of words at the beginner level. But now wasn't the time to try modifying anything. I took a deep breath, spoke the binding words, and began.

I spoke slowly, preferring to ensure I didn't miss anything rather than to work on impressing my examiners with my speed and competence. If I succeeded, that would have to be competence enough.

"End binding," I said, after what felt like forever, and I felt my released power drift away from me. As the healer rather than the patient, it didn't feel cool to me, but it still had a mist-like quality as the power settled over his arm.

As we all watched, the skin fused together, the blood slowing and then stopping as the skin knit back together. Within moments, his arm was smooth and whole, marred only by the leftover smears of blood.

"Incredible." Jessamine shook her head, her eyes jumping from her colleague's arm to me.

Casimir frowned, not giving me a chance to draw a proper breath before he also leaned forward.

"That's all very well for healing minor injuries, but there are plenty of situations out there in the real world that don't allow for long speeches." He pulled a parchment from his robe and ripped it, his eyes on me the whole time as if pointing out how much more quickly he could work.

A large bundle of sticks clattered onto the floor in front of me, appearing from nowhere. They looked damp.

"Burn them," the duke said. "I want nothing left but ash. Oh, and don't smoke us all out while you're at it."

I bit my lip, once again galvanized by my anger. Another request far beyond first year level. This was an examination—and with my life on the line, no less—not an exhibition for their entertainment.

And after this, I was still expected to do a third working. Any ordinary first year would be laid flat by these first two requests— if they managed to complete them at all. Thus almost guaranteeing failure. I had half-expected something like this from Casimir and Annika, but I had thought Jessamine and Lorcan would shield me. Apparently not. I was to be left on my own.

In which case it was a good thing I wasn't an ordinary first year. With a pang, I realized that it would be impossible to keep hiding my strength after this. But there was no point hiding it if it meant execution.

Thankfully we had covered fire in our regular composition

class, and I had come across a description of how to disperse and remove smoke in my armed forces studies. It was just a matter of combining the two.

I thought for a long time, running through the words in my mind twice to be sure I remembered them correctly and hadn't forgotten anything. A mistake on this one could end with disastrous consequences, and I had every intention of ignoring Casimir's comments on not making long speeches. I would use as many words as I needed to ensure the composition worked correctly. Especially when I was unleashing fire in a room full of mages, including four members of the Mage Council.

I spoke the binding words, and then the rest of the composition, using the same measured pace I had used previously. When I said, "End binding," I felt a stronger surge of power race out from me to explode into the wood. It went up instantly in flames.

All seven examiners drew back, but immediately the other part of my working took effect, the smoke wafting away from them and drifting out under the door. I stood back and let myself think with amusement of how it must look to anyone in the corridor, a steady stream of smoke emerging from the classroom and flowing steadily down the hall and out the front door.

But the wood had only been half-consumed when I felt something tug at the flow of my power. I frowned, looking around, but couldn't see anything visible. I looked back at the still-burning wood, only to feel it again. It was almost like another composition fighting my own.

And then, with a snap that reminded me of the backlash that had blown out my parents' store windows, half of my power pulled free of my working and washed back over me. I doubled over with a cry of pain, and the smoke from the fire immediately began to fill the room.

Still bent in half, I heard cries and sounds of disgust from the examiners, but already white clouds obscured the air between us. I drew a breath only to start coughing. I tried to clear my airways, so I could speak the broken half of the composition again, but I couldn't get a clear breath. And I could still feel the foreign power, guiding the smoke as it poured from the fire and billowed around me.

Then something heavy hit my head, and everything went black.

CHAPTER 28

I came to, coughing violently. Surely only minutes could have passed, if that, but I was no longer in the examination room. Instead I hung limply over someone's back, carted along like a sack of potatoes. Was I being carried to safety?

A voice spoke, immediately dispelling that illusion.

"She's awake already. Quick. Shut her up."

The giant carrying me dropped me carelessly to the ground, and a new round of coughing shook me as my lungs once again struggled to suck in air. I had barely managed to take an unobstructed breath before a soft round ball was shoved into my mouth, a piece of material placed over the top of it and tied around my head.

For a moment panic overtook me as my body screamed that it couldn't breathe. But terror sharpened my mind, and I pushed back against my instincts, focusing on my nose and sucking in deep breaths through my nostrils. Slowly my body calmed as air continued to fill my lungs, and my chest stopped convulsing in an effort to retch up the foreign objects.

By the time I had calmed enough to take stock, however, I had been picked up and slung back over my captor's shoulder.

Because it was now obvious that whoever these people were, this was a kidnapping.

A kidnapping or an assassination? I tried to push the thought away. I was still alive, and I had every intention of remaining that way.

They hadn't bound my eyes, and I tried to get my bearings, despite bouncing along upside down. We seemed to be outside the main Academy building but not outside the grounds. The curving edge of the Academy's arena told me we would reach the Academy's back wall soon enough, however. I had never explored back this far, but I knew from my room's view that the back wall was actually part of the ancient city wall. Like the palace, the Academy bordered the edge of the city.

I could only trust that whoever these people were, they weren't bold enough or powerful enough to have killed two members of the Mage Council. And that was assuming both Casimir and Annika were in on the scheme, otherwise it was four. No, my examiners must have been left behind, shielded by the smoke. Which must surely mean that someone would be pursuing us soon, if they weren't already.

The speed at which we crossed the grounds supported that idea, my head and shoulders bouncing uncomfortably against my captor's back.

"She wasn't supposed to wake so fast," the man said, speaking for the first time. "I don't like this."

"Don't worry, it doesn't matter. There's a reason we had to wait so long to make our move. She'll be exhausted and weak as a newborn kitten after all of that."

I tried to keep myself from stiffening. Someone had planned this attack very carefully indeed, taking advantage of the strange conditions of my examination. But who were they? And what did they want with me?

Fear sharpened every sense. After all my efforts and my success at my exams, this wasn't how it was supposed to end.

Today was supposed to be a success. It wasn't supposed to end like this.

A voice sounded in my head. *You're the first Spoken Mage in history.*

And again, from a different memory, this time in my own voice. *The other day I was the Spoken Mage—one of you. Now I'm one of them. Which is it, Prince?*

And the first voice replied. *I don't know. Tell me when you decide.*

The last time I had been attacked, I hadn't even remembered my ability to compose. But after my day of examinations, the knowledge burned in my mind. We might have been interrupted, but I had been about to pass. And at a second year level—at least. Most of the mages in the kingdom might think I had no place at the Academy, but they were wrong.

Because it was true that I wasn't like them, but I was still a mage. I was a Spoken Mage. And I was done running from it or fighting it. For some reason I had a power unheard of in recorded history. It was time I truly embraced it.

And if the other mages couldn't accept it, then they would see just what I was capable of. Starting with these two.

My heart rate had spiked, and I wanted to struggle and fight, but I forced myself to hang loosely, reinforcing their expectation. When the moment came to show them I was far from exhausted, I wanted the element of surprise on my side.

The second man, the one who had gagged me, sounded like he was walking just ahead of us. I couldn't see him until we stopped and my carrier turned to look back the way we had come. I got a brief glimpse of the shorter man opening a small wooden door in the wall before we turned back around and were swiftly passing out of both the Academy and the city.

I told myself I was imagining the finality of the thud as the door swung closed again, but I couldn't quite suppress a shiver.

For the first time since I had entered it, I was leaving Corrin behind.

The rushing of the Overon River sounded loud out here, and I knew from the hours I had spent gazing out my window that only a stretch of sloping grass separated us from it. The men didn't try to approach the swiftly flowing water, instead turning to follow the curve of the city wall.

They moved even faster now, with nothing to hamper their progress. We followed the wall as it curved away from the city, becoming older and more run down. And then they stopped again. I heard another door open, and we stepped back into the city.

I chomped down on the now disgusting, soggy ball of material in my mouth. I hadn't expected this. Hopefully whoever was pursuing us was more canny than me.

Tall gray houses rose around us as we weaved our way through a warren of dingy back streets. We were no longer in the mage's portion of the city, that was for sure.

"Time for a break," said the brute carrying me as we passed along an alley, and I was once again dumped hard against the ground.

"Better to press on," said the shorter man, eyeing his companion with disfavor.

The brute merely shrugged. "You carry her, then. She's heavier than she looks."

If it hadn't been for the gag, I would have grinned. All those new muscles I had been developing were paying off yet again.

The brute leaned back against a wall and closed his eyes, shaking out his shoulders. After a quick glance at me, still recovering my breath after being slammed to the ground yet again, the shorter man walked away, heading toward the end of our current alley.

As he scouted our position, I slowly swiveled myself until I faced away from them both. Then, not bothering to try to rise from the ground, I reached up to pull off my gag.

Everything in me screamed to hurry, but I kept my movements slow, not wanting a flash of motion to attract attention. As I pulled down the gag and spat out the ball, I wished I'd thought to practice how quietly I could speak a composition and still have it work. Too late now.

Whispering the binding words, I didn't bother to think of an existing composition. I barely paused to allow the words I wanted to fill my mind's eye.

"Incapacitate the brute and the shorter one." It was my power, so I figured it should understand the names I had assigned them. "And reveal our location to any friends who are following." I threw the second sentence in at the last moment, feeling a swell of pride for thinking of it. "End binding."

I spoke the last two words more loudly, and the brute pushed off the wall, with a bellowed, "Hey!"

The other man came running back toward us, but he was much too late. Power surged out from me, reaching for them both and, like with my previous attackers, they both went down fast, their screams cut off by unconsciousness.

I smiled and stood to my feet. Not so defenseless after all.

But the tug of power flowing out from me didn't stop, snaking away through the alley in the direction we had come. I bit my lip. Maybe that last addition hadn't been such a good idea after all.

I swayed and had to sit straight back down. Apparently I did have limits, and I could feel myself rapidly approaching them, my strength draining from me with terrifying speed. I needed to cut off this last composition, but I hadn't studied how to do that yet.

I tried to force my increasingly weary brain to come up with some words of my own, but I couldn't seem to form the right thoughts.

And then a figure appeared at the end of the alley, and the drain of power abruptly cut off. I reeled, gasping in relief.

"Well, that's one way to do it," said a familiar voice. "Showy, but effective I suppose."

I didn't bother to ask what he was talking about.

Lucas crossed the final distance between us and reached out a hand to help me to my feet. This time I didn't refuse it. A spark jumped from his fingers and raced through me, the fogginess in my mind lifting.

He looked at the two men collapsed near us. "As much finesse as ever, I see."

I wanted to protest and defend the circumstances, but my mind had stopped at the thought that his fingers still held mine. I looked down at his large firm hand, then down the alley, and then up into his face.

"Are you alone?"

One side of his mouth curved up into a lazy smile, and I felt momentarily dizzy again.

"I dare say they're following somewhere behind. But I didn't think you'd appreciate me waiting around for them."

I shook my head, and then nodded, and then tried to remember what I was responding to. His hand squeezed tighter, and he pulled at me. Gently at first and then with a hard, final tug that brought my body crashing against his.

He let go of my hand and gripped my shoulders instead, his emerald eyes glinting down at me.

"You are infuriating, Elena of Kingslee."

And then his arms wrapped around me, pressing me against him, and his lips came down hard against mine.

All thought spun away from me at the feel of his embrace. The strength of his body and the demanding warmth of his lips consumed me. Everything in me responded, pressing back against him.

I had never imagined that a kiss could feel like this.

And then a sound behind me made us pull apart. I spun within his arms, my own hands reaching up as if to block whatever attack might be coming.

Lucas cried, "Elena, no!"

But it was too late. A single word had already appeared in front of my eyes, and my mouth had opened to speak it.

"Shield."

A cat leaped back, hissing, as power surged out of me.

Dismay overwhelmed me as I instantly realized my over reaction to the non-existent threat. But my shield was already pouring out fast and strong, forming around the two of us, and I felt the last of my strength flowing with it.

Distantly I heard Lucas calling my name, but the darkness was rushing up to claim me. As it swallowed me whole, my last sensation was of strong arms catching me as I fell.

CHAPTER 29

$\mathscr{I}$ woke alone in an unfamiliar place. I sat up too quickly, and the room spun. After several deep breaths, however, the sensation passed, and I examined my surroundings. I recognized them, after all. Acacia's rooms at the Academy.

I shook out each of my limbs and gingerly felt my head. I must have been out for a long time because I felt no stiffness or even exhaustion. In fact, I felt quite energized.

"Oh, good. You're awake. It's about time." Acacia bustled into the room. "There are a few people who'll be very glad to hear it."

A green-eyed face immediately filled my mind, and I looked down to hide my flush.

"How long have I been…?"

"Two days."

"Two days!" I jumped to my feet.

Acacia gave me a stern look. "Over-extending yourself is a serious business, first year. And it can have disastrous consequences. You should consider yourself fortunate."

I nodded meekly, eager to be gone and willing to take whatever lecture was necessary to get me out of here faster.

Acacia sighed. "I don't know why I bother."

"Because you're a wonderful person." I grinned at her, and she reluctantly smiled back.

"Oh, go on," she said.

I hurried from the room, calling a thank you over my shoulder, and nearly collided with someone just outside the door.

"Elena!" Coralie squealed and threw her arms around my neck, squeezing me far too tightly.

I gave her a moment, and then protested.

"Let her be, crazy woman," said Finnian from behind us.

Reluctantly Coralie let me go. Saffron gave me a warm smile and, to my surprise, Finnian gave me a quick hug.

"I'll admit, you almost had us worried there," he said. "For a brief second."

"You wouldn't believe the commotion." Coralie tugged me toward the dining hall. "A trainee kidnapped during the exams! No one has ever heard of such a thing."

"We'd only just finished the written part of the exam when chaos broke loose. There seemed to be smoke everywhere, and Lorcan was running around bellowing, assembling a team to go after you." Finnian grinned at me. "Naturally I volunteered, but he almost bit my head off and ordered me back to the examination room."

Coralie rolled her eyes. "Show off. You were just snooping around, trying to find out what all the fuss was about."

"At your instigation, if I remember correctly," he said, without heat.

"Of course, we were dying to know what happened," said Coralie. "But Redmond came in and said the exams must continue, with or without Lorcan."

"The pompous—"

"Finnian!" Saffron cut off her cousin's muttered insult.

He just turned his grin on her. "What? He is, and you know it."

Coralie ignored them both. "So Walden had to take the head's place. It's a wonder we all passed given all the distractions."

A horrible thought washed over me. Exams. Passing.

"Except me." I swallowed. "I didn't get to finish mine. And Redmond was just waiting to fail me, too."

"Well, no one will give us any details, of course…" Finnian looked at me hopefully, but I just shook my head at him, having no intention of revealing Lucas's involvement if they didn't already know of it.

Finnian sighed. "But Lorcan managed to find and rescue you, it seems. And he said you did most of the saving yourself using all sorts of advanced compositions, so he declared your exam a pass."

I almost collapsed in relief, Coralie steadying me.

"Are you sure you're ready to be let out of Acacia's rooms?" she asked.

I shook her off with a smile.

"Of course. She said I've been out two days!"

Finnian clapped a hand to his heart. "The longest two days of my life."

"Don't listen to him," said Saffron. "He's spent the two days in utter bliss, lazing around doing nothing but eating and teasing us all."

"A man needs some pleasures in life."

Coralie shoved him.

"So we did it." I tried to take the thought in. "We all passed."

"Yes, yes we did." Coralie glanced at me sideways. "Although a certain prince disappeared just as the beginnings of the commotion broke out. He only got back in time to take his exam with the fourth years."

"The advantages of being royal," said Finnian. "Not a single instructor even questioned him, while I was soundly reprimanded for simply setting foot outside the examination room."

"You're lucky they didn't fail you on the spot," said Saffron darkly.

I felt my cheeks flush again at the mention of Lucas, the memory of our kiss searing across my mind. I quickly changed the subject.

"So I guess that means we'll all be back together for second year soon enough. Have most of the students already left?"

"I think at least half of them are hanging around to get a glimpse of you, to be honest," said Finnian.

I bit my lip. So I was once again to be the spectacle of the Academy.

Then I remembered my epiphany in the midst of my kidnapping. My back straightened. Let them stare. I was done trying to hide from it.

I entered the dining hall with my head held high and paid no attention to the whispering hiss that swept through the room. But one thing hadn't changed. My eyes still sought out a certain dark head.

He sat at his normal table, with the twins beside him, although there was no sign of Weston or Lavinia. He looked up at the commotion, his eyes moving to our group as we walked toward the first year tables. But his eyes didn't stop, traveling over me as lightly as he did my friends. Something in me deflated.

Coralie chattered on, glaring down Finnian's attempts to press me for details of my kidnapping and talking of her plans for the remainder of the summer instead. I barely heard either of them.

The smell of food hit me hard, and my painfully empty stomach made itself felt. I filled a plate and began to eat, despite my distracted mind.

"Acacia said no questions. She's supposed to have a chance to rest." Coralie glared at Finnian.

My eyes strayed down the line of tables of their own volition. Lucas listened to something Calix was saying with a bored expression. He didn't look my way.

Any desire to answer my friends' questions fled, and I was grateful for Acacia's orders. Apparently even I didn't know what had happened in that alley. Had I just dreamed it all? Because now that I was back in the Academy, nothing seemed to have changed.

"Natalya!" The voice from the doorway rang across the dining hall, and Natalya leaped to her feet and rushed over to embrace Lavinia.

"You'll come to visit me, of course," Lavinia said with obnoxious volume.

Natalya smiled and linked her arm with her friend's. "Only if you promise to visit me first."

I watched them stroll out into the entrance hall, leaving both doors wide open. No doubt so we could all observe the important looking retinue that had come to collect the Stantorns. I could see Weston, hanging to one side and looking bored by his cousin's theatrics.

But just as I was turning back to my food, something caught my eye.

I leaped to my feet, ignoring my friends' curious questions, and hurried across the hall toward the doors. Bursting out into the corridor, I strode the few steps to the entrance hall, but the Stantorn group had already swept from the building, carrying Natalya with them.

I hurried after them just as another group entered the Academy, filling the great doorway. Impatiently I shouldered my way through the crowd, ignoring their protests, and emerged at the top of the stairs.

"What do you want?" asked Natalya.

Two carriages were already rumbling toward the open gates.

"Who was that? With Lavinia?"

Natalya eyed me with displeasure. We didn't normally attempt any sort of conversation.

I turned to glare at her. "Well?"

She flicked her hair over her shoulder, having for once left it free of its usual practical style. "That was Lavinia's family, of course."

"Stantorns then? All of them?"

She frowned at me. "What is wrong with you? Don't tell me you've lived with us for a year, and you still don't know what families we all come from. Of course they were Stantorns." She turned on her heel and disappeared inside, leaving me grinding my teeth, alone on the top step.

But I wasn't alone for long. And I didn't need to turn to see who had come up beside me. I could sense his presence, although I wished I wasn't so attuned to it.

"Have you spoken to Lorcan?"

"Excuse me?" Now I did turn to face him. That was all the greeting I was to get?

His eyes held a warmth I hadn't expected given his earlier dismissal, but his words remained calmly practical.

"Have you spoken to Lorcan since you woke up?"

"No," I said stiffly, looking back out across the courtyard.

"They conducted an investigation while you were unconscious. The two men who kidnapped you died in custody before they could talk." He shifted. "Like the criminals who attacked you in the city."

"What? They died? No one ever said—"

He kept talking. "Lorcan has concluded the two attacks were connected. Perhaps the first one was a test, as you suspected. But I don't think these two were meant to be expendable like the previous lot. They left behind a bread trail to follow."

He paused.

"Well?" I asked, my mind still on the long-disappeared carriages. "Where did it lead?"

"Kallorway." His voice was grim.

"Kallorway?" I turned to stare at him. That wasn't what I'd been expecting. "It can't be."

"On the contrary." He shook his head. "I wish we were impervious to their incursion, but I am afraid that is far from true. It seems they heard we had discovered something new—a new way to wield power—and they thought to steal our secret weapon."

I wasn't really listening, my head shaking. "I don't think it was Kallorway."

He raised both eyebrows. "Oh? You doubt Lorcan's investigation? I suppose the two men confessed their whole plan to you before you knocked them both out?"

"You just said they died. The men who attacked me."

Lucas regarded me with narrow eyes, not bothering to confirm his earlier words.

"Well, that's impossible because I just saw one."

"Excuse me?"

"I just saw one."

"Is that why you leaped up and rushed out here like a maniac? Where is he then?" The prince looked around as if he expected the man to jump out from behind the fountain or something.

I ignored his condescending tone.

"I saw him through the door. He was with the group who had come to collect Lavinia and Weston." I looked at him significantly. "The Stantorns. He was a Stantorn, or one of their servants, I suppose. I rushed straight out, but they'd all made it into their carriages before I could get here. But if you sent someone after them, I bet you could still catch—"

"You saw him through the doorway, standing in the middle of a large group?" Lucas shook his head. "You've just woken up after two days of unconsciousness, Elena. No one's going to blame you if you're a bit wobbly at first. But they would certainly blame me if I pursued a set of Stantorn carriages and started making wild accusations. It sounds to me like you could have seen anyone."

I glared at him, tears springing to my eyes which only made me angrier.

"How can you say that? You weren't there in my exam. You didn't see the way Annika and Casimir looked at me. But you were there at that council meeting when they voted for my execution. Is it really so unbelievable that members of Stantorn and Devoras might have decided that I was going to pass my exam, and therefore they needed to take action of their own to be rid of me?"

Lucas hissed in a breath. If there had been warmth in his eyes earlier, it was gone now. "That's *Duchess* Annika and *Duke* Casimir you're talking about, remember. The council voted. They lost. Which means you just accused two of the most powerful families in the kingdom of treason. You need to watch your words, Elena of Kingslee."

I stiffened. "I know what I saw."

He shook his head. "You know what you think you saw." He looked at me for a moment, and something in his face softened.

"I know them," he said. "I'm half a Stantorn myself, so it's my relatives you're talking about. You don't need any special insight to realize that most of the Devoras family are hot-headed and that to be a Stantorn is to be intractable." His eyes lingered on my face. "Kind of like someone else I know."

I frowned and looked away.

"But for all their hot-headedness and intractability, both families are loyal. They would never work against the council."

Tears still stung at my eyes, so I kept my face averted. Maybe I *had* dreamed everything that had happened in that alley because clearly the prince had no great fondness for me.

Silence stretched between us before Lucas gave an exasperated sigh.

"Believe what you want, but I strongly suggest you refrain from any more accusations. We'll be back here for second year soon enough, and you have enough trouble on your head as it is.

We all do." He paused, but I neither spoke nor looked at him. He sighed again, before whispering his final words. "You are infuriating, Elena of Kingslee."

And then he was gone.

For a long moment, I couldn't move. So I hadn't imagined it then.

Hurt and anger fought for dominance, but neither could suppress the other. All those significant looks, all those words with their hidden meanings. The times he had seemed to step in to defend me. Even our silent study in the library. Somehow, when I hadn't been paying attention, I had allowed myself to believe he was on my side. That in his own strange and arrogant way, the prince of Ardann was trying to protect me.

And then I had let him kiss me, had spent my last energy to protect him. And even though he had subsequently ignored me in the public setting of the dining hall, he had sought me out the moment I was alone—and I hadn't been able to prevent the spark of hope and warmth I felt at the sound of his voice.

But I had been a fool. Whatever interest he had in me, it was the same interest that consumed Lorcan and Jessamine. Interest in the Spoken Mage, not in Elena the person. When it came down to it, I was just a commonborn girl to him. Someone to be dismissed rather than consulted. Naive and foolish in the ways of mages and of court. Someone who couldn't be trusted, who imagined enemies where there were none. Who insulted his family.

And now danger hung over my head, but there was nothing I could do about it. Because if the prince himself told me to let it go, if Lorcan had investigated and found some enemy far away in another kingdom, who did I have left to turn to? No one. My only friends here were as powerless as me.

I tried to remind myself that the existence of my friends was something of a miracle in itself, even if they could do nothing to help me now. Somehow, despite everything, I had made friends here at the Academy. I just had to remember that Lucas wasn't one of them. And he certainly wasn't more than a friend.

As if conjured by my thoughts, Coralie appeared beside me. She leaned her head on my shoulder and gazed out over the courtyard.

"I'm going to miss you over the summer," she said. "I would never have guessed that when I first heard about your arrival at the beginning of the year."

I shook my head, trying to shake away the memory of Lucas and hold on to the bright moments of my year. "And I never guessed at the beginning of the year that I'd still be alive at this point."

"Cheery," said Finnian, strolling out to join us. "You are—as always—our ray of sunshine."

I grinned at him. "I definitely never imagined I'd be friends with the son of a duke."

"Well, you can't hold that against me. None of us get to choose our family."

"Family!" I straightened. Somehow in all the chaos I had forgotten. "I get to go home now and see my family!"

Finnian slung an arm over Coralie's shoulders. "See how quickly we are forgotten, Fair Coralie."

She shoved him off. "Speak for yourself."

Sudden concern filled me. "That's assuming I'm even allowed to go home now."

"I'm sure you will be," said Finnian. "Lorcan was looking for you earlier and mentioned something about conditions you needed to agree to. So it sounds like you'll be allowed to leave, although no doubt these conditions will be ridiculous and over the top."

I wrapped them both into a group embrace. "Never mind that, you two. I don't care what they are. I'm going home!" I pulled back and gave them a broad smile. "But, come autumn, I'll be back. So don't go forgetting me."

Coralie shook her head, smiling back at me. "As if anyone could do that."

Finnian, however, didn't smile, his face unusually serious. "You're the change that is going to turn our kingdom upside down. No one will ever forget you, Spoken Mage. You mark my words."

Read *Voice of Command,* The Spoken Mage Book 2 to find out what happens to Elena and Lucas in their second year at the Academy.

To find out what Lucas was thinking when Elena arrived at the Academy, sign up to my mailing list at www.melaniecelli er.com for an exclusive bonus chapter retold from Lucas's point of view. My monthly newsletter will keep you informed of future releases and bonus shorts in the Spoken Mage world.

Want more fantasy, romance, adventure, and intrigue? Try *A Dance of Silver and Shadow*, the first book in my *Beyond the Four Kingdoms* series in which twelve princesses must do a lot more than just dance when they get caught up in a dangerous and magical competition.

Thank you for taking the time to read my book. I hope you enjoyed it. If you did, please spread the word! You could start by leaving a review on Amazon or Goodreads or Facebook or any other social media site. Your review would be very much appreciated and would make a big difference!

ROYAL FAMILY OF ARDANN

King Stellan
Queen Verena
Crown Princess Lucienne
Prince Lucas

MAGE COUNCIL

Academy Head (black robe) - Duke Lorcan of Callinos
University Head (black robe) - Duchess Jessamine of
    Callinos
Head of Law Enforcement (red robe) - Duke Lennox of
    Ellington
Head of the Seekers (gray robe) - Duchess Phyllida of
    Callinos
Head of the Healers (purple robe) - Duke Dashiell of
    Callinos
Head of the Growers (green robe) - Duchess Annika of
    Devoras
Head of the Wind Workers (blue robe) - Duke Magnus of
    Ellington
Head of the Creators (orange robe) - Duke Casimir of
    Stantorn
Head of the Armed Forces (silver robe) - General Griffith of
    Devoras
Head of the Royal Guard (gold robe) - General Thaddeus of
    Stantorn

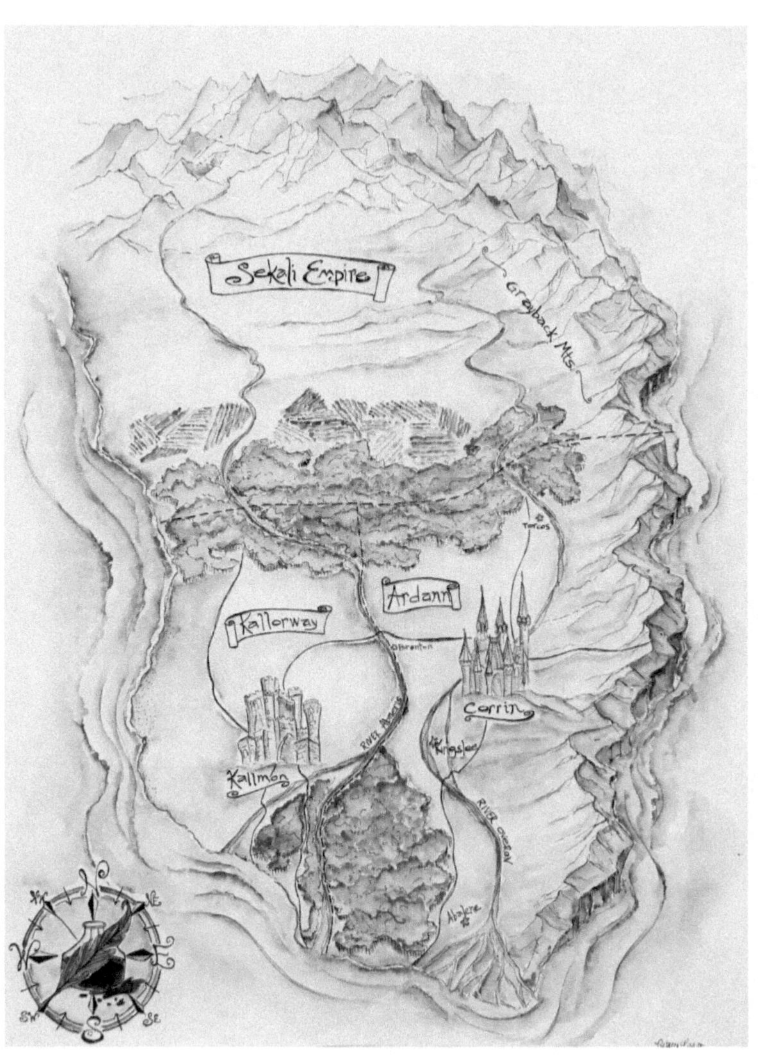

Sekeli Empire
Greyback Mts.
Tarcos
Ardann
Kallorway
Obrenton
Corrin
Kingslea
River Avonell
River Charon
Kallmon
Alakra
NW N NE
W E
SW S SE

ACKNOWLEDGMENTS

It was a long time ago now that my imagination was first captured by the statement that the tongue has the power of life and death. I'm excited to have finished my first book in a new fantasy world where that idea is true in its most literal sense, as well as my first non-fairy tale retelling. Although of course there are fairy tale elements there for anyone looking to find them—from the requirement of one soldier per family which is such an important element of the ancient tale of Hua Mulan to the handsome prince whose hair somehow manages to always look better than anyone else's. Given my love of happily ever afters, I can't imagine I'll ever entirely stray away from my fairy tale roots, but I've enjoyed the chance to explore a whole new fictional world.

Of course Elena and Lucas's journey is far from over, and I'm so grateful to the many people who have helped me get started and are continuing to walk with me as I see their adventures through.

My little family—now one person larger than it was when I wrote the last word of the first draft of Voice of Power—you bear the biggest burden of my authorly abstraction. I appreciate having you in my life more than I can say, even if it sometimes seems like I'm somewhere else entirely.

My beta reader pool expanded for this book since doing something new required more back up than ever. So I'm more than grateful to both my normal, faithful group of betas: Rachel, Greg, Priya, Ber, and Katie, but also to the newcomers I roped in: Marina, Cheri, Kristi, and Casey. They read and reread versions and were excellent sounding boards for both the characters and plot.

Getting this book finished required shutting myself away in my office far too intensively, and it made a world of difference to have colleagues right there beside me—even if they were only present in a virtual sense. Kitty, Kenley, Shari, Aya, Brittany, Diana, and Marina—it's so much easier to try something new with such awesome cheerleaders spurring me on. Thanks for all the chats, laughs, and gifs.

My editors have all followed me into my new genre for which I am utterly grateful. Thank you Mary, Dad, and Deborah for not running as fast as you could in the other direction! I couldn't have produced this book without your input and assistance.

My cover designer, Karri, also deserves praise for not just her skill but her unending patience as I dithered back and forth about what I wanted for my covers now that I was branching away from fairy tales. Thanks for walking the journey with me and never once even hinting I should make up my mind.

Rebecca is new to my team, but I could not be happier to have her on board as my map illustrator. She did an incredible job in a ridiculously short time frame and never showed anything but graciousness and talent as she did it. Thanks for coming to my rescue!

And perhaps I should have started this time with the thank you to my readers—both old and new. You're the reason I do this, and the reason I get to expand out to explore entirely new worlds from within my imagination. I am grateful for you every day.

And to God, whose voice is the first and only true source of power—thank you for giving us words and creativity and the chance to explore what we can do with them. May we always choose to follow in your footsteps and speak life rather than death.

ABOUT THE AUTHOR

Melanie Cellier grew up on a staple diet of books, books and more books. And although she got older, she never stopped loving children's and young adult novels.

She always wanted to write one herself, but it took three careers and three different continents before she actually managed it.

She now feels incredibly fortunate to spend her time writing from her home in Adelaide, Australia where she keeps an eye out for koalas in her backyard. Her staple diet hasn't changed much, although she's added choc mint Rooibos tea and Chicken Crimpies to the list.

She writes young adult fantasy including books in her *Spoken Mage* world, her *Mage's Influence* world, and her various *Four Kingdoms* and *Kingdoms of Legacy* series that are made up of linked stand-alone stories that retell classic fairy tales.

www.ingramcontent.com/pod-product-compliance
Lightning Source LLC
Chambersburg PA
CBHW030346200726

48286CB00013B/378